KEN ALLEN | SUPER SLEUTH SERIES

KING ME

KEN ALLEN | SUPER SLEUTH SERIES

KING ME

J. A. CRAWFORD

CamCat
Books

CamCat Publishing, LLC
Ft. Collins, Colorado 80524
camcatpublishing.com

Hardcover ISBN 9780744305760
Paperback ISBN 9780744305838
Large-Print Paperback ISBN 9780744306354
eBook ISBN 9780744306392
Audiobook ISBN 9780744306514

Library of Congress Control Number: 2023935964

Book and cover design by Maryann Appel
Floor plan illustration by Maia Lai

5   3   1   2   4

To Rob, who always asked for more stories.

And to the storytellers, crowded around their tables, dice in hand,

making up all the things that really happened.

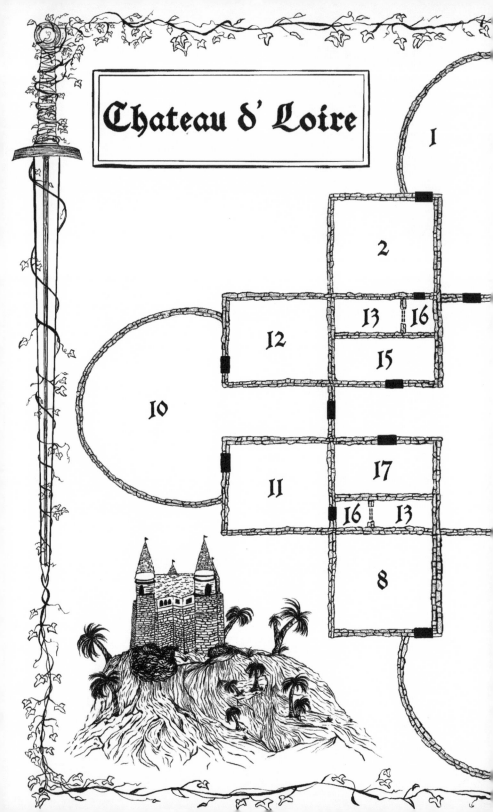

Chateau d' Loire

1

2

12

13 16

15

10

11

17

16 13

8

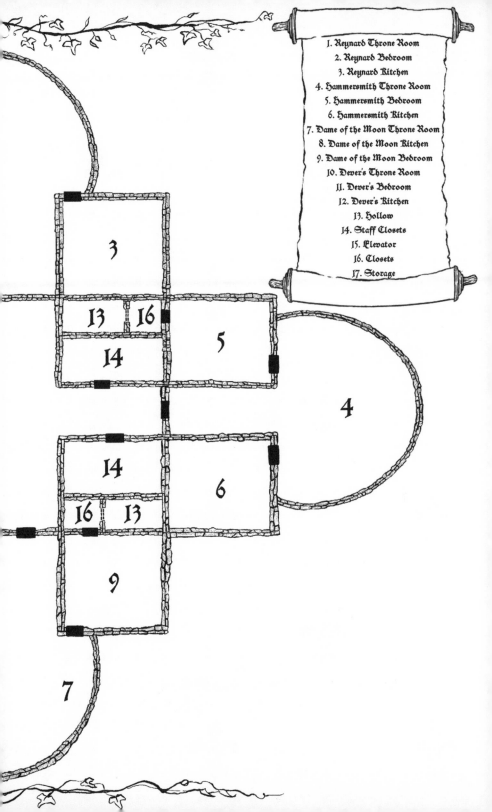

1. Reynard Throne Room
2. Reynard Bedroom
3. Reynard Kitchen
4. Hammersmith Throne Room
5. Hammersmith Bedroom
6. Hammersmith Kitchen
7. Dame of the Moon Throne Room
8. Dame of the Moon Kitchen
9. Dame of the Moon Bedroom
10. Dever's Throne Room
11. Dever's Bedroom
12. Dever's Kitchen
13. Hollow
14. Staff Closets
15. Elevator
16. Closets
17. Storage

WINTER HAD COME TO THIS TOWN, and boy was it a doozy. Record lows, day after day, with the thermostat threatening forty. The population combed their closets for cast-off garments. Scarves, once considered purely decorative items, found their true calling. Gloves and earmuffs, which only ever saw use as props for holiday photos, now adorned the natives. Faux fur of every hue and print abounded, transforming the masses into a menagerie fit for a zoo. As for this detective, well, I was in pure bliss.

The crisp climate was a godsend. Whatever the opposite of seasonal affective disorder was, I had it. It was all I could do not to *Ho Ho Ho* in the face of all the bah humbugging. I wasn't bothered a whit, being summoned forth by a potential client. Secret rendezvous were routine in my role as sleuth to the stars. My office had become a campsite for paparazzi posing the question, Why would So-and-so want to hire Ken Allen? If a client wanted privacy, clandestine meetings were required.

Which made their choice of setting puzzling. Chateau d'Loire was anything but inconspicuous. The luxury hotel was the closest thing my fair city had to a historic landmark. Architects often outlived their creations in This Town. The birthplace of showbiz was built on an evergreen graveyard, layered on the bones of those who failed in their quest for the immortality of fame.

The name itself, Chateau d'Loire, is grammatically incorrect, of course. It should be Chateau de la Loire. It's unclear whether Arnold Horowitz, the founder, was ignorant of this little detail or thumbing his nose at the French. Either way, I liked d'Loire better. Chateau d'Loire looked like what castles became after royalty stopped fretting so much over being besieged: a seven-story fairytale compilation of witch-hat towers and crenulated turrets, complete with meant-to-be-holy-but-actually-hot statuary. The arched doors and windows promised to transport you to another world. You even passed under a portcullis on entering.

The current visitors reinforced the illusion. The lobby was packed wall-to-wall with people decked out in armor of all varieties, from a knight's full suit to leather ensembles more suited to BDSM than battle. They carried an array of weapons: swords, axes, bows, and staves. While I wasn't familiar with this particular species, I knew the genus well: superfans.

The kind who traveled from far and wide to attend conventions like the one I was about to join: a celebration of all things *The Lands Beyond.*

The biggest television show ever. A cultural phenomenon that had exponentially gained steam over the last nine years, shaping pop culture from fashion trends to children's names. With the tenth and final season set to start filming in a week, the atmosphere at Chateau d'Loire crackled with anticipation. Prior to heading overseas, the cast and crew dropped by This Town for one last marketing hurrah. The most I'd ever charged at a con was forty bucks, and I had to be framed for murder to rate that. Photo op and autograph sessions from the stars of *The Lands Beyond* ran hundreds of dollars a head. Exclusive events, like sharing a meal, stretched into the thousands.

From what I gathered from the endless ads and ever-present merchandise, the show was a souped-up version of *Dallas* with sword fights. You'd think I'd know the basics about the program that had defined the last decade, but I'd somehow escaped its lure. Despite my past as a celebrity personal trainer, I didn't know any of its stars. It was shot overseas, with mostly foreign actors who went home after filming.

And to be frank, sword and sorcery wasn't my thing. But try explaining that to a diehard fan. They compare *The Lands Beyond* to Shakespeare, if only the bard had possessed the creative vision to include dragons.

While I managed to negotiate the labyrinth of humanity without contracting tetanus, I did catch plenty of glares. Cavorting around in slacks and a buttoned-up blazer was breaking their immersion. But to people in the know, I was also cosplaying . . . after a fashion: Once, and only the once, I played Jove Brand, superspy extraordinaire, which provided me with a gimmick for my second act as a private eye. Hiring a D-list super sleuth held a certain appeal among celebrities. I had been one of them, technically. I understood the tightrope they walked. And, more important, I knew how to keep my mouth shut.

The halberd-wielding security had been informed of my coming but still required I present my pedigree. Once they confirmed I wasn't an imposter—a claim I wasn't confident of myself—they parted their poles and allowed me to pass. I apologized my way through a bustling kitchen to the service elevator, where a second set of guards—this time the conventional kind with discrete holster outlines under unbuttoned jackets—also vetted me. They used a tubular key to provide elevator access to the penthouse level and ushered me in. When the doors opened at the top, I was staring into the smiling face of a guy who once upon a time might have killed me—nothing personal—if I had zigged instead of zagged.

Not too long ago, Alexi Mirovich was the top mixed martial artist in the world, before his career was cut short by a stint in a Siberian prison for involuntary manslaughter. A Russian oligarch arranged for a commuted sentence if Alexi competed in an illegal underground fighting ring. His opponent had been yours truly.

My goose would have been good and cooked had I not been able to suss out Alexi's big secret: the Bull of St. Petersburg—as he was known—suffered from labyrinthitis. At the time he was professionally competing, disclosing his condition was career-ending, as was treating it with corticosteroids, which would have shown on drug screens.

When confronted, Alexi agreed to work out a gentleman's agreement: he took a dive and I didn't expose him. Shortly thereafter, Alexi played the heavy in a Cherno Perun flick—the Russian version of Jove Brand. It got him noticed, and then he joined the swollen cast of *The Lands Beyond* as a naïve, unstoppable gladiator. Now Alexi was in full wardrobe in honor of the con. Or more likely, full wardrobe was contractually required.

In the past, Alexi's condition kept him from developing a notable physique. It's tough to do intense cardio when you have vertigo issues. Not that it stopped him from crushing the competition. When no one survives against you for more than two minutes, your VO_2 max is irrelevant.

But now that he was able to get proper medical treatment, Alexi could finally train the way he'd always wanted.

Underneath a costume of leather straps arrayed without rhyme or reason, Alexi Mirovich was absolutely jacked. Muscles like slabs of rock danced under paper-thin skin. Veins traced a roadmap up his arms and shoulders. He spread his spike-knuckled hands with a grin.

"Ken! Too long."

"Hey, buddy. Glad to finally talk to you. Wait, can you hear me?"

"Implant," Alexi replied, tapping his ear. He flushed slightly. "Sorry. Shy."

Deafness was a result of Alexi's condition, but he hadn't always been that way. It had been beaten into him via a grueling training regimen imposed by his late father. If there was one thing people in the entertainment and combat sports industries had in common, it was daddy issues.

"Don't be. Your English is better than my Russian. Or sign for that matter." I stepped out of the elevator. "So, what needs detecting?"

"Not for me." Alexi started down the hallway, waving that I follow.

The penthouse level had a weird layout. There were four penthouse suites, each centered in a rounded turret. The two hallways formed a cross, with the elevator in the middle. Each point of said cross ended in a suite entrance. The only other doors on the floor led to staff supply closets. Alexi steered us toward the turret with the swankiest view overlooking This Town: the chamber reserved for the guest of honor.

The hallway ended in a high-arched door, its brass knocker topped with a crown. Alexi produced an oversized vintage key from his woven harness. Electronic key scanners were a no-no here at the historic Chateau d'Loire. The lock opened with a satisfying click as Alexi gestured for me to precede him. The door had real weight to it. I applied some muscle and stepped into a throne room.

The broad, short hallway leading to the seat of power was lined by suits of armor, with the occasional ottoman in the event the visiting monarch wasn't ready to receive you. Bookshelves provided an entertainment option to pass the time while you waited.

The throne stood at the end of the red velveteen carpet, three steps up from ground level. The royal seat was classic midcentury medieval, America's Camelot period, when the emphasis was mood over historical accuracy. The man occupying the throne was dressed like the king of diamonds, in a primary color riot of an ensemble, though more svelte than the playing card implied. He'd leaned into the shtick, his white hair done wavy with a curling mustache and beard. The only off-theme accessory was his crown. It was in the gothic style: studded with high-reaching tips of what looked like sundered blades.

The king spoke, his eyes sparkling with amusement. "So you're Ken Allen."

He sat there with a faint smile while things got awkward. I had no idea who this guy was, and he had every expectation of being recognized. Realization began to settle in. A bead of sweat ran down my ribs. I had to say something, and I had to say it now.

"What can I do for you, Your, uh, Highness?"

The king laughed, thumping his scepter against the dais in a form of applause. Topped with an axe head, the rod matched his theme.

"I've spent too much time in a world of my own making, Mr. Allen. It took a complete outsider to bring me down to earth."

I gave a bow that would have been described as sardonic, back when the term was in fashion. "If you're looking for a jester, I got out of that business."

The king loosed another august belly rumbler, throwing his head back like a cartoon character. "I'm certain you're exactly who I'm looking for. You've gotten a lot of press over the last year, with the Jove Brand murders and the superhero sabotages. I'm in need of a shamus. There's a killer at large. One who is almost surely in this very building."

"Who's the victim?"

The king dinged his scepter against his crown. "Me. R. R. Reynard, at your service."

While I couldn't have picked Reynard out of a crowd, I knew the name. He was the mastermind behind *The Lands Beyond*. Its creator, showrunner, and sole writer. In the nineties, he'd helmed a show called *Never After*. Though it only lasted for two seasons, it gathered a huge cult following. After disappearing for two decades, he reappeared ten years ago with *The Lands Beyond*, his magnum opus. Most people didn't do their best work after qualifying for social security. Reynard was the exception who proved the rule.

"So what—" I'd exceeded my limit for standing at attention. Raising a finger to indicate a time-out, I dragged an ottoman over. Being vintage, it was heavier than it looked. I took a seat, unbuttoning my jacket. "If you've been poisoned, a doctor will do you more good."

"It's not poison, I've made sure of that. I have reason to believe someone has sabotaged my innermost sanctums."

"Which are?"

"I own a cabin in Maine. It looks like something out of *Walden*, but has state-of-the-art security. I was to visit with a colleague but changed plans at the last moment. While there, said colleague experienced a headache. But rather than take a pill, they decided some fresh air might do them good. When they came back from their hike, the cabin was burnt to its foundations. This was instance number one."

Reynard paused for questions or comments.

"I'm following along okay so far. Thanks for keeping the syllables down."

He toyed with his rod for a moment to make sure I knew who was at whose bidding. "On to instance number two. We leave for Scotland in a week. During filming, I reside in a custom trailer. On the heels of the fire, I sent my security team to prep it for arrival. They found the air mixture had been tampered with."

"Air mixture?"

"The trailer is mobile. When we film at elevation, I maintain a high oxygen environment, which I find conducive for creativity. It had been adjusted to emit a mixture more akin to rocket fuel. One spark, and I would have had an impromptu Viking funeral."

Reynard studied me intensely.

The guy was a storyteller, and his tale could appear to be the work of a speculative mind. He was expecting me to display some skepticism, maybe challenge him.

"The final season of *The Lands Beyond* starts filming in a week. You're the golden goose. Who would want to do you in now?"

"I've made my fair share of enemies in the last ten years. Most of the cast despises me. Maybe all of them." His grin went cold. "Some are better actors than others."

"Who's on short call?"

"Nobody. No matter how many episodes the players may appear in, every actor receives a full season's salary and is required to stay in residence for the duration of filming. So, even they don't know when I might give them the axe."

Reynard's scepter made more sense now. He was his own hatchet man.

"If you kick the bucket, who inherits?"

"I have no siblings and no children. Thirty years ago, when we were filming *Never After*, I successfully defended a false paternity suit. The lesson was not wasted. *Snip-snip* went my vas deferens. As for my estate, the exact details of my trust remain secret."

"So who profits from your death? Not the studio, and the cast is both in the dark and already paid. So, if it's not money, it's love. Who cares enough to kill you?"

Reynard reclined as much as his throne would allow. "*The Lands Beyond* has an extremely devoted following. Some might describe them as fanatical. A few even believe my yarns to be true, and that I am but the conduit who relays them. A prophet of sorts. And history tells us what happens to prophets."

"Could you foresee your way to a prime suspects list?"

"I knew you would ask."

Reynard went into his robes and came out with a metal-bound case the size of a tablet and a foot thick. A built-in lock anchored the reinforced hasp. He set his hand on the case, gesturing as if he were about to withdraw a rabbit, and the hasp popped open. He slipped a folded page from the interior and re-secured the case before beckoning

I approach His Grace. I had to put a foot on the bottom step to reach Reynard. He made no effort to meet me halfway. He was wearing a ring topped with a stamp.

As I stretched for the page, he let it drop from his fingers. I snatched it out of the air in a display of agility. Reynard's method approach was starting to wear thin, but I tried to give him the benefit of the doubt. Maybe he was worried about paper cuts.

The paper was dot matrix style, with perforated rails on both sides. The printer it scrolled out of could have had grandkids. A list was printed on the page. A long one. I had to unfold the next sheet. Next to each name was a percentage.

"You took a poll?"

Reynard grinned. "What is the point of loyal devotees if you don't make use of their free labor?"

"Looks like most of these aren't real names."

"Indeed. Those are the names the Edgelords have chosen for themselves, taken from the lore of Crucible."

I looked up from the list. "What's Crucible?"

Reynard made a face like he found a short hair in his soup bowl. "Crucible is the name of my world. The network didn't think using its formal name would work as a title, hence *The Lands Beyond*."

"And who are the Edgelords?"

Reynard gathered himself. If looks could kill, someone would have been investigating my murder. "I have had online forums in one form or another since the early days of the internet. The most dedicated fans of *Never After* were the earliest and most fervent supporters of *The Lands Beyond*. They became the first Edgelords. Others have joined them over the years, rising through the ranks to that innermost circle."

Reynard even had a feudal system worked out for his fandom. His creation had all the makings of a cult. I started to wonder if he ever took those robes off.

"I don't suppose you have these people's actual names."

"Indeed I do. Two-step verification is required before you receive the colée."

Being on thin ice already, I didn't ask Reynard to explain what that meant. In my short time as a detective, when it came to cases, I'd only had two big spuds among the small fries. Both times, I'd been lucky enough to have already been an expert on the subject matter. It looked like I was going to be spending a lot of time on the *Lands Beyond* wiki.

"Well, the sooner I get started the better. How long does the convention run? It's not often I get all the suspects in one spot like this. That's really going to cut down on the travel time. Most of this job is commuting."

"We are here through Sunday at noon."

Which gave me forty-eight hours before the convention attendees scattered to the winds and the cast and crew were an ocean away. I dug into my blazer for the envelope containing my standard contract. Reynard awaited me. I resisted the urge to fold it into a paper plane and launch it at him. He breezed through the contract before signing it. Reynard must have been a fast reader, because he didn't strike me as reckless when it came to putting his name on things.

I returned the contract to its envelope and tucked it away. As I did, my jacket parted enough to give Reynard a peek at the goods.

"You really use a Quarreler? I must admit, I didn't believe it."

I buttoned my coat before Reynard got a closer look. Along with dressing like Jove Brand, gallivanting superspy, I had become known for sporting non-lethal equivalents of his gadgets. The last thing I needed was Reynard requesting to take my sidearm for a spin.

"I don't like guns, and law enforcement barely tolerates me as it is. If I started trading bullets with the bad guys, they'd lock me up. Not that the bad guys care."

Reynard stared for a moment before a sly smile spread across his face. "I understand. You like to keep your secrets."

"Hey, could you swing me a room? It doesn't have to be anything special. I'm going to want to make the most of the weekend."

"That should be within my power."

"Do you have an assistant or someone I can coordinate with?"

"Bradley Corbett. He'll meet you at the elevator."

In a blatant breech of etiquette, I left without being dismissed. When I got to the doors, I turned around, scratching my head.

"This whole little world you got going is something else."

Reynard thumbed his axe. "It's good to be the king, Mr. Allen."

Bradley Corbett exited the service elevator thirty minutes after me. Like Reynard, he was also done up as a playing card, but a jack instead of a king. The look was less flattering on Corbett. I doubted the costume had been his decision, which scored an early sympathy point. He guided me out of the kitchen and into a side room with all the room-service trays and linens.

"I have some materials for you." Corbett struggled to holster the little axe he was carrying. His belt was too tight. I took it off his hands. It was heavier than it looked, and sharp. It occurred to me Corbett hadn't bothered with introductions.

"I guess I stand out in this crowd, huh?"

Either Corbett was wearing mascara or he had been gifted with naturally perfect eyelashes. "Oh, I recognized you from that viral video, Mr. Allen."

"Oh boy, which one?"

"When you and that female police officer fought those men in the street."

Corbett was referring to Special Investigator Ava Stern. After coming after me for a murder I didn't commit, each of our next big cases turned out to be the same case.

We ended up in a public dust-up recorded by about ten different bystanders. Stern saved my bacon and won another commendation she didn't care to pin.

"That was not my finest moment."

"Tell that to Mr. Reynard. He was rather impressed. Less so with your appearance on the silver screen." Corbett withdrew a tablet from his robes. Its slipcover was done up to resemble a leather-bound book. "When Mr. Reynard honors someone to the rank of Edgelord, a full background check is required. The dossiers are here."

Corbett shuffled next to me to provide a better view. He smelled like he'd done some reading about pheromones and believed all of it.

"Can you send this to me?"

"Part of the terms of service is that this information stays private within FoxRex, LLC."

"Of which I am currently a subcontractor. Look, Reynard didn't pick me for the way I pop on camera. I'm good people."

Corbett wavered, shuffling from one foot to the other. "I should ask Mr. Reynard."

He swapped to a messaging screen TMZ would have doled out seven figures for. Below Reynard were thumbnail images of every star from the show, as well as the chief executive of Home Drive-In, the dying cable channel *The Lands Beyond* had rocketed back into relevance.

We idled around awaiting a royal decree. The short back hallway was featureless, besides the two plainclothes guards. One door led into the kitchen complex, the other into the hotel proper.

"Mr. Reynard should have replied by now."

"Well, we can't wait around all day. Let's request an audience in person."

Corbett's expression was pained. "Mr. Reynard has a full schedule. He hates when his receptions are interrupted."

"Don't worry. I'll take the heat. It comes with the territory."

Corbett had the keys to the kingdom. Security cleared him up the elevator. He tapped on Reynard's door. When no answer came, I put the calluses on my knuckles to the test, to be rewarded with more silence.

"Open this, will you?"

Corbett produced an antique key from his robes. He cracked the door slowly, and softly inquired with a "Your Highness?" rather than Reynard's name. His posture and tone told me that in the past, Corbett had walked in on activities he'd rather not have witnessed.

Unconcerned about suffering Reynard's slings and arrows, I pushed past Corbett into the room. From twenty feet away, Reynard looked asleep. His bare head was sagged, his deep widow's peak pointing down toward the crown in his hands. But something was off. Humans are always in motion. Breathing, blinking, tensing, and relaxing. Reynard was too still.

I closed the distance, eyes peeled. Despite the reputation those in my profession had for being conked over the head, I'd managed to avoid being blindsided by living under the assumption a killer lurked around every corner.

Reynard's eyes were open and still wet. He wasn't bleeding much, what with the murder weapon still in his body, and the loud robe did a good job covering up what blood was present. The spiked crown had been driven into Reynard's chest, the circle of sword points deep enough to pin him to his throne.

Ding, dong.

The king was dead.

I KNEW YOU SHOULDN'T PRESUME DEATH, but Reynard was past resuscitation. He had blades through his heart, lungs, liver, and ganglion—the hub of the central nervous system. Good thing I had Corbett with me. It was getting stale, being framed for murder on every case.

Corbett mustered the courage to approach the throne. "Is the *Tome of All Tales* here?"

"What's it look like?"

"It's locked in a metal case."

So the same case that had held the list of suspects Reynard had given me earlier. I slipped on my gloves and searched Reynard and the throne as gingerly as possible.

"It's gone."

Corbett gulped. "It has everything in it. All the secrets. And the endings."

"You're kidding me."

"Mr. Reynard releases the scripts as they are filmed. He's the only one who knows what's going to happen." Softer, he added, "It drives the cast crazy."

That made the series bible the most expensive book on the planet. People killed for love or money. Now both motives were on the table. It was time to call the cops. I scrolled down my contacts until I hit *Cutie Pie,* the nickname I chose for Special Investigator Stern in anticipation of the day she seized my phone as evidence. She didn't pick up, so I texted:

R. R. Reynard dead. Get to Chateau d'Loire ASAP. Service elevator off the kitchen. Look for the Jack of Diamonds. Did you miss me?

It was succinct but covered the major points.

"Corbett, I need you to go down and wait for the lady cop you saw with me in that video. I should stay put. The killer might still be here, in one of these side rooms."

The situation was dawning on Corbett. His eyes were glassy to the point I could see myself reflected in them. "Okay, Ken."

I walked him to the door. "Breathe, Corbett. And don't lock your knees."

"Got it."

I closed the door behind Corbett and went back to Reynard. The way he'd passed a hand over the book stuck in my head. His signet ring was on that same hand. Up until a recent fallout, I had been close friends with Ray Ford, the top special-effects expert in This Town. From Ray, I knew a mundane object could conceal fancy gadgetry. I slipped the ring off Reynard's finger and tucked it into my pocket.

As tempting as it was to go hunting for the killer, there were two doors off the throne room, located on opposite walls. If the killer was still here, they could sneak out from one room while I was searching the other. The smart thing was to stand guard and wait for the cavalry.

I reached for my Quarreler before realizing there wasn't any point. At the end of my last big adventure, I took a principled stand that cost me one of my closest friends. But Ray Ford had been more than that. He had also supplied the gadgets that gave me an edge. There was no longer any super in my sleuthing. I was unarmed and unarmored. Thus far, I'd kept that development secret.

The Chateau was an old joint. It made a lot of little weird noises. Every one of them sounded like a murderer creeping about. I stayed put. Discipline, that was me. My whole life, what I lacked in brains, I made up for in dogged determination. I once stood outside a kwoon for three days to prove I was serious about learning. My prostate was fresher back then.

Fortunately, I only had to wait ten minutes before I heard a key in the door. Seeing as that was a suspiciously fast response time, I angled to watch all three doors. Special Investigator Ava Stern stalked over the threshold. She might have had her gun drawn, I couldn't say. I was too busy taking her in.

"What the hell are you wearing?"

Stern was gussied up for the convention. She had sculpted metal plates on her upper and lower arms, thighs, and shins, with a gladiator-style chest piece tying it all together. Anywhere that wasn't metal was oxblood leather, down to a strappy kilt thing made redundant by her leg plates. A pair of short swords were crossed at her lower back. Her auburn hair was up, bound in place by the gold coil she'd been wearing on our last case. In street clothes, it had looked out of place, but here it fit right in.

"Please tell me you're undercover."

"Quiet, Allen."

Stern moved softly for a person in sandals. I kept close, my eyes peeled. Both doors into the adjoining rooms were closed. It didn't take her long to come to the same conclusion I had about Reynard. Her eyes narrowed as she fished around the throne.

"No bible."

"Don't tell me you converted to this hokum."

"The series bible, Allen. The killer must have taken it." Stern surveyed the surroundings. "Tell me you stayed out of those rooms."

"I don't get by just on looks."

"No argument there. Okay. Keep watch."

Stern went in the left room first. A minute later she came out and went right. Another minute after that, she exited, shaking her head. "Killer moved quick."

"No one came out of the elevator since I went down and back up."

"Which means they're still on this floor."

"Unless they climbed out a window."

Stern gave me a namesake stare-down. "We're seven stories up."

"Parkour. We've seen it before."

"Why is it every time I get a weird one, there you are?"

I smiled into a shrug. "It's a gift."

Stern dug out her phone, started to dial, then stopped. When she talked, it was more to herself than me. "What's the right play here, Ahava?"

Stern was suffering a real crisis if she was busting out her Hebrew name. I figured with her on watch, it was my turn to poke around. She'd closed the doors behind her, but I was still gloved up. The left room was a deluxe bedroom, with stone veneer walls meant to echo the hotel exterior and a herringbone-pattern floor. There was a full fireplace, which was the first stop in looking for the book. The chimney was bricked up and the logs were polyurethane, with a built-in light system to fake flame. You couldn't have hidden the series bible in that space no matter how hard you tried. The bed was slightly disturbed, with the tucked covers bunched toward the end. I could make out where hands had gripped and pulled. There was nothing under the bed. The cushion on the chair was nudged forward, like someone had been on the edge of their seat. The book wasn't stashed in there either. Nor was it behind the curtains, which were open. The closet was big enough to rate double doors. Clothes were hung up on the bar. More period stuff, including a fur-lined bathrobe and cloak. There were negligees in two different sizes, both new, neither of which would have fit Reynard. Two wood boxes were stacked on the high shelf. There was a little crown in each, meant for a monarch-in-training or something. One was more feminine, like a tiara, and the other more masculine. Was there a word for that? A tiarzan maybe.

The bathroom was swank, with a quartz tub and sink. The water closet had a chain. Nothing was hidden in the tank. Reynard had a deluxe kit bag, the grooming implements tethered down. He'd brought his own toiletries in fancy bottles. He had prescriptions for both Viagra and Cialis, along with low-dose HGH, testosterone, and Adderall. The full anti-aging productivity package. One towel had been used, though the shower was dry. I stayed away from it. Stern for sure would want it DNA tested.

I crossed the throne room and headed to the other door. Stern was on the phone now, saying something about keeping it under wraps. When she tried to get my attention, I pretended like I had lost my peripheral vision in a tragic accident.

The last room was a combination dining room and kitchenette. I turned it over—well, I gently folded it over. There was nothing in any of the appliances. The cabinets came pre-stocked with dishes and cookware, none of which had been touched. There was a standing broom closet, the only contents being hotel-provided dry cleaning bags.

The book was nowhere to be found.

Stern was still on the phone when I came out. She had a tone I'd never heard out of her before. The sort you used when appealing to a higher-up. Corbett was leaning against the closed entrance door, barely holding on. I employed a soothing gesture from outside his personal space.

"Don't worry, the white hats are on the job."

Corbett took a breath. "Did you find the tome?"

Stern not displaying any emotion over Reynard being murdered was one thing. She dealt with death on a daily basis. But Corbett knew the guy. I hoped when I kicked the bucket, the first reaction of those closest to me wasn't to ask where my stuff had gone.

"The killer must have taken it with them."

Stern tucked her phone away. "Okay, Allen, get over here. Stay put, Corbett, you're next."

I jogged over with exaggerated arm pumping. "What's the plan, boss?"

"As the actual cop, I'll ask the questions. Why did Reynard want to meet you?"

I did my best to stay stone-faced, but the way she was done up made it hard to take her *just-the-facts* attitude seriously. "He hired me to find out who wanted to kill him."

"Great job."

"Cut me some slack. I was on the case for maybe half an hour. And I left my pavise in my other jacket."

Stern studied me. "Know why Reynard settled on you?"

"He received a referral from a mutual acquaintance."

"Who?"

"Alexi Mirovich."

My answer genuinely surprised her. "How is it you know Mirovich?"

"I beat him up once."

The way she looked at me. "You're testing my patience, Allen."

"Don't worry, you're passing with flying colors."

Stern exhaled through her nose. She wasn't normally so touchy. Me peeking into her private life had always been a soft spot, and now I was getting quite the gander. I couldn't help but wonder who she was here with. People rarely attended conventions alone. She looked past me toward Corbett, who had started to pace like he was waiting for an open stall.

"He's rattled," I said. "We better take the show to him."

"Wait." Stern walked me behind the throne. "Was he with you the entire time?"

I groaned at not having thought of it first. "No. He came down thirty minutes after."

Stern power walked toward Corbett. The getup did wonders for her silhouette. If I was Corbett, I'd be shaking in my pantaloons. I can say that with confidence, because when we met, I had been Corbett—the prime suspect in a high-profile homicide. I stayed two steps behind Stern, ready to play good cop.

"Corbett! Did you kill Reynard?"

Corbett was pale to start with. At processing Stern's question, he shifted toward blue. "What? No." He looked around, then turned inward in the quest for proof. "I couldn't have done that."

Stern spun him into the door and kicked his feet apart. She had mastered the move, another thing I knew first hand. She patted him down, tossing his laptop and scepter to the ground. "Did you steal the series bible?"

"No!"

"You know what a grace period is, Corbett?"

"Yes, I think?"

Stern spun him back around to lock eyes. "This is it. You currently exist in that narrow window after a crisis moment where people do dumb things nice cops like me forgive and forget. That window closes in ten seconds."

Corbett went quiet, unless you counted gulping.

"Tick tock, Corbett."

"I didn't . . . I need to sit down."

Corbett melted down the wall until his butt hit the red carpet. Stern kept on with the stare.

"Okay, here's the plan. Right now, there are only four people who know Reynard is dead: me, you, Allen, and the killer. If word gets out, this place is going to riot and after an hour there's going to be more press here than guests."

It started to dawn on me what Stern was getting at. "Which means the killer can slip out no problem."

"Now you're getting it, Allen. The department is setting up a perimeter. Anyone who leaves the hotel gets logged, questioned, and searched. Forensics is coming up in disguise to deal with the scene and body. Meanwhile, I get on with the investigation."

Stern was a lone wolf. The fact that she got away with it spoke to her results.

But no way was I going to get squeezed out of this one.

I batted my lashes. "You mean *we* get on with the investigation."

"Sorry, Allen. Professionals only."

"I am a professional, with a client and a signed contract."

Stern dug around for the antique cigarette case she kept her gum in. "Yeah? Can your client Venmo you from the afterlife?"

"That's for Reynard's estate to sort out."

"No dice, Allen. Thanks for doing your civic duty."

It wasn't only that I felt like a boob, signing up with Reynard only to have him killed on my watch moments after. The case was also too juicy to let go.

There had to be an angle Stern could stomach.

"You interrogating people raises questions. A badge tells them something has happened. But I'm not a cop. As a private eye, I could be investigating anything. It doesn't have to be a crime."

Stern didn't say *hmmm*, but she thought it pretty hard. I'd run out of carrot.

It was time for a little stick.

"And I already know what I know. Boot me now and who can tell what I'll get up to. I'm either on a short leash or no leash at all. That's up to you."

"We've been getting along so well, Allen. Why ruin it?"

"A detective needs cases, and cases don't get any bigger than this. If I let you chase me away from every gig I land, you're going to run me off the map. And you keep cribbing the credit for all my solves."

Stern looked to the heavens to gather herself. "Fine."

"Consider me the Hutch to your Starsky."

"More like the Lacey to my Cagney." Stern went over to wait by the door for the stealth forensics team. "And I didn't want your thunder, Allen. If I could hand it over, I would in a second."

———

An hour later, forensics showed up dressed like caterers, the tools of their trade stashed in rolling carts. Stern handed the scene over, and Corbett along with it, and we went into the hallway to strategize.

"Command has the elevator locked down," Stern informed me. "Stair access is for emergencies only. I need to talk to hotel administration, confirm the fire alarm is working, and find out what the surveillance camera situation is like."

"There aren't any. Chateau d'Loire is a no-tell motel. It's part of the appeal for celebrities." The look Stern gave me made me defensive. "What? I'm a trivia buff."

While Stern called the desk, I checked out the maintenance closets. Both were locked. When I had all my gadgets, a lock-picker thingy had been among them. Now all I could do was jiggle the handle. The only other doors on the floor led to the three remaining suites, none of which had bloody footprints leading to them.

Stern kept her voice low. "Staff says the fire exits are alarmed. Maintenance checked them right before the con. We have to take their word for it, because if the alarm goes off from us confirming, the whole building will clear out."

"I tried the maintenance doors, but they don't take Diner's Club."

"I'll have a key sent up."

"So that leaves the other suites. What do you say we go left of the elevator first and work counterclockwise?"

Stern froze. "The killer didn't come from that suite."

I didn't bother asking how she knew. It was all over her face.

"Ah, that's how you got here so fast. No commute. You were already here, with whoever is in that suite."

"KEEP IT DOWN, ALLEN."

Stern got close enough where I could smell her gum was wintergreen. "No one knows about us. And I mean no one."

"Does he or she know? Because that's two people right off: you and them. Then one more minimum because you had to get penthouse clearance, so he or she had to tell someone to put you on the list. I'm guessing that someone is Corbett. He's the high gofer around these parts."

"He or she is not a suspect, discussion over."

"And you were calling me unprofessional. You're snuggled up to one person of interest, and another person of interest has leverage on you. I don't have my copy of *Criminal Justice for Dummies* on me, but I think that constitutes a conflict."

"I'm their alibi."

"Yeah? Were you with them the entire time?"

Stern opened her mouth to give me guff, then ground her teeth.

"I was in the other room, going through my morning routine and getting all this on. It took a while."

"Was the door open or shut?"

"I like my privacy."

"Oh, come on." I threw my hands in the air. "This is all very uncoplike of you."

"I'd like to think I'm a good enough judge of character not to screw a killer, Allen."

"So it's serious then. Have they met your parents?"

"Grow up." Stern took out her phone. On principle, I don't like to eavesdrop, but as an unbiased investigator, it was my duty. She typed: *Stay put, don't talk to anyone.* The contact name was *Blank*. Not vacant, but the word *Blank*. She put her phone away and said, "Let's go clockwise."

Which was the exact opposite of my suggestion.

"Sounds great." I followed her as she strode off. Two steps from the door, I tapped her pauldron. "Aren't you going to deputize me?"

"If you want to see stars, I can oblige, Allen."

The door was arched and thick, like the others leading to suites, with a peephole and a knocker shaped like a horse head with a ring in its mouth.

Stern's first three knocks were ignored. She took out her phone and said, loudly, "Desk will bring up a key."

The door opened ten seconds later. A guy twenty years younger than me who could have posed for a Greek sculptor peeked out through the chained crack.

"Yes?"

"There's been a theft." Stern wedged her badge into the gap. "We're questioning everyone on this floor."

A masculine voice projected from inside. The words were clean and clear, the sign of someone stage trained.

Stern answered him.

"I don't need a warrant. I have cause and there are exigent circumstances. But if you insist, I can hold you here until a judge gets around to it, then bring in some more cops."

The unseen voice bid the doorman admit us. We stepped into a turreted room much like Reynard's, transitioned from the sixties to the seventies. The low-backed carved wood throne stood at the far side of a conversation pit with a circular firebowl in the center. Being in fire-phobic California, the bowl was stocked with fake coals glowing from a cherry light source below. The pit was ringed by a circular couch, broken up with inset tables, including one on each side of the throne.

The man occupying the royal seat was of senior age but not yet elderly. The only thing he had on besides a blue velvet robe was a watch, turned so the face was inside his left wrist. He was sharp featured, with precise cheekbones and a thin nose. His widow's peak was receding, the platinum locks swept back to shoulder length.

As usual, I couldn't contain myself. "Hey, I know you. You were Dust in *Star Searchers*."

"Wonderful. A fan."

I laughed at the dripping sarcasm. "That's such a Dust thing to say. Have to admit, that movie still holds up after thirty years."

"Mr. Hammersmith, I'm Special Investigator Ava Stern. This is Ken Allen, a private dick. A theft has been reported."

Hammersmith looked good for a guy in his seventies, with rangy muscle on all four limbs. I watched him spin his wheels. There was no reaction to hearing about a theft. He stopped to drink from a silver cup whose dimensions were normally reserved for someone winning a championship.

"Whatever it was, it must have been valuable. You didn't even stop to change clothes, Special Investigator." Hammersmith took another sip. "Even with your things so near at hand."

So much for Stern's clandestine relationship.

She handled it pretty well, but went for more gum, which was her tell. I stepped in to let her regroup.

"When is the last time either of you left the room?"

"Not since the evening prior. We ordered in. I would be overwhelmed, were I to brave the masses below."

"Anyone else here? Anyone show up in the last hour?"

"I'm sure the front desk can confirm we are alone."

"So far, so good. Any way you can back your story?"

"Well, how fortunate for us that we've been filming." Hammersmith rested his lips against the rim of his cup. "Would you like to review the footage?"

Stern snapped her gum case shut. "Queue it up."

They were playing a game of chicken. Hammersmith wasn't about to blink. "Fairchild, if you would."

That put a name to Hammersmith's boy toy, who retrieved a tablet from a side table. Fairchild looked less than enthused about a forced postmortem of their intimate moments.

"Don't worry," I told him. "You aren't being graded."

Fairchild brought up a folder titled *Raw*—possibly a reference to the footage, possibly not, from what I saw next—which had a few dozen files in it. He tapped the latest one and a video came up.

The shoot was set in the room we were standing in. Hammersmith was still in the robe, with nothing underneath. If I looked as good at seventy, I'd probably want video documentation too. He stayed where he was, on the throne. Fairchild did all the work, and the man didn't cut corners. As demure as he acted about sharing the footage, he had nothing to be ashamed of. Hammersmith either. No wonder he didn't mind fresh eyes on their home movies.

As gripping as the acts depicted were, I focused on everything but the coitus. The frame stamps confirmed the date and time. The room looked the same, at least what the camera showed. They hadn't cleaned up or stashed anything in the moment it took to open the door.

With the viewing party wrapped, Stern rebroke the ice. "Mind if we look around?"

"Greatly, but I cannot envision my privacy violated any more egregiously than it already has been, so do what you must."

Stern went right for the bedroom. I broke the opposite way but didn't get two steps before she heeled me.

"Over here, Allen."

The bedroom was the same dimensions as Reynard's had been, but this one had more of a cozy country-manor theme, with a low king bed, hearth, and in-room stone jacuzzi. Fairchild, at least I assume it was Fairchild based on the dynamic I had thus far witnessed, had been busy. They were fully unpacked and into bubble baths enough to bring their own caddy. Stern turned the place over with a soft touch. I watched her technique closely. Not only did I loathe snooping, which was a negative trait in my chosen profession, but I also had come to sleuthing later in life. It was always good to improve one's skill set.

We didn't turn up Reynard's book or a pair of bloody gloves. They had all the markings of a long-term couple: matching luggage, shared toiletries, overlapping personal spaces.

We crossed to the other room. The kitchenette in this suite was set up as a formal dining room. The pantry was stocked with elegant spread supplies: artisan carbohydrates, cheese, nuts, cured meats, fancy fruit like figs, and caviar. I didn't know enough about wine to comment, but the labels were yellowing so I'm guessing it was quality stuff. The unopened champagne was from the proper region to not technically be sparkling wine.

Some dishes were drying in the rack: three mugs, two juice glasses, a spoon, and a butter knife. Stern found the trash and went digging. No book, but I caught a glimpse of an energy bar wrapper. I knew the brand. It was not something you'd find in a vending machine. There were no matching bars in the pantry or closet. There was also an empty artificial sweetener packet, a monk-fruit blend. Again, not something you'd find on a room-service cart, and no others of its type were present.

Stern strode back to the throne room. I rushed to keep up. A fresh silence lingered in the air. Fairchild's robe swayed slightly, as if he had suddenly stepped away from Hammersmith. Stern got close enough to them as to be inhaling their exhales.

"Okay. This floor is on lockdown until we've cleared it."

Hammersmith leaned back. His knotted belt performed its job admirably. "Somehow we shall endure."

"If you get any visitors, contact me."

Stern handed Fairchild a card. I added one of my own on top, saying, "And if I could get the number of your robe guy, that would be great."

Neither man graced us with a reply. We let ourselves out. When we hit the elevator intersection, I broke the silence.

"Are we comparing notes?"

"Sure, you first."

"Whoever else was in there is into fitness, namely hitting their protein goals. It will be someone with muscle. Probably over one hundred eighty, so either a male or a pretty jacked woman."

"Why one eighty?"

"Normal protein bars are twenty grams. Enough for a smaller person, but not someone my size. There are thirty grams in those bars."

"Not bad, Allen."

"Good enough for you to take a turn?"

Stern stopped and thought. She had more than one nugget and was deciding which one to share. "There was a scent when we came in. A cheap one, like body spray. No matching can in their bathroom. I got close enough to get a whiff; it wasn't from either of them. Back to you, Allen."

"There were two of everything but mugs. The extra mug goes with the single sweetener packet. Whoever used it probably brought more. A person who totes around their own sweetener doesn't just bring one for the whole weekend. Back at ya."

Stern contorted to reach a well-armored itch. "I'll admit this one is soft, but they were being weird. Hammersmith's squeeze is on the show, in a nonspeaking part. Fairchild isn't his real name. It's his character's name."

"That is weird. Is Fairchild an Edgelord?"

"He could be," Stern decided. "I thought you didn't know thing one about the show."

"Reynard gave me a summary. He thought maybe an Edgelord was the potential killer. Hammersmith rates a penthouse, which makes him important. Who does he play on the show?"

"Potens of Wythane, patriarch of a banished line who were cheated out of the throne. He overthrew—"

"So a villain, got it."

Stern squinted. "*The Lands Beyond* doesn't really have villains. I mean, the Wythanes have done some egregious stuff, but they were wronged. They had a legitimate claim—"

Normally I couldn't get five consecutive words out of Stern, now she wouldn't shut up. "What's Hammersmith got to lose, if Reynard offed his character?"

"Not much," Stern said. "The show reignited his career. He does movies in the off-season, and now he's a theater draw."

"Well, the footage clears him and Fairchild anyway."

Stern winced, weighing the disclosure.

Surprisingly, she spilled.

"The time stamp was changed. It didn't match Hammersmith's watch in the footage."

"That's what took so long. They were staging the room. Hey, thanks for sharing."

Stern kept chasing that itch. "It felt wrong, letting you labor under a misconception."

"Still, I don't think either of them did Reynard in. I can get that for you."

Stern shook her head. "What makes you so sure?"

"Their hands. Reynard's crown is a mess of blades. Whoever used it for sure cut themselves, shoving it so deep. Which eliminates Corbett too. His hands were clean, so to speak."

Stern weighed that thought and approved the heft. "Then the killer must be behind the last door."

"Second to last. We're going to have to talk to your not-so-sneaky link."

"Don't push me, Allen."

"Hammersmith knew your big secret, and he was literally the first person we talked to. No way you aren't exposed. Might as well get it in under the wire. When your boss finds out, you're getting yanked."

Glaring, Stern knocked harder than she needed to on the next door. The knocker was a dragon this time. We didn't have to wait long. The door swung wide to reveal Alexi Mirovich.

"Ken! Is this your woman?"

Now, in theory Alexi could handle Stern. He was an ex-world champion who outweighed her by eighty pounds. In practice, I scrambled to save his life.

"English isn't his first language," I told Stern.

"If he keeps it up, it's going to be his last."

A feminine voice from the throne room intervened. "Let them in, Alexi."

Alexi thumped his own forehead a few times at his lack of decorum. He moved aside to unblock the way, closing the door behind us as we passed.

Reynard's suite had been midcentury; Hammersmith's leaned Lloyd Wright. This suite was pure Victorian. Everything looked equal parts aesthetic and uncomfortable. The throne was high-backed and wide-bottomed, to allow for a gown—the seat of a queen.

Said gown was in an unusual design: green lace over silver satin. The lace was custom, a blend of crescents and circles. Silvered armor speckled her ensemble: a gorget, one pauldron, one bracer, and a girdle. There was a karambit, a sickle-shaped Indonesian knife popular in self-defense circles, sheathed on her girdle. The ensemble made it hard to judge her height, age, or anything else. Her skin was beyond pale, her eyes silver gray. Her hair was a cascade of black waves. It had to be extensions. No one had that much hair. Maintaining it would be a full-time gig on its own. She wore a circlet that met with a V on her brow, with a crescent pointing up like bull horns.

"So, who are you, the Moon Queen?"

She either chuckled or scoffed. "We didn't think there was a person in this building who hasn't seen the show."

"We?" I looked to Stern. "Is this a bit?"

Stern was locked in a trance. Her cheeks were as red as her hair. I resisted the urge to rib her. The truth was, none of us knew who was going to make us starstruck.

"I'm Ken Allen, a PI. This is Special Investigator Stern. There's been a theft from one of the suites. We have reason to believe the thief and stolen property are still on this floor."

The queen stared into me with those wolfish eyes. They had to be colored contacts. Peepers like that were not naturally occurring. I held real still. Stern hadn't found her voice yet.

"This is more serious than you are presenting," the queen decided. "It has to do with Reynard."

"What makes you say that?"

"Alexi was not surprised to see you, and he had an audience with Reynard earlier. We found that unusual, but Reynard is a combat sports enthusiast. It's why he sought Alexi out. He likes proven warriors."

"Pretty good. Look, when this show thing wraps, ever think about detecting? 'Ken Allen and the Lunar Lady' has a ring to it."

Stern found her voice. "Dame of the Moon."

"Welcome back. What's that?"

"She's the Dame of the Moon, not the Moon Queen."

"Dame? Now there's a word we ditched. And *gunsel*. I miss *gunsel*."

"It's the *Tome of All Tales*," the Dame of the Moon interrupted. "Someone has stolen the series bible. And you two are trying to recover it before the hundreds of followers in the floors below learn it is missing."

Jesus Christ. "Lady, you are something else. How'd you get on the show? Walk into the audition and foresee Reynard would hire you?"

"No one knows who she is," Stern informed me. "She came out of nowhere."

"Spooky. Look, uh, Dame, you got us. I don't suppose you have the book or know where it is."

"We do not."

I caught Alexi's eye and raised my hands like I wanted to play patty-cake. "Do this."

Alexi complied. His hands were pristine, which was a relief. No doubt he had what it took to pin Reynard to the throne, but his mitts were so big, no way he wouldn't cut himself on the crown. I really didn't want it to be him, and not just because he could have flattened me. I had a soft spot for the guy.

"Has anyone been around this morning?"

The Dame of the Moon shook her head.

"You hear anything?"

Again with the head shake.

"How about your crystal ball? Anything come up?"

The Dame of the Moon gave me a slow blink. Maybe, just maybe, the corner of her mouth twitched upward. What can I say? My irresistible charm had done it again.

"Would you like a reading, Mr. Allen?"

"Sure. Personally, my favorite is *Where the Wild Things Are* but I'm guessing you're big on *Goodnight Moon*."

Her jaw clenched, but she didn't break. The woman could keep in character. "Alexi, would you bring our table over?"

Alexi retrieved said table from the room that had been a kitchenette in the previous suites. It was a circle of ash, stained black, inset with a large mother-of-pearl crescent moon and carved with chimeric animals: winged wolves, a stag with horns made of briar, a crystal lion. Probably a prop from the show. The Dame of the Moon produced a deck. I use that word because she set her hand on the table, and when she lifted it, the cards were stacked there. She turned her hand over, gesturing for me to approach.

"Shuffle the cards to your satisfaction, then cut the deck."

I picked up the cards. They were old timey, with deckled edges. The backs had star patterns centered around a crescent moon. Another prop from the show, by my guess. The cards were too thick to riffle. I shifted them around as if it mattered, then ran my thumb along the side, like I was deciding, and cut the deck shallowly. I was standing, and she sitting, but it felt like the Dame was looking down on me.

"Are you satisfied?"

"Happy as a clam."

The Dame of the Moon passed her hand over the deck three times, each time leaving a card facedown on the table. Her nails were almond shaped, the polish a luminescent pearl that caught the light like oil on water.

"This reading passes through the three phases of your life, Ken Allen. The first card speaks to your past."

The Dame flicked her fingers over the card, turning it face up without appearing to touch it. On the card, a man hung upside down from a tree, his head surrounded in a halo of light.

"The Hanged Man. You have sacrificed deeply, but gained knowledge."

I did my best not to make a spooky ghost noise. So far, I wasn't impressed. My past was public record, the broad strokes at least. Even before the Jove Brand killings, I had my own Wikipedia entry. Now that I'd switched careers and been cleared of murder, it had gotten revised and relocked:

> *Ken Allen is an American private detective. A one-time actor and martial arts expert, he is best known for playing Jove Brand in the foreign-only release* Near Death.[1][2] *Chosen for the famous role based on his strong resemblance to the character, as well as his physical ability, Allen was an unknown at the time of his casting. A cultural oddity, Allen's sole film credit to date is the lead role in one of the largest movie franchises of all time. He was also once known as the Sensei to the Stars.* [citation needed]

On top of that, I'd made the news cycle twice in the last year. While the details of each case were hazy, I had a reputation for being in the eye of the storm and keeping quiet about it, when talking might have won me fame and fortune.

"The second card represents the present." There was something musical in the way she landed on the words. The Dame had voice training.

She flickered her fingers again, revealing a tower topped with a crown being shattered by lightning. Flames danced in its windows as people fell from its heights.

"Destruction, danger, and unforeseen change. The situation is far more dire than you reveal. Beyond a simple theft. Our world is set to crumble."

"If my quest doesn't succeed, of course."

The Dame looked from the card to me. "No. Once it has fallen, the tower cannot be raised. What has been done cannot be undone."

I looked down at the final card. "I know I should stay, but you only live once. Hit me, dealer."

The Dame revealed the last card, which depicted Adam and Eve in the garden of Eden, an angel filling the sky above them.

"This card glimpses into your future. The personal change you have experienced is all-encompassing. You have gained and lost. What relationships have survived now flourish. But you must be willing to bare yourself fully to find the connection you crave."

I exhaled in thought. "Dame, I gotta tell you, I don't think baring it all is the way to go, when it comes to courting."

"You jest because you sense the truth in our reading."

Stern found her sea legs. "If the book isn't here, you wouldn't mind if we looked around, would you?"

"We mind greatly. Our mysteries must remain our own."

"You're the only guest to say no."

The Dame stared into Stern.

"You and your beau are a good match. Both of you are skilled manipulators. I wonder if you also share his cavalier attitude toward fidelity."

First Hammersmith, now the Dame of the Moon. So far, we hadn't run into anyone who didn't know about Stern's supposed secret relationship.

It was as close as I ever witnessed Stern come to breaking. She took a step forward, hands clenched, then checked herself, coming to a stop so fast she almost stumbled. "Guess we'll have to get a warrant."

The Dame didn't blink. "If you wish."

The four of us lingered until I broke the silence. "Any hot tips before we get out of here? The spirits whispering something that might help?"

The Dame swept her cards from the table with a single motion. They disappeared back to wherever they had come from. "Chateau d'Loire is a storied location. What you say is true. Spirits roam its passages. Secrets dwell in its shadows. Alexi, if you would see our guests to the door."

Alexi's English was a work in progress, but the Dame of the Moon included a magnanimous gesture, which Alexi took as a cue. As we walked out, he put an arm around me.

"She has very good magic."

"It was something else all right. Are you and her . . ." I struggled to find words Alexi would understand. "Are you her man?"

"No. Not with *gadalka*. She is . . ."

Alexi moved his hands like he was holding an invisible slinky, at a loss for the English word. I would have asked for Alexi to spell whatever he had called the Dame, but Russian letters wouldn't do me any good.

"Buddy, you gotta keep quiet about Reynard."

"I never say, Ken. Gadalka knows. When I return, she knows."

He closed the door gently behind us. Stern was in her head. I stopped her at the intersection.

"Quite the act, huh? She's going to clean up this weekend. Imagine what a fan would pay to get a tarot reading from the Dame of the Moon herself."

"You didn't seem too impressed."

"The cards are marked. You can feel which one you're getting from the edges. The Dame showed me the cards she wanted to show. Speaking of which, her hands were free of injury."

"Alexi would have been able to do Reynard in. And he's already got one murder under his belt."

"If Russian media is to be believed. And Alexi wouldn't need a weapon to take Reynard out. Anyway, whoever killed Reynard, the way they did it speaks of something. Hate. Or symbolism."

Which was odd, because the prior attempts on Reynard's life had been the opposite: distant and technical rather than up close and personal. Not that I was sharing that with Stern. "Anyway, if Alexi was going to do it, why refer me to Reynard, then kill him after I was on the job?"

"Maybe he estimated you."

"You mean underestimated."

"I know what I meant."

As much as I was game for a good roasting, I had other things on my mind. "Back in there, what did you say about no one knowing who the Dame of the Moon is?"

"She was an unknown before the show. Not just uncredited but nonexistent. She didn't audition. Reynard hired her out of the blue. The fan base has been digging for ten years and all they've come up with is conspiracy theories."

"Reynard's core fandom comes from his old show *Never After*. Maybe the Dame slid in that way. She has a fairy-tale feel about her."

"You know about *Never After*? I'm surprised, Allen."

"Yeah, I also use my ears."

"But she would have been only what, three or four years old back then."

"Some people look way younger than they are."

Stern went for her gum. "Your first two cards checked out, but what was she trying to say with that last one?"

"I dunno, maybe she likes me."

Stern's phone went off. I'd never heard it make a sound, but a vintage police cruiser siren blared to life. She dug for it like she had three seconds before it blew. "Quiet, Allen. I mean it this time."

After a quick, "I'm here," Stern went silent herself. As requested, I kept my trap shut. Anyway, I was too busy trying to listen, with mixed results.

She was getting chewed out something fierce. The tone was clear enough: *I'm not mad, but I'm disappointed.*

The dressing down went on for maybe three minutes, but it felt like three hours, and I was getting it second hand. Stern had to say she understood twice before she was hung up on. She stared at her phone, thinking hard.

"There's already been a leak. A big one. And I've been outed. I'm off the case." Stern grabbed me by the lapels. Her eyes were a deep blue. The color of troubled waters. "Look at me, Allen. Do you really know what you're doing, or have you just been getting lucky bounces?"

I didn't trust my ability to lie to her. I wasn't much of an actor, and that's not modesty. About a hundred million people shared the same opinion. "It's half and half."

She rubbed my lapels between her fingers. "What happened to your bulletproof coat?"

"Left it at the cleaners."

"This is on you now, Allen. Do not leave this building. Stay away from anyone who looks like a badge. And change your outfit. You stick out like a sore thumb."

Stern tapped a fist against my chest, then jammed the elevator button hard enough to break it. "Check your phone. I'll be in touch."

I nodded as the elevator doors closed. When I was sure they were staying that way, I spun around and went right for the fourth door.

THE LAST DOOR HAD A KNIGHT'S-HELM motif for a knocker. I stepped to the side of the peephole and clapped it at a steady pace. Stern had told whoever was inside to hunker down, but incessant tapping was like water torture—a sane person could only endure it for so long. Fortyish taps in, the door whipped open, and I might as well have been looking into the mirror.

The occupant of the final suite was a few inches over six feet, with thick, slightly wavy blond hair and cobalt-blue eyes. He had a solid frame, fit enough to have a triangular silhouette in street clothes without crossing over into bulky. His skin was pale but glowing with health. His teeth were precisely off-white enough as to not shine distractingly under production lighting. There was no glimmer of confusion at my appearance in his doorway. He knew me on sight. His eyes flicked from my head to toes and back.

"Very good." He turned his back on me, waving me in. "I've been hoping to meet you."

The fourth suite shared the same layout of the other three. This was the most fairy tale of the lot, done in marble with shining brass accents.

The throne was wing backed, literally, designed so the occupant looked like an angel. My host waved at it in dismissal, turning toward the kitchen.

"Let's not stand on ceremony."

The kitchen was a cottagecore dream, holly and stone with a faux hearth that could double as a hockey net. My host went right to the retrofitted woodstove.

"Please sit and partake of my frittata."

It smelled too good to be true. "There any potatoes in there?"

"Not if I wish to fit into the increasingly outlandish costumes wardrobe devises. I've begun to suspect production is devising a fabric that will somehow display my abdomen."

He tilted the cast-iron pan to show a cross-section from where two pieces were missing—his and Stern's breakfast.

"Then sure."

He stocked the table with two reasonably portioned plates, a pair of stone mugs, a carafe, and no less than three awkward apologies. Sitting down, he dug right in. "I'm embarrassed to admit my meals are strictly scheduled. And equally so that I enjoy it that way. I find comfort in routine."

The frittata was dynamite. The feta was gooey without interfering with the fluffiness. Three bites in I reminded myself I was here on a mission.

"Since we're sharing, I gotta admit I have no idea who you are." The coffee was strong, with cinnamon notes. "Never seen the show."

"Then that makes two. I can't bear to watch myself perform. My name is Blake Dever. Pardon me for not offering a hand. If I escape this contractually required weekend without contracting diphtheria, I will count myself fortunate."

Dever's deprecating energy was making my skin crawl. I had to wonder what the heck Stern saw in this guy. I mean, besides being incredibly attractive, successful in his field, presumably wealthy, and a great cook. "What did Stern tell you?"

"Only that I should remain in my room and not speak to anyone."

Yet here we were, conversing. Whatever his motives, I wasn't about to talk Dever out of providing me the opportunity to grill him. It was time to build trust, and he'd figure out what I was up to eventually anyway.

"Reynard is dead. The killer is on the loose and the story bible is missing."

I watched Dever closely, wishing I knew more about his acting. As in, was he any good at it and what were his go-to moves when called upon to feign surprise.

Dever flinched as if being struck before descending into consideration. "Are you sure he was murdered?"

"I guess he could have tripped."

Dever quirked an eye. "You're delightfully acerbic. So Ava was attempting to protect me, due to my proximity to the crime."

"And keep a lid on your relationship."

"I've told her more than once it is only a matter of time before we are outed, and that it would be best to do so on our own terms. Ava is the most headstrong person I have ever known, which is admirable, but she refuses to accept inevitabilities."

As much as I wanted to delve into the secret life of Ava Stern, there were more pressing matters at hand. "What do you say to a game of pretend?"

"I'm sorry?"

"Pretend I'm a real cop, come to question you. Did you have a motive to kill Reynard?"

"Dear Lord, no. He rescued my career, casting me as both the prince and his rook."

"Wait, you play two parts?"

"Yes. Mallory, heir to the Crucible throne, and Greystone, who was robbed of all memory of his life prior to being magically transformed into a double of the prince. Sort of a play on *The Man in the Iron Mask.* You see, the prince had a twin who died when they were children—"

Again with the show. "Let's stick to the real world. I understand the cast has been paid, whether Reynard kills them off or not. Can you think of anyone who would murder him over their character being offed?"

Dever let that thought have a full lap around the track. "Well, it could affect possible spin-off productions. Such a thing is not in the cards for me. It's doubtful either of my roles will survive the season. If they did, then they would be king. Which doesn't allow for tangential adventures."

The key to a spin-off was to involve as few prior cast members as possible to keep the costs down. A story with Dever as king couldn't swing that.

"Okay. Who could go off on their own?"

"It's almost too long a list. Reynard is an expert at unspoken story. It creates fervent audience interest in the most minor of roles. The fabric of *The Lands Beyond* is an interweaving of a dozen bloodlines and organizations, which serve as source of a popular recurring theme: the choice between duty and family. One could envision a tale surrounding any of these factions. The House of Wythane, for example. Or the Sect of the Moon."

"What about the Edgelords?"

"A very viable possibility. They have a fervent base. The dream of rising through the ranks of fandom to eventually become officially canonized is a heady brew. A fan becoming a star would also make for good marketing."

"Reynard ever hang the possibility of axing someone over their head?"

Dever poured himself a fresh cup. "He threatened to kill all of us, at one time or another. His public humiliations became a rite of passage. It was when he requested a private audience that any of us truly worried. Serious discussions were always held individually and behind closed doors."

Dever got startled by his phone vibrating in his pocket. While he studied the screen, I studied him.

"Including salary negotiations?"

"Indeed."

"The cast ever try to bargain collectively?"

Dever quirked at my question. "You really don't follow the show, do you? Refreshing as that is, I'm afraid you'll have a lot of catching up to do. I'll attempt to be succinct. Initially, core cast members signed a three-year contract. Reynard fought for more, to get us while we were cheap, but was unable to convince the network. Even in the beginning, the production cost was exorbitant. The setting itself demanded it: costumes, sets, special effects. We actors were the smallest portion of the budget."

I joined Dever for a second cup. There was sweetener in the coffee, but not sugar. "So going into season four, the cast finally gets to renegotiate, with three hugely successful seasons behind them. I'm following."

"Henry March played my father, the king of all Crucible. He was our senior statesman, a veteran of both stage and screen. As the king, he was believed to have the most secure role. Rather than exploit his position, he attempted to unite the cast. Henry was no fool. He acted covertly, approaching us each in secret."

The pain on Dever's face told the tale.

"Someone squealed."

Dever gave the ghost of a nod. "To this day, the identity of the perpetrator remains secret. Reynard's retribution was terrible. Henry's character was killed offscreen, his remains slowly devoured by Potens

Wythane in a ploy to absorb the king's divine right, using sorcery to restore his body each day, as if he were Prometheus. Scenes with the captive king were shot using a body and voice double. Henry's character was humiliated and broken over the course of many seasons, turned into a disfigured, simpering madman who betrayed every confidence."

"None of this riled the rest of you up?"

"At that same time, Reynard negotiated generous long-term deals with key cast members, including sharing merchandising rights associated with their characters. It removed the teeth from the jaws of the whole. And the king's fall plot was hugely successful. The audience ate it up, if you'll pardon the pun. It demonstrated to both the viewers and cast that none of us were irreplaceable."

"How does the cast get along these days?"

"Poorly. There is tremendous jealousy over pay disparity, along with interpersonal conflicts. Try to understand, we've shot remotely, in sequestered isolation for ten years."

"You're talking about showmances."

"We're an incestuous bunch. Many feathers have been ruffled beyond any hope of smoothing. And Reynard delights in the conflict. The dissention only adds to the cutthroat nature of the beast. The fandom is equally enamored at rumors of us hopping beds while at each other's throats."

Dever's phone went off again. He kept it under the table while sneaking a peek. I kept him on course.

"The Dame of the Moon said something like that. Your name came up."

Dever scooped up our plates and took them to the sink. "I'm not proud of my past behavior. My journey has been rags to riches. A career saved from the brink and catapulted into stardom. You're aware actors are often conflated with the parts they play."

Looked like Dever knew more about me than I did about him. "It happens."

"I play two parts. One is forceful and steadfast. Unwavering in his duty, honorable in word and deed. The other is tortured with angst over his forgotten past and tasked with atrocities to keep the prince's hands clean."

"If the ladies don't like one, they love the other."

"Indeed. I fell prey to the temptations of fame. My romantic escapades over the last decade have been a dream for the tabloids."

And a nightmare for your current squeeze. "If you were forced to pick a name, who was capable of offing Reynard?"

"I don't feel comfortable accusing someone of murder."

"I'm not asking you to testify. This is a whole new world for me. I'm trying to get my bearings."

Dever went to the window and took in the scenic parking lot. It was the first whiff of acting I detected out of him. Here's a tip: When someone doesn't want you to see their mouth when they are talking it's because of what's coming out of it.

"When an unsavory act is required, Reynard turns to the Edgelords. Many of them have checkered pasts. And, if given the choice of worlds, they would rather live in one of Reynard's making."

"Any of them good with edged weapons?"

Dever laughed. "All of them. Their society requires expertise in such. They train in full panoply, with no holds barred. Long ago the Edgelords replaced the stunt performers. Reynard's personal army surrounds us on set, always listening, vying for their master's favor."

"Bradley Corbett was my point man on this, but the cops have him. Who's next in Reynard's hierarchy?"

Dever affected thinking about it. "Sheila Polk. She is the prototypical Edgelord—the first fan who became canonized as Acacia Wythane, the prodigal daughter—"

"Sheila Polk. Got it."

"And if you could neglect using me as reference that would be lovely. Polk has been attempting to pull me into the fold from the jump."

"Mum's the word." There was one more thing I needed from Dever. I hated to ask, but he was the closest fit. "You got an extra surcoat on you?"

———

Dever was forced to serve as squire. The straps and buckles were not self-explanatory. When he was finished, he stepped back to give me free reign with the mirror.

"I look ridiculous."

Medieval was not my style. Dever lent me what he called a gambeson: a button-up, quilted three-quarter length jacket the color of dried blood with a high collar.

A thick brown belt cinched my waist, with a convenient pouch for the essentials. Underneath were tight off-white leggings, then a pair of boots that matched the belt.

He wasn't kidding about wardrobe accentuating all his discipline when it came to calorie counting.

"You cut a fine figure, though I'm concerned those below will recognize the ensemble."

"I'll tell them I'm cosplaying you."

"I might have a larger satchel for your crime-fighting effects."

I didn't want to let on that since parting with Ray Ford, my arsenal was depleted. "Don't worry about all that. The whole point of wearing this getup is to blend in."

"As you wish."

I turned to and fro to ensure nothing would get caught in heavy machinery. "Okay, I'm off to do some sleuthing. Hey, I appreciate the assist."

"Any friend of Ava's is a friend of mine."

I tried to control the wattage in my expression. "She said we're friends?"

Dever gave a hearty chuckle. "Not in so many words. But she possesses a grudging affection. It's why I was curious to speak with you. I must confess, I was a bit jealous over how often your name crosses her lips. But I see now that you're no threat."

"That's me in a nutshell."

"Oh dear, that's not what I meant." There was a small stammer of apology in Dever's voice. "What I mean is that it is clear you are a man of honor. Old school, I believe is the term."

"Yeah, back in my day, computers had disc drives."

Dever saw me out with a pat on the shoulder. "Good luck, Ken. And be careful. The Edgelords are dangerous."

"If they weren't, they wouldn't be worth the effort."

"Fortune does favor the bold."

The penthouse tour completed, I headed back to Reynard's suite. Caution was required. My status quo with any non-Stern law enforcers was shaky. The cops hadn't locked the door behind them. I peeked in to find Corbett hovering on the threshold, fiddling with his tablet. Three techs in paper coveralls were processing the scene. Reynard was still on the throne, getting photographed six ways to Sunday. I spoke through the crack in the door.

"Keep looking at your screen. They go at you yet?"

"Only cursory questions."

"Tell me about Sheila Polk."

Corbett's pallor shifted from blue to red. "What do you want with her?"

"You're tied up at the moment and I need a local guide."

"You can't tell her about any of this."

"I'll be discreet."

"Sheila Polk is not to be trusted."

I busted out Reynard's list of prime suspects. "Her name isn't anywhere in this poll."

Corbett sighed. "That's because she conducted the poll."

"Okay. What about this Kurt Hooper? He's number one with a bullet."

Corbett went into his minimized windows, pulled up a directory of dossiers, and brought up a gallery of all things Kurt Hooper. Hooper was in his mid-thirties. He had ashy brown hair and really needed to give up on the ponytail. His thin face could have been carved from a pumice stone, with dark eyes and the telltale lines of a lifelong smoker ringing his mouth.

Next were the wardrobe tests. Hooper's getup resembled those spiked dog collars but expanded into a whole bodysuit. He was on the thin side, but tall. Gangly was the term. Gangly guys could be dangerous on their feet. They had reach. Gangly guys trained in edged weapons made me nervous.

"Is he on the show?"

Corbett nodded. "As one of the Blackguard—the king's assassins. The studs on his outfit are made of nullinium, a metal which negates magic."

"Good to know. I won't waste my time casting spells at him. What do you have on his actual past?"

Corbett brought up a file. "He claims ex-military, but stated due to the clandestine nature of his missions, the details were classified. Despite this caveat, he's never had an issue boasting about the lives he took for queen and country."

Which meant Hooper had the technical skills to sabotage Reynard's cabin and trailer. "Criminal record?"

"Weapons charges, which are common among his kind. If an Edgelord is pulled over, law enforcement officials are almost certain to find some sort of weapon."

"What's this assault charge?"

"Oh, I remember this. Reynard had it investigated. Hooper had romantic interest in a woman with an abusive boyfriend. Hooper beat him with a flail."

"You mean like nunchucks? That's promising. What rated him the number-one suspect spot?"

"He had a falling out with Mr. Reynard last year, after his character, Sir Wring Tailor, was, um, violated by someone under the Fenris curse."

"Fenris? Like the wolf?"

"Yes. A person cursed in such a way transforms into a bestial man."

"Hooper's character was raped by a werewolf? What the hell kind of show is this?"

"The scene cut away before the act took place. Regardless, Mr. Hooper did not take it well."

A text alert from someone named Norman flashed on Corbett's screen. He swiped it away before I could read the message.

"You're the leak. Shame on you Corbett. No one likes a tattletale."

Corbett turned sullen. "You don't understand. I had no choice."

"Who is Norman?"

"Head of programming at Home Drive-In. He had a right to know. The longer I went without telling him, the worse it was going to be."

"More like you were reaching the next vine after this one snapped."

"Mr. Norman wants to speak with you."

"He can schedule an appointment. Get it in your head, Corbett. I'm the best friend you have right now. These cops, they are going to nail you to the wall if they get an inkling you're holding out on them." I dug my phone out of my pouch and slipped it through the crack. "Text yourself so I have a line open."

While Corbett did that, I formulated a harebrained plan. If the killer wasn't on this floor, and they hadn't used the elevator or emergency stairs, they had to have another way off the penthouse level. Based on what the Dame of the Moon had told me, I had a theory as to how this was possible, but the only way to test it was to get past the forensics team. The key was going to be confidence. I took my phone back from Corbett, rapped on the door, and burst in like I was late for the party.

"Sorry, I got here as fast as I could."

Everyone turned toward me as I closed on them.

"Ken Allen, private eye. Corbett and I found the body together. Figured you'd want a word with me." I stopped suddenly, as if I'd just realized I was striding through a crime scene. "Tell you what, I'll wait in there."

Before anyone could protest, I strode off to Reynard's bedroom in search of secret passages. The Dame of the Moon had tipped me to the idea. Having been built in a more romantic age, one where space wasn't at such a premium, Chateau d'Loire was the sort of place to have hidden secrets. Especially the penthouse suites, so a VIP could sneak people in and out without anyone knowing.

The flimsy bedroom lockset wasn't keeping anyone out. I dragged the chair over and wedged it under the knob. Satisfied I'd bought myself a few minutes, I surveyed the room again, this time with an eye on its architecture.

The bathroom didn't make sense. The wet wall would have posed too many problems. The closet had potential, but all its contents had been in their proper place. Someone leaving that way would have disturbed them.

That left the hearth as the most likely candidate, both dramatic and practical. Plus, the fireplace had once been real, which meant there was room in the framing for a chimney.

It took me a while to find the switch. I started at the top, checking all the stones. The cops outside started knocking as I explored the firebox. It had become full-fledged pounding by the time I got to the base. A cornerstone stuck out a little. I stepped on it and a pocket door popped open.

The cops gave up on knocking and started kicking. Fortunately for me, the officers on scene didn't have a full-fledged riot load-out. I eased the pocket door open.

My phone's flashlight gave me a preview of the secret exit. It had once been a concealed dumbwaiter. The cab and mechanism were removed, replaced by a rope ladder. I ducked inside and stepped onto a rung. The ladder wanted to twist. I used a free hand to brace against the wall and halt my rotation.

The doorknob snapped, ringing like a bell. I maneuvered the rest of me onto the ladder and looked for the inner switch. There wasn't one, just a handle mounted on the inside of the pocket door. I tugged the door shut a hot second before the propped chair tumbled over. Through the wall, the cops exchanged heated words as I lowered myself down. While the content was undecipherable, the tone was unmistakable. I'd heard it plenty since pivoting careers. It's always a good day when you make new friends.

As tempting as it was to hurry down, I stopped to take in the surroundings. The rope ladder was new: aluminum rungs over paracord. No dust on either rungs or rope, nor sign of wear. The carabiners on the end were too small for the horizontal support pole. Whoever had hung the ladder knew knots and had secured it with cordage rather than trust the carabiners.

The question was, Had they hung it from inside Reynard's suite or from the secret passage? Coming from below meant free climbing. As I went down, I found no signs pointing toward that theory. No hand or footprints, no stress cracks from bracing. Either Reynard knew who hung the ladder, or they had done so before he occupied the room.

The ladder extended down several floors. The sixth floor's Sheetrock was cut into. The marks were ragged, with a fresh layer of drywall dust. The panel had been wedged back into place. I took note and kept descending. The ladder went down one more floor. I found the same deal on the fifth floor's wall: a door cut into the drywall, then covered up. Whoever had hung the ladder had given themselves two exit options.

I took out my phone. There were text alerts from Stern. She'd have to wait. I snapped a photo of the lower opening, then climbed back up to compare it to the higher one. There was no discernable difference. Now I had to pick. Would I get the lady or the tiger? What was on the other side of the drywall, I had no idea. I decided to start at the top, on theory that being up higher meant you were more important.

Dangling on this ladder left me a sitting duck. The only way forward was with my metaphorical guns blazing. I put my back to the newly cut opening and braced my legs against the opposite wall. Kicking hard, I shoved through. When I hit the floor, I kept rolling, using my hands to bridge to my feet. I swiveled, ready to face off against a killer.

I was in a bedroom one-and-a-half stars below Reynard's above me. It had a single king bed, a desk, and a chair. The décor was on theme but updated, with glass-cloth walls and busy carpeting.

I wasn't alone. There was a man facedown on the bed, with an axe in his back.

IT ISN'T EASY TO TAKE YOUR eyes off a corpse, but a dead body isn't going to kill you. I put my back to the wall and focused on my five senses. This was also a suite. The door into the bathroom was open, the door to the sitting room closed. I swept the bathroom first. It was recently remodeled in fieldstone veneer tile and absent any axe murderers.

Once I was assured there was nothing lurking in the closet but clothes, I burst through the bedroom door into the sitting room, feeling the stress over my complete lack of a ranged weapon. The outer room boasted a wrap-around leather couch opposite a large standing cabinet. A galley sink and hot plate occupied the space between a small bank of upper and lower cabinetry. Nobody tossed a hatchet in my direction. I was all alone with the corpse.

To report a murder or not to report a murder? That was not the question. The real question was exactly when to let the cops in on this one. After I'd had a look around, at minimum.

I decided to start with the corpse and work my way outward. Now would be a good time to mention I am entirely untrained. Before becoming a detective, I was a personal trainer. Before that, I was a semi-professional martial artist who stumbled into a movie role.

With that in mind, the dead guy on the bed seemed fresher than Reynard. I used the back of my hand to touch him. Still warm. He was a black man, around my age and height, but built like a powerlifter— lots of muscle with a fluffy layer.

In terms of wardrobe, he was dressed like a leatherboy version of the grim reaper. Metal studs adorned a thick vest. His arms were bare. Always lead with your best feature. He wore reinforced studded wrist guards and a belt so wide you could use it for dead lifting. It kept his waist cinched. His boots had lifts in them. His hands were calloused but free of cuts.

There was no ID to be found in his getup. A hooded cloak hung in the closet, along with a full-face mask and two hatchets that matched the one in his back. A pair of giant suitcases and a guitar case were tucked into a corner. I was reaching for them when the deadbolt started turning.

I crept toward the door as it eased open. A black-clad figure slipped through a gap just wide enough for their slim body. Since I already had the momentum, I transitioned to a stepping side kick.

Something warned them. The pad of my steps, a peripheral sense of movement. Whoever it was retreated rather than forge ahead. I completed the kick anyway, putting all the steam I'd built up into the doorplate above the knob. They got clear by a quarter second. The door slammed shut with a boom that shook the frame. I ducked back as I tore it open. The slipping motion saved my life. A blade slashed through the air where my neck would have been, had I been fully upright.

My would-be killer was dressed like a medieval ninja: a combination of silk and suede in all black. Their tunic or whatever you called it was hooded, and their face covered by an animal mask. What animal I couldn't say. I was too busy watching the knife.

It had a short, curved blade with a chiseled tip. The ninja led with it, their other hand open, positioned underneath their chin. Their stance was balanced and loaded. The cut that could have ended me had been expert: a short arc at the end of a thrust. Whoever was under the hood knew what they were doing.

They feinted toward my eyes and then slashed at the inside of my wrist on the withdraw. It was a tricky maneuver, and one I was utterly unfamiliar with. I saved myself on instinct, ripped my right hand away while seeking out their forearm with my left. They slipped the knife under my outstretched hand, then jabbed upward toward my armpit, another completely alien technique.

I twisted away to avoid being skewered and tried a turning kick in hope they would lunge into it, but they stayed on the far side of the threshold. Holding the doorway was smart. It kept me from circling, and they had reach with a thrusting weapon.

Stymied, I backed into the room. If I still had my Taser gun, I would have dropped them. Instead, I took out my phone and held down the camera button.

They took off running.

I gave chase. Three steps into the hallway they whirled back around to stab me. Unable to hit the brakes in time, I dove into the takedown, the knife passing close enough to trim my hair. We hit the ground and I put all my focus into controlling their knife hand. I latched onto their wrist and was setting up a keylock when they blasted me with pepper spray.

I twisted away, eyes closed. Most of it missed me, but it was the good stuff. I growled in pain and kept on seeking the joint lock. When they realized they also had to breathe the air around us they laid off the spraying. If my opponent had another knife I was in big trouble, and chances were they had another knife. It was a race: either I secured the lock or got stabbed. Voices shouted from down the hall. I did the heroic thing and yelled for help.

Something metal clubbed the side of my head. I wrenched for dear life. It clubbed me again. Hands were tearing me upward, away from safety and into prime stabbing territory. They were sure to grab my arms, in case I had the bright idea to stop myself from being impaled.

Through the tears, I watched the ninja roll to their feet and dash away. I set a hip on the Samaritan holding my right arm and tossed them, then hooked the other one under the elbow to set them up for the trip. The ninja hit the stairwell door. By the time I got there myself, they were long gone.

Behind me, a helpful couple who'd broken up the fight were cursing me out. Behind them, the room door leading to a fresh corpse was wide open. It was stick around and attempt to explain myself or run for it.

I went with run for it.

———

Dying to rinse out my eyes and bereft of options, I made my way to the lobby level to seek a public bathroom. Reynard had never gotten around to checking me in. Blake Dever may have tolerated a squatter, but the authorities seeking me were also located on his floor. I stumbled my way down the staircase, half expecting round two with the medieval ninja.

Two flights down, I remembered about vending machines and exited the stairwell. The machines were tastefully stashed in a nook. It being early Friday meant there was still water in stock. I bought two bottles, lay down on my back, and poured them over my eyes, using my thumb to direct the flow.

All in all, it could have been worse. My right cornea felt sanded down, but my left eye was almost entirely spared. If ever there was a place to score an emergency eyepatch, this had to be it. But I had other plans first.

I went back up one floor, which was under the second murder scene, and worked to orient myself. The secret ladder ended in a room on this level. In my tear-filled egress, I hadn't gotten a chance to scope a room number. It was either the third or fourth door. I pressed my ear to the third door.

Sounds bustling inside, with the muted, comforting back-and-forth of a couple. *Did you get the thing, honey? Grab that for me, dear.* Interactions like that felt fictional to me. Let's just say that growing up, little Ken had a lot of uncles. My father was English, I was aware of that much from my dual citizenship. The rest was up in the air. For all I knew, I was a prince.

The fourth door was quiet. This floor had replaced the original doors. The tight seal prevented any sense of the temperature or hint of suspect odors. I had no way of busting in. The hard truth was that I was spoiled. From the start of my second chapter as a gumshoe, I had always had support. Ray Ford and his daughter Elaine not only had supplied me with the gadgets, but Elaine also had the internet at her disposal, including monitoring emergency responder channels for minute-by-minute updates as to how hot the water I was in had become. But this gig took as much as it gave, and now I was on my own.

And time was limited. My masked sparring partner knew that I knew about the dead guy in the suite above. From that, they could extrapolate I knew the ladder in the wall extended down to this room. If there was anything they wanted inside this room, chances were they'd come here to get it immediately. There was also the possibility they were lying in wait for Ken Allen to stumble into another ambush.

Chateau d'Loire had no security cameras. I could kick down the door. Maybe get a once-over before the happy couple next door reported the break-in. I backed up a step to load up when my phone started buzzing with a call from Corbett.

"Hold on." I backtracked to this floor's vending nook and got an angle where I could keep an eye on room 513. "Okay, go."

"Mr. Norman would like to speak to you."

"I'm in the middle of a thing here, Corbett."

"I feel it could be beneficial. He's well connected. His father is Bill Norman."

"As in Bill Norman the billionaire who owns Pan-Global Media?"

"Yes."

Corbett was right, but I had my hands full. "I'm on something time sensitive. The only way I'm seeing Norman is if he comes to me."

"Where are you located?"

"Fifth floor, vending nook."

"Give me a moment." Corbett had the sound turned off on his tablet, but I could hear his fingertips dancing. "Hold on, Ken."

"No problem. Hey, can you multitask me some *Lands Beyond* lore? Is there a character that dresses like an executioner? Wearing all black, with a hood, axe, all that."

"Sounds like a member of the Blackguard."

Of which Kurt Hooper was also a member. "Go on."

"Each of them has a specialty. The Blackguard Cleave is sent forth to deal with masses of foes. He wields an axe."

"Is he on the show?"

"In a minor capacity. It's a nonspeaking role."

"Who plays him?"

"Wallace Bowers."

"Describe him."

"Black, five foot eight. He is an ex-boxer and competitive power-lifter. Before joining the Edgelords, he was featured in the world's strongest man competitions."

"This Blackguard, you said they do the king's dirty work?"

"Yes, as opposed to the white guards, who act as his personal protectors."

I hmmed the *hmm* of a man politely tolerating a story. The important bit had been Wallace was an Edgelord, and part of Reynard's private army.

"Mr. Norman has agreed to come to you. He'll be there in ten minutes."

"Great. Do the cops still have you on lockdown?"

"Yes, but they have been clear I am not under arrest."

Corbett seemed a sensitive soul. I decided not to tell him that if he couldn't leave, he was under arrest, whatever the cops were calling it. Which meant he was safe enough for now.

"If they let you off the hook, steer clear of this Blackguard."

"It's hard to believe they would be involved as a group. They were among Mr. Reynard's most devoted followers."

"There's a thin line between love and hate, Corbett. Trust me here."

"If you say so, Ken."

Corbett didn't sound like he believed me. After we said our goodbyes, I googled Will Norman. There was plenty on him, on account of his father owning a media empire, including Home Drive-In. Ten years ago, Norman had graduated from Stanford and immediately became an executive at the flagging network. His first swing had been a huge one: He'd greenlit *The Lands Beyond* to the tune of 50 million dollars.

It had been a big story: Daddy's boy dips deep into the family fortune and potentially bankrupts the network. Except that first swing had been a home run, and all of a sudden Will Norman had proved he was his father's son, a true wunderkind who moved Home Drive-In from being a digital video store into premium original programming.

There were plenty of pictures of Norman, but they changed from year to year. Norman had gone from beanpole to bodybuilder. But it was more than a growth spurt. His features had also slowly transformed. If you jumped right from twenty-year-old Will Norman to the thirty-year-old version, they looked like two totally different men.

I had my suspicions as to the cause but withheld judgment for the face-to-face. The vending machine was calling to me. Life-and-death battles really left you famished. Pickings were slim. I went with some heavily salted almonds and another bottle of water. This gig sure made you guilty about your carbon footprint. My eye still felt like it had sand in it. I let the tears flow, confident I'd ingested enough sodium to replenish my natural saline supply.

The stairs and the elevator were on opposite sides of the floor. Norman came, by himself, from the elevator side.

On paper, he was around a decade younger than me. But all the work he'd had done imbued him with a timeless quality. His face was a road map of plastic surgery: an impossibly even hairline, a shaved-down brow, prominent cheekbones, a nose as slim as its nostrils would allow, a cleft in his chin.

Plastic surgery could be a slippery slope. Get one little thing done and the next seems like an even better idea. In the end, you're left with a face that's an assemblage of society's most desirable traits, the sum of which leaves the recipient residing in the uncanny valley.

Norman was dressed like he'd walked out of the Richard Harris version of *Camelot*—in multiple textures with every surface etched. His efforts didn't stop at his face. His body strained under the suit of armor. Broad shoulders, a deep chest. Peaks had been sculpted into the metal sleeves to allow room for his biceps.

Add together the plastic surgeries with Norman's physical transformation, you came up with body dysmorphia. No one was immune to societal pressure. In This Town, go ahead and square and cube that pressure. You looked into the mirror and all you saw was coal begging to be a diamond.

I leaned into the hallway and gave Norman a thumbs-up. He perked but didn't alter his stride. When he got to me, I gestured that he join me in the nook.

"Please, step into my office."

Norman's voice was deep and clean, with a transatlantic bent. The voice of a kid raised by television. "My room is a little nicer."

"I'm on a stakeout. Forgive my lack of eye contact. They are currently peeled. Nice outfit."

"Reynard insisted I dress up. I'd shake your hand, but getting these gauntlets on and off is a pain in the ass."

I waved him off. "Hand shaking needs to go the way of the dodo."

Norman laughed. "It's a good way to be sure the other guy isn't holding a knife."

"Last time I checked, people had two hands. Enjoying the convention?"

"Tolerating it. Keeping an eye on Reynard is a full-time job. He's prone to announcing developments to his little cult before consulting those who hold the purse strings."

"It puts the pressure on you to cough up."

"You got it in one. We've entered every negotiation with Reynard already on our heels."

"Yeah, golden geese are known for being finicky. Did Reynard have walking power?"

"We bought the show, but not him. If he ever departed, we had no show. The market research is clear. The fans would reject any substitute. He knew it, we knew it. That's why I'm here, actually."

The door to the room next to the one I was watching opened. The happy couple exited, a pair of witches in matching forest-green cloaks and lunar-themed accessories.

"I'm listening."

"Home Drive-In wants to hire you to recover the series bible."

"Hot commodity. And also key evidence."

Norman folded his arms, an act that sounded like a mechanical press. "Let us sort that out with the authorities."

"Thing is, I only brought the one agency agreement. Which Reynard managed to sign prior to getting perforated."

"No contract is required. I'm authorized to pay you ten million dollars on delivery of the authenticated item."

That turned my head. Norman had crystal green eyes. Nothing in them said he was joshing me.

"Tell you what, if I come across the thing, I'll keep you in mind."

Norman nodded, as if satisfied with my response. "I have a feeling I picked the right horse."

"Well, you won't find me naysaying. Do you have any pull with the hotel?"

"I might. What do you need?"

"A place to stay, off the books. I've put a target on my back with both the cops and the robbers."

"That should be doable."

I pointed down the hall. "And access to that room. 513."

Hotel staff showed up fifteen minutes after Norman left. Certain considerations were made for a successful producer with a billionaire father. The porter looked like he sold caskets in Dodge City on the side. He held up a ring of keys.

"Each one of these keys is the master for a separate floor. They are appropriately numbered. Suite keys have heads matching their door ornamentation."

The porter handed the keyring over like his hand was magnetized. "I'll expect these to be returned in a timely fashion. And please exercise restraint. The suite keys are certified historical artifacts."

"I'll keep them under lock and themselves."

The porter scoffed and turned away before I could decide if I should tip him or not. I waited for the distant sound of the elevator doors closing before easing the appropriately numbered fifth-floor key into room 513. I held the knob tight and rotated the tumblers with a firm tension, silently praying there would be no audible click. Once the key stopped turning, I repeated with the knob.

Having been recently attacked, I decided discretion was the better part of valor. I stood off to the side and shoved the door completely open.

Call me imaginative, but I exist in a world of possibility. When I check the backseat for serial killers, part of me expects to find one. It's not like I believe in ghosts, but if one showed up in my kitchen, I wouldn't waste time denying its existence. Bigfoot and the Loch Ness monster are on the table, as far as I'm concerned.

So when I step to the side prior to opening an unknown door, it's because a little part of me believes something could be waiting to pounce. That's why I was only slightly miffed when a crossbow bolt shot past me, close enough that I felt the wind of its passing.

SHOOT A CROSSBOW AT ME ONCE, shame on you. Shoot it twice, shame on me. Rather than stick my neck out, I eased my phone into the open doorway to scope the suite. Its layout was identical to the one above. The crossbow was set up six feet from the door, supported by a bipod on top of a side table. Fishing line connected it to the inside doorknob. Besides that, the room appeared hazard free.

A crossbow bolt sticking out head height in the hallway was bound to attract attention. Gloves on, I worked it free. It didn't have an arrowhead as much as a spike. I slipped into the room and immediately out of line of the crossbow.

Loaded or not, I'm not fond of projectile weapons pointed at me. I closed the door with my foot before taking in my surroundings. The air was cool and heavy with a scent, like peppermint mixed with anise.

The furniture was rearranged to face the blank wall opposite the television cabinet, as if they were studying the hotel paintings. Except the painting was taken down and a rectangle of double-sided tape was in its place.

I tore myself from speculation to give the adjoining room a once-over. In the bedroom, the bed had been stripped down, the bedding piled in the corner behind the lounge chair. A selection of ancient weapons was laid out on the bed, their hafts and hilts blackened. A check showed each of them was functional, with a practical heft and sharp blades. They were arrayed by size, with a few missing spots between the daggers and long swords. The weapons that filled those gaps would have been ideal for fighting in enclosed spaces, such as hallways and hotel rooms.

There were similar gaps with the throwing knives and hatchets, which was either really good or really bad news. When it came to throwing weapons, you were either delusional or an absolute expert to believe they were effective. Or both. In this situation, it was probably both.

Open suitcases on hotel-provided stands lined the walls, providing all one's tactical needs. There were a lot of belts, pouches, and sheaths, along with enough rope to climb Everest. What was it with tactical nuts and cordage?

The bathroom was next. It was a duplicate of the one above with one critical exception: there was a body in the bathtub.

It was under a hotel comforter and then one of those foil survival blankets, stripped and covered in ice. From the state of the ice, it had only been here a few hours. There was a black hood over the corpse's head. Underneath was an Asian man who could have won a mustache contest. Besides being dead, he was in great shape. The cause of death was not immediately apparent. I leaned in and took a whiff. He had a strong, musky cologne scent. As much as it was a bad idea to disturb the body, I had to check his hands. No crown-shaped cuts. I snapped a picture of him with my phone and put everything back where I found it.

An essential oils diffuser on the wall pumped out the cloying pseudo-freshness. There were no personal hygiene effects in the bathroom. There was, however, an extensive first-aid kit, including a purported remedy for eye damage. If the weekend continued on its current trajectory, I was going to need medical attention. I threw the whole kit in a duffel bag to take with me.

Back in the sitting room, the concealed mini-fridge was stocked with insulated bottles filled with water. In the top drawer, small tubs of powder were labeled by compound. I recognized the mixtures: electrolyte mix, a nootropic blend, and a stimulant-based formula for physical performance commonly found in pre-workout supplements.

The next drawer was dedicated to food. Vacuum-sealed bags of jerky, a medley of nuts and seeds, granola, and dried fruit. There were also two boxes of protein bars, the same brand as the wrapper I found in Hammersmith's suite. One box was open, half of them missing. The bottom drawer was dedicated to cleaning supplies. Like the tubs of powder, they were custom mixtures in generic bottles rather than off-the-shelf purchases. I added some jerky, nuts, and protein bars to my duffel bag. To the victor went the spoils.

There was a power block in every outlet. Each block had two device chargers in it, making six total. The power blocks and chargers were identical, with no signs of wear on their cords. Charger cords were built to break. These had been freshly purchased for the mission, which told me their matching phones were likely burners.

I stepped next to the door and took in the scene. Knowing what was there, I tried to focus on what was missing. The good news was the utter lack of modern weapons. It was hard to imagine a group that would haul around a mile of rope would not also bring surplus ammunition. There were no files, no notes. Nothing on paper at all. No devices. No personal effects. This room had been rented for one purpose:

I was standing in a war room.

Six chargers meant either six people with one device each, or three with two, or two with three. As much as the latter two options would have been nice, the food supply said six. So did the load-out. If you wanted to stock the room in one go and not attract attention trafficking in and out, you'd need a half dozen people to carry all the luggage.

Almost everything was still present. Some weapons were missing. The plan, or map, or whatever had been taped on the wall for briefing was gone. One person had been back here, grabbed the essentials, and ditched. Whether they were pros or just pretending to be, this room had been written off. At least I'd denied them that much.

Satisfied I had gotten what I could out of the location, I threw the duffel bag over my shoulder and left. After putting a floor between me and the latest crime scene, I took out my phone and texted Stern the update she'd been requesting:

Dead guy in 613. Maybe Wallace Bowers. War room in 513. Second dead guy in the tub.

Her reply was nigh-instantaneous. *Two more? It's only been a couple hours.*

I think they were after Reynard. The game is afoot.

Leaving you alone was a mistake.

I could practically feel Stern pacing. If this kept up, she was going to kick down the door.

Don't worry, you're always in my thoughts.

I needed to know more about the cast, but when it came to information, Corbett was a last resort. The guy was as leaky as a waterbed. He'd gone right up the ladder first chance he got. Anything I brought to him more than likely would end up directly on Will Norman's desk. The fact that he was so strongly against Sheila Polk leaned her toward the plus column. What I needed to know was where to find her. Fortunately, events like this provided such resources.

The convention had officially begun an hour ago, blissfully unaware that its guest of honor was dead seven stories above. The lobby had become congested as the crowd dispersed in the direction of their activities of choice. Excited voices echoed in the big marble square. A fountain of winged victory stood in the middle. The lady was in full armor, stretching a sword to the heavens. The service desk was built into the wall to the left as you entered, with the offices behind. Opposite that were the elevators.

The entry doors were double-sliding automatics, the only concession Chateau d'Loire gave to the modern world. Even then, they were disguised inside arches, with a portcullis hanging above. Light was provided via arched windows, sconces, and a giant round chandelier with about a thousand fake lanterns hanging off it.

There was a broad mezzanine above the lobby, bordered with an iron railing so you could spy from both levels. The mezzanine was the social center, with a bar, café, and open dining. A woman dressed half-Cleopatra, half-Mark Antony walked by me. Holding her phone in front of her face, she stopped at the doors, causing them to open and close, over and over.

"—texted me. If you leave, they won't let you back in. They won't say why. Okay."

Other people came to the doors on their phones, speaking with their friends who hadn't made it past the gauntlet. Word was spreading about the lockdown. Once people knew you couldn't get back in, no one was leaving. The convention was a once-in-a-lifetime event. I felt for the kitchen staff. They were in for it.

I stopped at the desk, where Will Norman had arranged a convention pass and room reservation. I wondered who he had booted in favor of me. Probably a gaggle of production assistants. Those poor souls got stacked like cordwood at these things.

The room came with a VIP package: access to all areas, two photo ops of my choice, and seats at the premium events. My status was displayed by wearing an amulet the size of an Olympic medal. The same spiked crown that had done Reynard in was cast in relief on its surface. Instead of tickets, there was a pouch with fake gold coins, each with a symbol matching an event. The coins were actual metal, with trace nubs from being in a casting mold. A scroll of parchment bore instructions to download an app and enter the included redemption code. I passed on that for now and consulted the program, which was also a premium item: leather bound on thick parchment with deckled edges.

One of the big draws of conventions like these were the panels. Some were presentations, where announcements were made and teaser clips aired to stoke anticipation and speculation among the fandom. Others were Q and A sessions with the cast and crew—hundreds of people crowded into a room to bask in the aura of their favorite performers. But The Last Beyond Confluence—the convention's official name—was more than the typical fan event.

Reynard's fandom had its own subculture. People super into the show strove to live in its world. So along with the standard fare, there were lectures on homesteading and how to make chain mail and brew beer. There were poetry readings and role-playing game sessions. Full-contact duels, conducted under official WMA rules, whatever those were. Knighting ceremonies and something called Revels capped each day.

All of it was hosted by the Edgelords. Ranks were clearly delineated, though it was Greek to me. Hopefully there was a chart on the wiki. Future Edgelord events were advertised throughout. Wednesday meetings were held in your local fief. On the weekends were tournaments, complete with shops and feasts. You could even spend two weeks on a commune, living the *Lands Beyond* life.

The program had an index in the back. Thank the universe for pedantic superfans. I looked up Sheila Polk. She was active in the community, with a dozen appearances over three days. If Corbett was Reynard's behind-the-scenes assistant, Polk was his publicist, the front-facing portion of the equation. Polk had a small bio, which told me nothing Corbett hadn't, minus his bias. She had been Mistress of Ceremonies at the opening event and was due to appear on a *Secret History of Crucible* panel. Concerned about finding a seat, I put on some hustle. I needn't have bothered; my VIP amulet granted me the equivalent of boxed seats. I'd made it with a minute to spare and took the time to survey the audience. It was a Nielsen dream of age groups, genders, and ethnic origins. Reynard had done the impossible and created a world that appealed across the board.

The panelists entered through the service hallway, the same one that ended in the elevator with penthouse access. Will Norman arrived first, with Bradley Corbett on his heels. Oh, to have been a fly on the wall when the cops were deciding whether or not to turn Corbett loose. Sheila Polk was the last to arrive. She was dressed in in an eggshell gown with armor accents that made it look like she was carrying a swan on her shoulders. She was all of five feet tall and Rubenesque, fair skinned, with hair like spun platinum and gold, long enough to accidentally sit on. She sat in the middle, flanked by Norman and Corbett.

A moderator dressed up as a monk conducted the panel, the content of which was a mythologized oral history as to the origins of the show. Norman started by saying Reynard had showed up in person at the Home Drive-In offices, where no one recognized him. Polk one-upped Norman by stating that Reynard invited her to his personal writing retreat to reveal he had been working in secret on a whole new world.

The pattern continued. Norman would make a statement, then Polk would jump in to make it clear he was last in the chain. Corbett didn't speak unless spoken to. When prodded, he supplied details of early casting, including Reynard's original picks for roles, which drew the intense interest of the audience. The usual litany of pie-in-the-sky A-list names was offered, as always, as if there was a chance in hell a fledgling show on a cable network could afford them. After that came several actors who, I gathered from context, had been players on Reynard's previous show, *Never After*.

The last fifteen minutes of the panel were reserved for Q and A. Having sat on about a hundred versions of the same panel, this was the part I dreaded the most. I started to sympathetically sweat. The questions were all the same, either designed to demonstrate the asker's expertise in the subject, intended to show their adoration of the answerer, or covertly advertise the asker's hustle of choice.

Norman, Polk, and Corbett fielded it well, with Norman emerging as a dark horse favorite. He was engaging, personable, and had begun the panel framed as the villain—the evil network Reynard had to battle every step of the way. Polk scrambled to keep up, but the truth was that she was essentially an outsider—a fan who had risen through the ranks into Reynard's inner circle.

She possessed no special insight into the nuts and bolts of production. She could only relay anecdotes.

Everything was going smoothly until a young woman asked a question. She was dressed in forest green, with accents made to look like her body was host to brambles and moss. Her cloak was held in place with a silver crescent. If her English accent wasn't legitimate, she was a heck of a budding actress.

"Was Lynn Chambers ever considered for a role? There have been whispers, one might say. Please and thank you."

As innocuous as the question appeared, Norman, Polk, and Corbett froze as if the girl had pulled out a pistol. Corbett was the fastest to recover.

"Miss Chambers retired from acting before the second season of *Never After* was completed."

The moderator jumped in to wrap the panel, urging a round of applause from the audience. Polk stayed behind to soak it up, while Norman and Corbett made their exit. Polk had her own guards: two men dressed in quartered red-and-white surcoats. They moved to intercept as I drew close. Each presented a stiff-arm while their free hand went to their sword hilt. I didn't take offense. Polk started toward the exit.

"Miss Polk. I'm Ken Allen, a PI. Reynard hired me."

Polk stopped but didn't turn. It was time to butter her up.

"You seem like the expert around here. Corbett is pretty much useless."

Polk about-faced with a soft grin. "Do you have proof of your claim?"

I produced my agency contract with Reynard's signature on it. Polk perked at Reynard's signature.

"I have a few minutes before lunch."

"We can walk and talk."

"What did Rex hire you for?"

Not wanting the guards to overhear, I got close enough to whisper. "He's had death threats."

Polk nodded as if it was old news. "How might I help you?"

"What can you tell me about the Blackguard?"

"They traditionally number eight, each with their own specialty."

Eight made sense. If six of them were in the room, then two members had been on the outs from the get-go. One was Wallace Bowers, who was on the floor above the war room with an axe in his back. The other was the mustachioed Asian man in the bathtub.

"Are they all featured on the show?"

"Oh yes."

"Any of them come up through the Edgelords?"

Polk gave a nod of respect at the question. "All but two, John Cannon and Mikail Chelovak. They were cast for speaking roles. Being a member of the Blackguard doesn't often call for dialogue."

"Silent but deadly."

"Indeed."

"Any of them have a beef with Reynard?"

"Oh, most of them, surely. But vendetta enough to threaten his life? This I doubt."

"What about Kurt Hooper?"

Polk was big on verbal reactions that weren't words. She emitted a pitched *Hmm!* at the thought. There must have been something in my manner. Polk's eyes flickered in calculation. "Is Rex all right?"

"The police are with him now." Which technically was the truth. I followed up with another technical truth. "He won't be able to keep to his schedule, I'm afraid."

It was a shade too far. Polk fell silent at my words, delving deeper into thought. Worried I might not get a second swing at her, I soldiered on.

"You said Reynard told you about the show at his retreat? Where might that be located?"

"Ask, and I will confirm."

"A cabin in Maine."

Polk bowed her head.

Time for a little white lie.

"He said you were there, when the cabin burned down."

Polk's *Uh-huhs* had *mmms* on the end. "Uh-huhmmm!"

"He said you got a headache, went for a walk."

"Mmm. I realized later it was from the gas."

I hmm'd back. Polk's onomatopoeia was contagious.

"If you'll excuse me, I have a luncheon."

The guards stepped between us to signal I should not follow. Not wanting to escalate things, I let them go. All in all, Polk had learned as much from me as I had from her. About everything she shared I could have gotten off the *Lands Beyond* wiki. I wondered if detectives had the equivalent to the Razzie awards. If they did, it would look nice on my shelf next to my actual Razzie.

It was time to cut out the middlemen. I consulted the program, circling appearances by members of the Blackguard with a purloined hotel pen. If the medieval ninja I'd tangled with was a member of the cast, I'd recognize them. I never forgot a fist. When appearing on panel, the character name was listed first, followed by the actor in parenthesis.

For example, in two hours Sedek Grane (John Cannon), the Blackguard Point, was hosting a workshop called This One's On Me: Slaying With Style, which sounded promising. Right after that was Jand Makarov (Mikail Chelovak) The Blackguard Reach, with a lecture called Cold Fury: A Killer Mindset.

The big event was a Saturday-evening panel with the assembled Blackguard. Wallace Bowers would not be in attendance, that was for sure. Of the other listed names, Fernando Denoso stood out. Denoso was a Pinoy name. Filipino names leaned Spanish, on account of them occupying it before America.

My phone vibrated in my pocket. I was expecting a terse reply from my favorite law enforcement official. My heart skipped a beat when instead, there was a message from Elaine Ford.

Come to the lobby. I'm here.

The lobby was a lunch break madhouse, but Elaine was impossible to miss. She was wearing a jeweled tiara, her hair high like a smoky explosion, with platinum filigree earrings styled to suggest elven ears. Her outfit was the *Lands Beyond* core aesthetic: Elizabethan with random pieces of armor on a shoulder or wrist. She'd converted her chair into a throne, adding carved panels of chimeric beasts to the sides and back, along with a deep red velvet lining.

When she saw me, she smiled. A half ton of guilt evaporated off my back and disappeared into the ether. I smiled back and negotiated the bustle toward her.

"Wow, you look great."

"Same to you. From the back, you could be Blake Dever."

"He's an okay guy, if you were wondering."

"I know." Elaine looked adorably busted. "I, uh, I heard."

"Ha-what? How?"

"Back when you had the smart watch and Bluetooth, when I paired them to your phone, I may have put a teensy tiny ghost app on there."

Part of the deal in accepting the aid from two of the world's foremost special-effects experts was being their guinea pig. The other part had been them living a life of vicarious adventure in exchange for their support.

The loss of my privacy was outweighed by preventing the loss of my life.

"I haven't always been listening. But when I got a location alert that you were at the Chateau . . ."

"It's fine, Elaine." I was just happy she was talking to me. Then it occurred to me: Elaine was out. In public. By herself. "So you're into all this, huh?"

"Heck yes, I am. And this is my only chance."

"Chance for what?"

Elaine bit her lip. She was up to something mischievous enough to cause her to suppress a smile. "Let's talk about it in my room."

She led me into the elevator. Her chair wasn't much of a deterrent when it came to preserving personal space. Being two of six crammed into the cab, we stayed quiet on the way up. On the third floor, everyone shuffled to let her pass. One other person exited on our floor. She had green hair and a silver crescent necklace. Another Dame of the Moon acolyte. I faked having to check my phone to text Elaine:

Don't stop at your room.

She shot me a slight nod without checking her phone. A close glance showed her elven earrings extended into her canals. My message had been transferred as text-to-speech into her dressed-up Bluetooth buds. The two of us ambled down the hall, the green-haired girl trailing behind, sandbagging by pretending fixation on her phone. When we turned the corner, I motioned for Elaine to stop, then spun around and leaned against the wall, my arms crossed with my hands untucked. Casual, but prepared. The green-haired girl ducked her head around the corner. I smiled back at her.

"Hey there."

Wide-eyed, she turned on her heel and skedaddled, her pace on the line between power walking and jogging. When she hit the stairs, she took them.

Elaine turned around to join me. "What was that about?"

"The Dame of the Moon runs a cold-reading routine. Part of that con is having eyes everywhere."

"That girl didn't look dangerous."

"I doubt she was. The Dame's followers probably don't know the score. They just get word if they see me around, scope what I'm up to. And I'm betting it's not just me the Dame is spying on. Speaking of which, how much of this morning did you overhear?"

"All of it." Elaine flashed a fox-in-the-henhouse smile. "I know I should have said something sooner, but I was worried you'd be mad at me after what happened last fall."

Oh humanity. Elaine and I'd been avoiding each other, both of us assuming the worst, rather than talking it out and discovering we were on the same page.

"Me too."

This time her smile was genuine. I almost asked about her father, but then I chickened out. "We're in the clear."

Elaine doubled us back to her room. The fourth floor only had suites in the corners. Being the silent partner in the world's premiere practical effects duo, she could afford it. Once the door was closed, Elaine took the lead.

"So Reynard is dead, the series bible is missing, and you think the Blackguard is involved."

"Right on all accounts. Except I don't know if it's the actors cast as the Blackguard on the show or a group dressed up as the Blackguard. Right now, I'm leaning it's the actual cast."

"Why?"

"Wallace Bowers was on the show. He was an ex-fighter. Reynard liked fighters. It's how Alexi Mirovich ended up in a role and was probably a factor in hiring me. The dead guy in the bathtub could be Fernando Denoso."

Elaine brought his picture up from the Wikipedia entry, which I should have thought to do. It was indeed Denoso.

"Reynard had a cult thing going with these Edgelords. He used his superfans to do dirty work, promoting them up the ranks. The big prize was appearing on the show. My guess is if you made the Blackguard, you earned your spot the hard way. And I think Bowers knew his killer."

Elaine was a great audience. She rubbed her hands together. "No way. Why?"

"Bowers knew his killer well enough to turn his back on them. And got caught off guard, despite being a fighter." I loosened my girdle and flopped down on the sofa. "The room below Bowers was set up for six. Bowers was number seven, and on the outs, though he didn't know it. Denoso was number eight. Sheila Polk said the Blackguard was eight strong. That accounts for everyone."

When you give a superfan free reign to unload on you, buckle up. Elaine leaned in, excited. "So, the identity of the eighth member of the Blackguard is a secret. None of the others know who he is. He always wears a helmet that covers his face."

"Wait. Is his identity secret on the show, or secret in real life?"

"Both. He's uncredited."

"He's probably just a random stuntman."

Elaine shook her head. "It's always been the same person. People compared screengrabs from all the seasons."

"I mean, the eighth Blackguard member could end up being any-body, retroactively."

Elaine soldiered on like she didn't hear me. "I think it's Blake Dever. They've never been in the same scene, which is weird because the Blackguard answers to the prince."

"Doesn't Dever already play two characters?"

"Yes, but one of them has no memories. I think the eighth member is whoever Dever was before they wiped his mind. His former self that sometimes takes control of his body. Also, there have been hints that the secret member has royal blood, and Dever plays the prince."

I rubbed my eyes to clear my head. My right one exploded in pain. "Okay, so, let's put the fan theories aside. What I'm dealing with in real life is enough. The current agenda is tracking down the other six Blackguard members and seeing if any of them fit the bill for being Reynard's killer. Figure out which of them both have the know-how to sabotage Reynard's properties and also the ability to do him in with his own crown. Could be all of them were in on it."

Elaine pursed her lips in frustration. She had just been getting warmed up. "Okay, but why would they band together to kill Reynard?"

"Maybe to ransom the series bible. It has no value with Rey-nard alive, outside of extorting over the threat of dumping it online. Will Norman offered me ten million for the thing, and that was his opener."

"That feels thin. The Blackguard is like royalty. With Reynard gone, they lose everything. Ten million divided six ways isn't a lot."

She had a good point. "Maybe when we dig enough, we unearth a better reason. One more thing." I dug one of the pilfered protein bars out of my bag. "I found a few boxes of these in the suite the Black-guard was using as a war room. There was a matching wrapper in Hammersmith's garbage. Does he have a link to the Blackguard?"

Elaine lit up. "Oooh. There's a theory that Potens Wythane has a spy close to the king. I thought it might be—"

"I'm talking about Hammersmith here, not the character he plays. He was shacked up with Fairchild, one of the Edgelords. How wrapped up with the Edgelords is Hammersmith?"

Elaine sighed a patient sigh. "I know you don't want to hear about the show, but I think it matters. There are a lot of parallels between the real-life actors and the parts they play. Reynard mines the lives of the actors for story. It's controversial, even in the fandom. Some people defend it, because it kindles very personal performances."

"And others say it's exploitation."

"That's right. Potens Wythane is gay, so is Hammersmith, for one."

"That's just accurate casting."

"But Hammersmith wasn't out before the show. It was also Potens's biggest secret. When Potens was outed, Hammersmith came out in real life. There's a bunch more like that."

"Okay, I'm listening."

Elaine brightened. "On the show, Potens married and fathered children out of duty. He does everything for his family. It tells me Hammersmith could be involved in this because of Fairchild. On the show, both of Dever's parts are in love with the same woman, but she doesn't know he's two different people. The Dame of the Moon, her big deal is no one knows who her father is. In real life, no one knows where she came from."

It was information overload. I stood up and stretched. "Crime waits for no man. Off I go."

"Wait." Elaine's gaze was steady. "I want in. And I come bearing gifts."

I SKIPPED RIGHT PAST ALL THE things it was better not to say and went straight to the big one: "Everyone who helps me eventually hates me for it."

"Oh, I'm not doing this for you." Elaine gestured two thumbs at her crown. "I'm doing it for me. This whole situation is too juicy. I love the show, and people are for real killing each other over it. This time, you're the one doing me a favor."

I unwrapped a protein bar and thought about it. It was pretty decent but could have been improved by fifteen seconds in a microwave. "I hope you happened to pack a bunch of helpful gizmos."

"Ken, if I knew you were coming, I would have baked a cake. How offended are you by the concept of regifting?"

"As long as no one has eaten out of it, not one bit."

Elaine withdrew to the bedroom and returned with a wooden box. "I made this for Blake Dever, but it should fit you."

The box was beautiful. Red oak with a winged lion carved into it. The hinges were smooth, but the lid stood up without support. Inside, a crown rested on a hill of velvet. The electrum circlet was thumb-thick, with a small stylized lion's head at the center of the brow. Four fire opals dotted the circumference, with small wings swept back along the ears.

"Each of the opals is a combination camera and parabolic micro-phone," Elaine explained. "I have a spare earpiece. We can pair it to your phone. The wings will cover it."

My brain locked for a moment, processing the implications of Elaine's regift. "You were going to bug Blake Dever?"

Again with the mischievous lip bite. "I don't mind spoilers."

"What if he never wore it?"

"The box is also wired."

My laugh could be described as incredulous. "Absolutely shame-less, Elaine."

She put a hand over her heart. "I was going to keep everything to myself. And I didn't know he was with Stern until this morning. The shock about knocked me out of my chair."

"Okay, you sold me. I guess I can let you tag along and do all the real work." I finished the protein bar and stuffed the wrapper in my pocket. "Look, I'm not going to tell you to stay in your room. You spent enough of your life locked up. But people saw us together. The dangerous kind."

Elaine lounged in her throne. "They can try me, but they won't like it."

"Roger that." I stopped short before opening the door. Most of my life, I'd gone it alone. But at a key time, I'd had Ray and Elaine in my corner. Having support spoiled me. "I'm glad you're here."

"You should be. I'm pretty great."

With two hours to kill before any Blackguard-hosted panels, I decided to walk the floor. The public areas of the convention were divided among the lobby level and mezzanine. Lectures and panels were in the smaller conference rooms. Vendors were located in one of the big ballrooms. Special Guest tables were in another.

I veered toward the ballroom with the Special Guest tables. It being early Friday meant key cast members wouldn't be present, but the midlist players might already be staked out, taking advantage of every opportunity to hawk photos and autographs, and members of the Blackguard were firmly midlist. Don't take that the wrong way. During my convention days, I was chained to my table bell to bell. When you're low on the totem pole, you're making fans rather than maintaining them. Conventions were great outreach for those of us far from the top.

The thoroughfares were a trip fest of cloaks, banners, and scabbards. The halls were abuzz with rumors surrounding Reynard's absence at the opening ceremonies. He wasn't the sort to pass up the spotlight. It was rare, for a behind-the-camera person to rise to celebrity status. But here, Reynard wasn't just a cog in the wheel. He'd invented the wheel.

My loaner outfit held up. I caught several double takes, ending in the disappointed realization that I wasn't actually Blake Dever. The deflated reaction struck a well-calloused spot on my spirit. I'd been the guy you recognized from somewhere for the better part of a decade, since my one and only movie appearance leaked online. When those who recognized me finally realized exactly where in their memory they were being tickled from, they were inevitably let down.

The congested hall limited vision to arm's reach. I got bumped around like a pinball. An eight-year-old could have knifed me. I should have asked Dever for a chain-mail shirt.

The Special Guest ballroom was arrayed in a familiar formation. Long, collapsible tables lined the walls, with more dividing the room into aisles. Banners were draped over each of the tables, running a muted spectrum. Each was decorated with a fantastic animal. The animal thing kept coming up. It must have had to do with the show. If it turned out to be important, I was going to be kicking myself. I was being forced into learning all about *The Lands Beyond* against my will.

I posted up next to the entrance and waited for a solid ten count. This time, no tail. The flow of traffic was steady, building into a jam. Usually at these things, half the tables were ignored, but here even the most minor cast member was deluged with fans.

My heart rate spiked on sighting a member of the Blackguard, only to tank on realizing it was a cosplay. Everyone was dressed up. Not almost everyone. Every single guest and attendee. The costuming quality was off the charts. It made it impossible to filter out phonies. I covered my mouth and whispered, "Okay, which of these people are worth talking to?"

Starting on my immediate left, I did a slow sweep of the room. Before I was a quarter of the way through, Elaine chimed into my earpiece.

"You can stop. The table layout is in the program. Give me a second."

I passed the time performing allegorical analytics. The fans were basically color coded. Fire red, ice blue, leaf green, and lightning yellow were the most common, covering the four elements. The second layer was the animals. So you could be a fire bull or an ice one. An earth elk or a lightning eagle. Reynard had combined crayons and creatures into a new zodiac.

It was fandom 101: create subgroups for each different type of fan to identify with, offering enough room for individualism inside the greater group. Circles within circles that promised something for everyone, while also allowing fellow fans to easily sort you for their socialization needs. The followers of the Dame of the Moon wore green, accented with silver crescents, their points facing one of four cardinal directions, which probably meant something. Every one of them was a woman. It might have been my imagination, but I felt more glances off them than any of the other groups. The twinge of recognition, as if they had spotted me. Had the Dame sent out an all-points bulletin on Ken Allen?

While I'd changed clothes, a quick internet search would provide my face. Once one of them noted my current ensemble, maybe snuck a picture, they could distribute it through the group.

Besides the four colors, a small number of others were dressed in white or black. White looked like your stereotypical noble knight: shining armor, chivalric bearing. Black was the medieval ninja garb I'd identified with the Blackguard: studded armor, hoods, small blades, and slinky postures. A few of those scoped me out, but they were scoping everyone out. The shady assassin thing was their whole shtick. Elaine cut in to save me from my building paranoia. "The Blackguard has their own table, left of center on the far wall."

Now that I had my bearings, I could see the room was also divided by color. The four elements were at the cardinal points in the room, a physical representation of the settings' factions. Red was at the north point, with a white table to the right of it and a black table to the left.

I wove my way there, apologizing with each unintentional contact, whether it was my fault or not. The four-figure admission price hadn't detoured diehard fans. This was like a trip to Disney for adults. While the police cordon was no doubt turning away the newcomers, the attendees who had booked rooms the night before had awoken inside the gauntlet. The mass grew denser as I got closer to the red section. Red was the color of the king. My loaner duds from Blake Dever were red. Stern had also been wearing red.

The Blackguard table was to the left of the royal red one. Being on the back wall, it had immediate access to the service hallway. I eyed it from the cover of the crowd. There was only one person manning the station. He looked exactly like the guy who informed you were about to get audited: white, mostly bald with a band of close-trimmed hair around the ears. Average height, with no defining features and built like a distance runner. I inched close enough to overhear him, doing my best to stay clear of his peripheral vision.

He was having a conversation surrounding how to kill various characters on the show. Whether a spear or mace was the right choice for Lord Hawksgrave, or why apple brandy would be the preferable poison delivery system for Lady Constance. On its face, the topic should have been interesting, but all the imaginary people, places, and things mucked it up. It was like listening to two people debate how to hang wallpaper.

"Elaine, who is this guy?"

"Lord Rance Hyde of Bondskeep. His—"

"Got a real name?"

"Archibald Thelen."

"That's his real name? Sheesh. How much screen time does he get?"

"Only a few lines a season. His signature phrase is 'It will be done.'"

Thelen's protracted discussion with a pedantic fan led to some crowding. I joined the mass, maneuvering toward the front, and spoke softly to Elaine.

"What's Wallace Bowers's character name?"

"Lord Javak Nunn of Pathsbreak. His Aego is the Felumbra."

I understood exactly as many of those words as I needed to. The front line of fans held their positions. Fortunately, I had a few inches on them. I was probably doing something dumb here, but doing something dumb was underrated in my line of work. Dumb got results. Whether you liked those results or not was a topic of future conversation. I broke into the discussion, projecting my voice.

"What about, uh, Javak Nunn? How would you kill him?"

The outburst brought silence. Thelen looked at me, craning his neck like an owl. His eyes didn't move. I soldiered on.

"Thought exercise: You need to off one of your own. How do you give Nunn the axe?"

Thelen's mouth shrunk to a puncture mark. His eyes held at room temperature. "Poison. Lord Nunn is known for the prodigious amount of food he consumes."

"Huh. Why not just sneak up on him? Go with the good old stab in the back?"

The fans surrounding us found that proposition preposterous. Two portly fans with matching beards offered their opinions.

"No way you're catching Lord Nunn off guard. He's the Blackguard Cleave, dude. He's taken out rooms full of soldiers."

"Yeah, uh, he's the best axe fighter in the entire realm. Close-quarters fighting is like his whole deal."

Thelen kept his owl gaze locked on me.

"But doesn't he trust the rest of the Blackguard?" I asked. "Couldn't they exploit that?"

Another round of laughter. The left beard beat the right one to the punch. "Nunn's Aego is the Felumbra. It would alert him to any surprise attacks."

"Ah. Didn't think of that."

"Shuh, yeah."

Having completed one angle of study, Thelen cocked his head the other way. "And who might you be, sir? You wear Mallory colors."

"I'm Lord Allen of Kenland."

"Curious." Only Thelen's lips moved. The rest of his body was motionless.

The silence lasted two whole seconds before someone jumped in with another homicide hypothetical. Thelen addressed them, ignoring me utterly. I turned away and whispered to Elaine.

"He look back?"

"Yep."

"Thelen wasn't in Hammersmith's suite. Neither was Wallace, or whoever I mixed it up with in the hallway."

"Why?"

"The bars are high protein, low carb. My sparring partner and Thelen are both too slight to require protein bombs, and Wallace wasn't cutting carbs."

The royal red section was next. A sign outlined when big players from that faction would be present, starting with Blake Dever. Dever was also listed at the white table under his other character's name. He was a true man of the people, making two appearances a day per character. Over in the blue corner, Hammersmith was appearing only for one hour on Saturday, outside of special events and premium personal photo-ops.

Out of curiosity, I cruised by the Dame of the Moon's table. She was equally mysterious, her sign explaining she would appear as the cards foretold. I had been right about her giving private readings. What boggled me was the pricing.

"What are *gots*?"

"The coin of the realm," Elaine explained. "And it's pronounced *gots*."

"Reynard is minting his own money?"

"Yep. It's a digital currency, though you can 3D-print the coins. They have redemption codes on them."

That's what the scroll in my VIP kit had been about. The app was for managing and transferring Reynard's digital coins. "What's the exchange rate?"

Elaine told me. Twenty minutes with the Dame of the Moon ran three grand.

"Good work, if you can get it."

"Maybe the price is part of the draw."

As a former celebrity personal trainer, I concurred.

Lowballing a service could cut into your bottom line. You had to charge enough to make people believe you were worth it.

"Reynard wasn't the only one. The Dame's also got her own personal army blooming. Why are all the moon units women?"

"Uh. How can I put this delicately? They are based on the Amazons. Any male thralls are gelded."

"Yeah, I can see where that might limit guys running around wearing moons. It's announcing to the world you've been fixed. What's this drama about the Dame of the Moon's father?"

"She claims to have no father. To be fully a creation of a woman's bond with the sacred moon. But fans think it's a misdirect."

"So who's the leading lunar sperm donor?"

"The king. Which potentially gives her a claim on the throne, if she was born before the prince."

"And no one knows where the actress who is playing the Dame comes from. So art imitates life."

"Exactly. Proud of you, Ken."

"That makes one of us." I completed my circuit, exiting the Special Guest room, and set course for the vendors, thankful to have eyes in the back of my head. "Anyone on my heels?"

"Hard to tell. Zigzag a little."

I detoured a left at the lobby and made for the bathrooms. Six feet in front of the entrance, I stopped to check my laces.

"Someone in a black cloak, hood up. Maybe."

"Thelen put a tail on me. Good. It means my allusions had an effect."

Having made the trip, I kept in character and used the facilities. Aware Elaine had a camera between my eyebrows, I kept my eyes forward, washed my hands thoroughly and tried not to think about how many others going in and out didn't after doing their business.

"Remind me to pass on the complimentary mints," I whispered to Elaine.

Outside the entrance to the vendor ballroom, she chimed in.

"You picked the tail back up. Same guy."

"He look like he works out?"

"Hard to tell if it's even a him, with the cloak."

I took the stairs up the mezzanine. The cafeteria was a midcentury medieval dream, all wood, leather, and brass. Buffet-style dining ensured the guests would maintain a strong immune system through the unseasonable winter. I made a note to bomb some vitamin C and zinc tablets at my first opportunity.

A demolished breakfast buffet was being swapped out for lunch. The eggs were scrambled, which was the worst option away from home, with all the cream and butter dining establishments threw in with them. There was some decent-looking ham, with a brown sugar crust over a layer of congealed fat. After that was all the stuff I didn't eat: potatoes, pancakes, French toast, muffins, cereals. A neat contraption stuffed full of oranges with a hand crank allowed you to press your own juice, for people who liked their water with extra fructose. I was reaching for the ham tongs when I spotted a stout fellow in a chef's hat manning a cart with a hot plate. A woman dressed the same was stationed at a second cart.

Be still my beating heart. I practically jogged over. "Are you an omelet guy?"

The stout fellow beamed. "That I am. And she's the crepe lady. What's your pleasure?"

"Tell you what, you know your business. Dealer's choice, minus any carbs."

He perked up at my permission to employ creative freedom. Requesting a low-carb dish wasn't unusual for This Town. It was probably half the reason he had a job. The crepe lady was the yin to his yang, serving up a little guilty pleasure on your vacation.

The omelet chef surprised me by going with cream cheese, smoked salmon, and dill—a combination I never in a million years would have asked for. It was fantastic. I failed at eating it slowly but managed to not go back for seconds. Omelets were the way to go for folks like me, who were always watching their macros.

It might have been the calories, but my brain managed a good idea for once. There was an ATM on the mezzanine. I withdrew the maximum and tucked a twenty in my savior's tip cup, becoming the majority donor. "Bet you had a hell of a morning."

The omelet guy grinned inside his beard. "It's been eggstra special."

"You here all weekend?"

"Making custom breakfasts for strangers is my passion."

I held up a hundred bucks. "Up for a side hustle?"

He squinted dubiously. Omelet guys probably don't often get propositioned. "Doing what?"

"There are going to be a few health freaks here. Egg-white omelets. Four ounces of lean protein, that kind of thing."

He nodded at me. "I know the type."

"Keep an eye out for ones with a lot of muscle, my size or bigger. Especially any dressed in all black." I passed him my card and the money. "I'll be back tomorrow to show you some pictures, see if you recognize anyone."

He took a moment to analyze how my request might be illegal and came up empty. "Okay . . ."

I tipped my crown. "Don't worry, you aren't breaking the hallowed code of breakfast chefs. This is on the level. I'm a prince among men."

"If you say so. We wrap up at two."

I tossed him a thumbs-up and headed back to the stairs. Elaine didn't inquire, but I was too proud of myself not to explain.

"The Blackguard lost their stash. Which means whoever is behind the protein bars is panicking over keeping to his macros. If we get lucky, he'll turn to omelets. How's the tail?"

"Still on you, hiding behind every plant."

Live music met me as I passed into the ballroom where the vendors had set up shop, stringed instruments accompanied by light drums. The source was a band of troubadours who anchored the room on a low stage.

"Pretty mournful for a party."

"It's the *Lands Beyond* theme song," Elaine informed me.

I started on the left and moved clockwise around the room. Being right-handed, I wanted to turn in that direction in the event I needed to deflect a broadsword.

"I like the cellos."

Elaine laughed. "You would."

"What's that supposed to mean?"

"Cellos are the dirtiest instrument, Ken. I mean look at them."

"I take exception to that. I have never conducted myself as anything less than a gentleman."

"I've noticed. Riding shotgun on you, it's not like you haven't had the opportunity. Plenty of gals have shown interest, not to mention some guys. But you never bite."

"Cavorting with people involved in a case would be unprofessional. The same applied when I was a trainer."

The way Elaine clicked her tongue told me she was unconvinced, but she dropped the subject, which was A-okay with me. The booths on the immediate sides of the double doors were the biggest in the space. One was dedicated to ancient weapons, the other to armor and gowns. The big ticket items, for those looking to treat themselves to a medieval makeover on a magical weekend.

Those spots next to the entrance demanded the highest rent, but it was worth it. Folks who came to such things had dollars, or in this case gots, burning a hole in their pouches. Vendors warred to clean them out early. You had to take advantage of impulse buying before another merchant did.

The weapons were divided into two categories: sharp and not.

The sharp ones were moving at twice the rate as their blunted counterparts. Of those, some were labeled as competition safe, with flat tips and rounded guards. I waved down the booth worker with the thickest forearms.

"I'm new to this. What's with these swords?"

"Each one is for a different event." The guy had a shaved head, a healthy mustache, and serious burn scars down both arms. "It's structured a lot like HEMA, with a Crucible twist."

"Yeah? Are the fighters any good, or is it more a hobby thing?"

His forearm muscles rippled at my tone. "Society people make it their whole life. Some of them are the best in the world. Former champions, summoned by Reynard. You wouldn't want to draw steel with them in an alley."

I took a step back, palms up. "Gotcha, gotcha. I mean, I'm sure whoever stunts for Blake Dever is a pro."

"Ha!" the guy barked. "Dever doesn't use stunt people. He practically sleeps with his schlager."

"He the best?"

"Hmm." The guy stroked his beard, running hypotheticals. "With a long blade, maybe. Short blade is probably John Cannon."

"What about Hammersmith? He's been swinging a cutlass since the eighties."

"Yeah, he was legit in *Star Searchers*. But he's pushing seventy. Game's changed a lot since then."

I inspected price tags like I was weighing my decision. It wasn't ten seconds before the booth worker was called away, giving me time to tap Elaine.

"Who's John Cannon again? I've heard too many names the last few hours."

"He plays Sedek Grane, the Blackguard Point," Elaine informed me. "Before he was on the show, he was front man for that band Emotional Weathermap."

"What is it with England and all their pop stars becoming actors?"

"Blame the BBC. They run a racket over there. By the way, your tail broke off and started perusing chain mail."

"Loosening the leash. There's only one way out of this room. Sticking to my heels isn't important. What they really want to know is who I'm reporting to and where I'm shacking up."

The next booth was dedicated to books. It was split between fiction and nonfiction. The fantasy genre dominated the fiction section. Nonfiction was dedicated mostly to manuals, with some history and behind-the-scenes volumes on both *The Lands Beyond* and *Never After*. There was also a Reynard autobiography. If you asked me, autobiographies belonged in the fiction section. The central display was a trifold shelf dealing with the fictional histories of the Crucible lands. I scooped up an omnibus.

"Sire Press. Never heard of them."

"It's Reynard's own independent publisher. He had total control of the publishing rights: all print versions, eBook, audio."

To maintain the illusion, fictional authors were listed on the spines. I leafed through a dozen different ones. One name dominated the byline: Bradford Ravenlore. Or, in our world, Bradley Corbett.

"Corbett is more than an assistant."

"He's the *Lands Beyond* Laureate," Elaine said. "After Reynard, no one knows more than him. Except maybe Sheila Polk."

"And Polk is the OG Edgelord."

"Yep. She's been around since the *Never After* message boards. We're talking the prototype internet days on USENET. People love her."

"Home Drive-In is going to be all over her and Corbett. Even if they recover the series bible, the fans are going to riot at anyone but Reynard penning the scripts."

"The scripts should be done," Elaine countered. "Shooting starts in a few weeks. Reynard always has the story locked before cameras roll."

"That's what he says. But writers aren't known for working ahead of deadline. That goes double for the successful ones. I've never been on a set that didn't have script pages still warm from the printer."

Shelved with the manuals were a bunch of rulebooks: tournament dueling, mass combat, table-top, and live action role-play. Fans of fantasy sure loved their rules. One of the manuals was a guide on how to determine your *Aego*.

"I'm going to regret asking this, but what's an Aego?"

"Okay." Elaine was so elated she needed a moment to gather herself. "Aegos are like spirit animals. Every lord or lady of the Lands Beyond goes on a quest to discover their element or humor and what beast holds their bond."

"Ah. Reynard's version of the horoscope. Got it."

The next booth over was a pop-up video store, which was more my speed. I'd never been one for the written word. It took too much focus for a chronic multitasker such as myself, and audiobooks made me sleepy for some reason. Maybe trying to visualize things was too much for my gray matter.

The pop-up store had *Lands Beyond* series collections of all varieties: boxed sets, deluxe boxed sets, super deluxe sets with bookend statues.

The IMDb family tree spread roots from there, with films and television series featuring the key cast members. The selection was mostly illegal pirated copies of BBC productions, with the exception of Sven Hammersmith, who had used his *Star Searchers* nerd cred to scrape by on some sci-fi stinkers before his career resurgence.

As for the king himself, Reynard possessed only a smattering of official credits outside of *Never After* and *The Lands Beyond*. To someone not familiar with This Town, it might seem unusual that a creator had been the driving force behind one show, disappeared for twenty years, then reappeared, again at the helm. But it was an old story. The public-at-large didn't realize how many creatives worked uncredited in the industry. Script doctors who demanded high fees to "fix" projects from the shadows, the secret hands behind the throne.

As a result of the massive success of *The Lands Beyond*, Reynard's cult hit, *Never After,* had received the VIP remaster treatment, with the box design changing to suggest it had more in common with its younger sibling than it really did. I had vague memories of the show. The basic concept was that iconic fairy-tale characters were based on actual magical beings who had been reborn in the modern day, unaware of their mythical roots. As living archetypes, they were doomed to repeat their secret histories.

I perused the boxed set, my memories crawling back. The show had been a big idea on a small budget. They had done what they could with makeup and costuming. It had only gone two seasons before its big star, Lynn Chambers, disappeared from the spotlight. Some said health issues, others addiction, but that was all conjecture. The show had a memorable cast, many of whom went on to greater success, but Chambers was the breakout star. A haunted woman who slowly discovers she was the evil witch featured in all the fairy tales, destined to be swallowed by darkness and turn on her friends. Dark haired and pale skinned, Chambers was on the back of the box, looking as ephemeral as ever, with melancholy eyes under nineties-style bangs and blow out.

After the video booth, the merchandising began. Think of a thing, anything—guaranteed there was a *Lands Beyond*-branded version to be found here. Clothing, mugs, bedsheets, toothbrushes—you name it—the products ran the literal spectrum. Reynard's Technicolor world was the medieval version of a sports league. That was before even getting into the action figures, stuffed animals, and prop reproductions.

Sanctioned services lined the back wall. For a fee, you could become an official member of *The Lands Beyond*, either joining an established family tree or, for a larger fee, creating your own lineage. An additional fee allowed you to tie your line to an already established one through fealty. Then you could pay to schedule an official Aego hunt, have heraldry designed and printed, and enroll in both virtual and live events.

All of it was controlled by the Edgelords. Reynard was a true entrepreneur. Past the show, past the products, he was creating a culture. And you couldn't spell *culture* without *cult*. In the vacuum created by Reynard's death, revenue in the hundreds of millions was looking for an heir. But beyond that, there was also power up for grabs. Who stood to inherit the throne?

8

REYNARD CLAIMED TO HAVE KEPT THE identity of his heir under wraps, but someone had to know. An empire like this didn't exist without paperwork.

"Elaine, when you get a chance, can you look into Reynard's legal representation?"

"Will do."

"Exciting weekend for you, I know."

"Are you kidding me? I wish I got my camera crown on you the second you walked through the door."

The rest of the vendor circuit was devoted to handcrafted artisanal goods. Dried food, premium jerky of every imaginable animal—including a few that were made up—honey, and craft beer. A large booth featuring gowns going for wedding-dress prices tapered into the armor shop.

I surveyed the options with professional interest. As someone who had broken most of their fingers and toes, it was always good to get an idea where not to hit an opponent. Skinning your knuckles on a bulletproof vest was worlds apart from punching someone encased in metal.

A barrel-chested man a head shorter and belt size wider than me ambled my way. Up top, his armor was the full knight's deal, but on bottom it ended in a long metal-reinforced skirt. It made him look like a bell.

"My lord, might I compliment your gambeson? It is finely made indeed."

"Thanks. My ma, she really does a bang-up job."

"Might I suggest a brigandine vest? It provides the ideal protection for urban assemblages such as this one."

He gestured to a rack where a high-collared tan leather vest stood. It looked like the fantasy version of Kevlar. Brass studs dotted its surface. I'd seen the design before. It was standard issue among the Blackguard.

"What's brigandine?"

Rather than be annoyed by my newbie question, the guy lit up. "The outside layer is thick leather, with a more supple fleece-lined leather inside. Small steel scales are sandwiched between the layers, riveted in place."

"So the studs on the outside, those are the rivets."

"Indeed."

I took a close look. It wasn't going to stop a bullet, but it would turn a blade. The chest, back, and neck were covered. I thought back to my scrap with the medieval ninja. They'd gone after my face, my armpit, and my wrist, while avoiding the easier to hit torso. The Blackguards' entire fighting style had revolved around avoiding armor. But then we'd tangled up on the ground. They'd felt my form, up close and intimate. Which meant the bad guys knew I was running around as good as naked.

"How much does this stuff run?"

The armorer provided the price in gots. I had to use my phone calculator to convert. When I saw the number, I ran it a second time, sure I had screwed up a decimal.

"Let me mull it over."

"Consider in haste, my lord. Our best stock will not last the morn."

Different world, same sales tactics. Act now, while supplies last. I put my phone to my ear as cover and spoke to Elaine. "Honey, how mad would you be if I came home dressed as Lancelot?"

"Mad? More like the opposite."

"Seems like it would chafe. Any eyes on my tail?"

"They shifted over to the video booth when you got close."

I looked back at the armored vest. "I can't believe I'm considering this. I have to admit, I miss the peace of mind that comes with being bulletproof."

To buy anything here, I would have to download the *Got Pouch* app, link it to my bank account, and convert funds. But it was the coin of the realm. Maybe I could expense the whole deal to Reynard's estate.

I was thumbing my address into the touch screen when the bearded bell of the booth tapped me on the shoulder. "Your payment has been received, sire. If you would but follow me into fitting."

A quick check on my screen confirmed I hadn't halfway completed the process. I didn't have to linger in suspense. As I stepped into the dressing booth, Elaine chimed in.

"Happy birthday."

The quarters were too tight for me to reply that my birthday had been two months ago. The stout armorer brought in forearm and shin guards along with a vest, all of them the same butter-colored leather. I made like a scarecrow while the armorer bolted everything into place. He started with the vest.

"Expand your lungs while I fit this, sire, as to not restrict your breathing."

"Sure. The last thing I want is a bout of the vapors."

The vest was around twenty pounds, most of it supported by my shoulders. I had enough of a V shape where the rest of the load was distributed evenly throughout my torso. The tail end of the vest had a slight curve to it, tapering to a point to cover my lower stomach but still allowing full range of motion for my hips. It also meant equestrian events were still on the table.

The bracers fully encased my forearms, with a thumb loop to keep them from rotating. The shin guards were a little fussier, being opposed by gravity and reliant on the size of your calves. It was a good thing I literally kept on my toes. Train long enough, and a loaded stance becomes second nature.

When he was finished, the armorer rotated me to face a trifold mirror. I looked ridiculous, which meant I fit right in. In my earpiece, Elaine whistled a catcall. The armorer seconded her emotion.

"Quite dashing, if I do say so myself, sire. A cloak, perhaps, would complete the ensemble. Or a stole of fine fur."

"Nah. I've fought a few guys in capes. They always get tangled up in them."

"Ah, are you a seasoned sellsword? If so, methinks it strange you do not carry arms."

I'd already been pulled in far enough to start wearing armor. Strapping on a sword was going too far. "I'll manage. Thanks."

The guy waved me off as I went for my pouch.

"A gratuity was already included, sire. Fare thee well."

"Back at ya."

I exited into the hallway, checking the time. Elaine lasted all of thirty seconds of me being alone. "My knight in shining armor."

"I'll admit I am less worried about getting shivved in the yard."

"What can I say? Gift-giving is my love language. Where to next?"

"Attending some panels to get a closer look at the Blackguard."

"Aye-aye, Captain."

The workshop didn't start for thirty minutes, and there were already two dozen people lined up ahead of me. It was an even mix of men and women, all of them on the younger side, including some whose parents had to have driven them to the hotel. Almost all the men were dressed to emulate the Blackguard, in tactical medieval style. I was the only guy without at least three bladed objects strapped to me. As for the ladies, it was evenly divided between that aesthetic and the armored princess route. After assessing my peers, I spent the rest of my time in queue on my phone, doing background on John Cannon.

Cannon was twenty-seven, having joined the show five seasons prior. As a teenager, he'd been in two different manufactured boy bands, a time-honored UK tradition. Once he was no longer a minor, he'd formed his own group, Emotional Weathermap, and produced two albums. Each had done well, though his success was attributed to his established audience carrying over. From there, Cannon had pivoted to acting, appearing in a few indie films before being cast as Sedek Grane in *The Lands Beyond*.

His character was described as an impetuous hothead, quick to anger and known for publicly calling his enemies out, confident his skills in combat would win the day. The prevailing opinion was that his character would eventually mouth off to the wrong badass and not survive the final season.

Five minutes before showtime, the line started to shuffle inside. Everyone did their best not to trip on everyone else's scabbards, with mixed results. Those things were a real menace. Had there been personal injury lawyers in the Middle Ages, they could have made a career off scabbard-related falls.

The workshop space immediately set off nostalgic sensations. Four sixteen by sixteen-foot squares of painter's tape had been laid over the industrial grade carpet utilized in hotels and casinos. I knew those dimensions instinctually. It was the martial art standard. Small for a ring, but at amateur events space was a premium. Event managers had to jam in as many simultaneous bouts as possible. As an up-and-comer, I knew all my efforts were paying off as I literally graduated into larger arenas.

The room was bereft of furniture. The attendees sorted themselves according to their eagerness to participate. Those who had come solely to see John Cannon live and in person hugged the walls. The ones who fancied themselves fighters toed the tape. Some took a knee, others sat folded in traditional poses, their hands resting on their thighs as if at attention for the shogun.

I parked near the door, a blind spot to anyone entering, and crossed my arms. Crossed arms read as defensive, but this getup had no pockets to speak of. What did people do with their hands back then? Rest them on their pommels or hook their thumbs into their belt, if a survey of the room was an accurate sample. I tried the belt thing. It felt contrived. Crossed arms it was.

A musician at heart, John Cannon showed up fashionably late. He was a white guy, average height, with thick, wild red hair and sparkling eyes. His mouth had a permanent quirk, as if he were continually thinking of something funny. The Blackguard's schtick was head-to-toe sable, and Cannon was no exception. His outfit was the medieval equivalent to a finely tailored suit: a sleek three-quarter-length jacket and tapered trousers. The jacket had blackened metal panels on the shoulders. Underneath the jacket was an armored vest like mine. Cannon carried a slim-bladed sword as if it were a walking stick. A scabbard would have broken up his lines.

Two men came in flanking Cannon. Both wore hooded black cloaks with sword bulges underneath. Neither was taller than him. Some celebrities were touchy about that when it came to their security. They didn't want to look dwarfed in photographs.

"Well, hello!" Cannon slapped his palms together, his gloves muffling the sound. "Welcome to Slaying with Style. Want to learn how to kill someone?"

The crowd didn't know what to do with him and checked each other for cues. In the back, one girl unleashed an excited *wooo!*

Cannon pointed at her. "She gets it. Come on, let's hear it for murder!"

Cannon motioned with both arms like a conductor and people started to cheer. "That's better. You'd think someone died around here. Sheesh."

Cannon hovered on the edge of laughter. It was hard to judge if he was making a little inside joke or existed in a permanent state of self-amusement. "Okay, so, I'm sure many of you have studied the choreography used on the show. It's not like any other show you've seen, because the moves are all based on actual historic techniques. Some people use longswords or axes or spears, but my character is different."

Cannon drew his weapon with a flourish, tossing the scabbard aside as he swept the blade clear. Its tip stopped a hair short of slicing the carpet. "My character, Sedek Grane, is an artist. Death is his medium."

He started to move inside the square, his footwork precise. His body coordination was first rate: feet, hips, and arms moving together. Power was mass times velocity. Cannon didn't have the mass, but he knew how to generate speed. He worked mostly with the point. Any cuts were tight arcs, delivered with a minimum of windup. Either he had been studying since childhood, or the guy was a prodigy. It happened sometimes. Some people who sat down at the keys could just play.

He was also left-handed. The sinister hand, Romans had called it. Lefties were always a problem. It was like fighting a mirror. Everything was backward. You had to employ a whole different set of techniques. But orthodox fighters trained against very few lefties, while lefties spent all their time fighting right-handed people.

Cannon spoke as he whirled through techniques. "Bob Hobbs, the lead choreographer, explained to me that Sedek's fighting style was unique. It wasn't designed for the battlefield. It wasn't for tournaments. It was kill or be killed. Sedek races death with every strike." Cannon came to a sudden halt, his last blow shifting to a fencer's salute. "I'll need a volunteer."

Hands shot up faster than a starter pistol. Crossing blades with a cast member was a once-in-a-lifetime opportunity for a superfan. Cannon pretended to survey the crowd.

Somehow, I knew what was coming. I used to get the same feeling back in school, willing myself into invisibility as the teacher determined who would least like to perform algebra in front of the whole class.

Cannon was a performer first. His eyes settled on me as if he had only now registered my presence. He pointed me out with his sword, the tip perfectly aligned with my right eye. "You sir. The one garbed in the house of Mallory."

The crowd whirled toward me. I joined them, craning my head, even though my back was to the wall. When I looked back, Cannon's eyes were waiting.

"You talking to me?"

"Oh yes. I've been eager to cross swords with Blake Dever, and you're the closest thing to him within reach of my blade."

I patted myself down. "Ah heck, I left Excalibur in my other surcoat. I'm always doing that."

The sound of drawn steel echoed through the room as a dozen helpful attendees offered up their swords. The remainder of them dug out their phones. Wonderful. I might have been the only person in This Town who viewed going viral as a bad thing. It had been all of two months since it had last happened. Maybe one day it would be for something I was proud of.

I kicked off the wall and ambled over, perusing my options when it came to cutlery. As I was passing one of Cannon's bodyguards, I spun around and shot a hand into his cloak. He tried to step into me, but I shoved him away. His sword I kept. It whisked free of his scabbard as he stumbled backward.

"I'll use one I'm sure works, thanks."

The sword was a lot like Cannon's, which wasn't a surprise: more Zorro than Conan. Bodyguards often also served as instructors and sparring partners. Our clients loved to practice on us, and we had to grin and bear it to salve their egos. Though if either of these guys were better than Cannon, they ought to resign and try out for the Olympic team.

Cannon made an inconspicuous two-fingered gesture with his free hand. The guards backed off. Interesting. He had signals for his guys, and they listened. Bodyguards often had to do the opposite: it could be exhausting, saving someone from themselves.

Cannon started to circle. Being left-handed, he moved right, to keep me outside his profile.

Though I was right-handed, I followed his lead, maneuvering to keep his guards in view. But they circled with us. No matter which way I was turned, one was always going to be at my back.

Cannon started narrating the lesson. "Distance is key. Knowing when you are in the killing zone, and when you are safe from death."

Hyperbole aside, Cannon had the goods. He was intimately familiar with his weapon. He knew its reach to the millimeter. Conversely, I had no clue. I tapped the ground like a blind man, noting the point on the carpet, and brought the sword up. It was fairly light, less than two pounds, and well balanced.

Still, holding the point level and moving it took effort from the shoulder, forearm, and wrist.

Sword fighting was like any other athletic endeavor—the muscles employed were sport specific. Your standard push/pull split wasn't going to do much when it came to thrust and parry. I kept my sword close to my body, like I was trying to tap my opposite shoulder with the blade, in a stance more akin to stick fighting than fencing.

"Don't worry, you're perfectly safe," Cannon said. He lunged, flicking his sword upward into a thrust. I read it as a feint and ignored him. The thrust stopped six inches short of my Adam's apple. He slid back out, ready for a response. His expression shifted from playfulness to respectful surprise. The performance wasn't for my benefit. He was catering to his fans.

His next attack was a low/high switch, with a false thrust at my groin flipping up into a cut at my face, delivered backhanded, so the flat would slap me across the cheek. I didn't try to parry with my sword. Instead, I used my armored forearm to deflect while coming up from underneath with a cut of my own, aiming for his armpit.

Cannon was fast. He reversed direction with his sword and intercepted my cut. He sprang from the parry to deliver a slap at my opposite cheek, but I followed his sword upward with my own, sweeping his blade away.

Cannon broke off with a spin. "Well, well. The king's man has hidden talents. What a delightful surprise."

He came in again. He kept his mouth quirked but his eyes were ice cold. He wove a pattern of thrusts and cuts, mostly from the arm, determined to score. I kept my guard tight, focused on his point and steadily withdrew, circling out with each attack to force him to chase.

There's a world of difference between wanting to win and trying not to lose. Even experts could be held off by determined turtling. A total commitment to defense was easier than attempting to score. Attacking someone created openings your opponent could exploit.

But the end was inevitable. I couldn't hold Cannon off forever, and there was no way I was going to land a touch. I'd taken my one shot at surprising him. The second I extended, he was going to skewer me.

But that didn't matter to the audience. The onlookers thought they were witnessing a battle for the ages. They gasped and roared as if they were watching a trapeze act. To the layman, a long fight was a close one, even if one side had no chance. By surviving for all of thirty seconds, I was making Cannon look bad, which was never a good thing. It showed on his face. His smile faded into a sneer.

Cannon locked blades with me and drove in, taking hold of my sword hand with his free one. I returned the favor. He angled to step into a trip, but swords or not, I knew that game and rotated with him. While we were hugged up, Cannon whispered into my ear.

"You sully the name of Jove Brand."

Ah, boy. I figured Cannon had decided to give me a public flogging by way of a warning. Let me know I was in over my head, going after the Blackguard, in an attempt to scare me off. But I was in more trouble than I thought. Way more. Allow me to explain.

To Americans, Jove Brand is an iconic character. A suave superspy who travels the world, seduces beautiful people, and eliminates anyone in his way. A household name, for sure, but just one among many other action stars. On the other side of the Atlantic, Jove Brand was something greater. He represented England's national identity. Gave them fictional relevance in a time after the sun had set on their empire and they were sandwiched between superpowers. To Brits, Jove Brand was akin to a deity.

Which meant my dismal performance was sacrilege.

I had played the role exactly once, in my sole film appearance, in order for the producer, Calabria Films, to satisfy a contractual requirement. The film was meant to be buried forever, but in the internet age, nothing stayed dead. Had the Calabrias the choice, they would have fired the print into the sun.

Could it have really been that bad, you ask? Well, I'm the only non-UK actor ever cast in the role, as well the only actor never to be knighted for playing Jove Brand. And I'm eligible, having an English father. Chances were, if John Cannon ran me through, he'd be Sir John Cannon by the end of the week.

Cannon spun out of the bind to get his distance. He'd lost his head there for a moment but recovered quickly. Swords were what he was good at, not wrestling. Me, I wasn't looking to win. Surviving was victory enough.

I chose my moment. Cannon came in with an overhead cut. I saw it for what it was and brought my sword up obliquely to block it. There's a difference between parrying and blocking. Parrying was a redirection of energy. A deflection. Blocking was a total stoppage, a meeting of force versus force.

In almost all cases, parrying was preferable. You could end in a better place than you started through parrying. Blocking just battered you. You could break your forearms, your shins, absorbing damage. It had happened to me on more than one occasion.

Cannon's sword never touched mine. He went right around it, his blade reversing to sweep up under my chin. His mouth stayed amused, but his eyes were calculating. The smart thing to do would have been to pretend surprise, to sell that he'd caught me off guard. But, as explained above, I wasn't much of an actor.

"You got me."

Cannon's expression flickered, but people were watching. He broke off, throwing his arms wide to soak in the applause, before turning back to salute me with his blade. As I returned the gesture, we locked eyes. His look said it all.

This wasn't over.

9

CANNON LAUNCHED INTO A TUTORIAL USING moments from the show as examples, which gave me the opportunity to slip away. I returned my borrowed sword on the way out the door. The guard angled their face down when I tried to peak under their hood. Less distracted, I noticed he or she was downright petite.

"Well, that was a moment," Elaine said into my earpiece. "Is Cannon the killer?"

"He might be. He'd know how to use Reynard's crown as a murder weapon, and he's wearing gloves. On the other hand, it's hard to imagine him crawling around in the walls. But he's not whoever I fought outside room 513. Totally different style, down to the dominant hand."

My early exit secured me a prime spot in line for the next panel hosted by a Blackguard member. According to the internet, Mikail Chelovak had been an amateur mixed martial arts fighter prior to playing the heavy in a series of European action films. Reynard was repeating himself. Alexi Mirovich ended up on the show the same way. After being cast on *The Lands Beyond*, Chelovak parlayed his platform into becoming an influencer, surfing controversy to expand his base.

The demographics of those in line mirrored that following. It was all men, almost exclusively young. Those who weren't fancied they were. As a type, they were well-groomed, with precisely calculated facial hair. They flashed jewelry and wore cologne. Those who were talking were doing so loudly and over each other. Those who weren't were staring at their phones. Their screens showed nothing I ever wanted in my search history.

A few minutes before the doors were scheduled to open, a second wave of the same breed arrived, ignoring the line to crowd by the door. Those looking at their phones looked harder, but those who were talking took exception.

What came next was the typical pretending-you-wanted-to-fight-while-absolutely-not-wanting-to-fight performance. The involved parties addressed each other with a myriad of synonyms for friend—bud, pal, chief—and declarations of brotherhood. Both sides had serious doubts the other knew who they were dealing with, or what they were made of. They got in each other's faces close enough to rub noses.

The doors opened before I got a chance to evaluate Chateau d'Loire's security policy. The knot at the threshold shoved in all at once. I started to worry the room would reach capacity before I got there, while also kind of wishing it would. My wish was not granted. I was one of the last attendees in.

The room filled up starting at the back, everyone angling for the cool seat. I pondered standing, but after being publicly singled out by one Blackguard member, it was probably best to do what I could to fade into the crowd. Unfortunately, all that was left was front and center. The guys on either side of me, neither of them old enough to rent a car, spread into my seat space. Rather than shoulder myself some room and perhaps cause another disturbance, I leaned forward, which I hoped would keep me under Chelovak's eyeline.

Chelovak arrived aggressively on time. As the hour rolled over, he barreled in from the back hallway reserved for VIPs and staff traffic. Unlike Cannon, he traveled alone. He was an ex-fighter, not a pop star. The role of security was to play the bad guy: to enforce space, to plow a path, and to refuse access. Chelovak appeared to have no problem being his own bad guy.

He used every step up to the stage, moving to the center without haste. The podium and house microphone were pushed off to the side. Once Chelovak hit his mark, he surveyed the crowd. I looked down at my program to avoid eye contact. Chelovak started off with something like, "We're men in a world that doesn't want men to be men." I repressed a groan and snuck a peek at him.

He was six-four or -five and built like Charles Atlas. He looked like an artist was told to draw a face with no further elaboration. He had thick brown hair identical to what you see on Lego figures. He was decked out in Blackguard gear: armored vest and shoulders, bracers, shin guards. A combination of a hammer, axe, and spear was angled across his back.

No chance Chelovak was the guy in the hallway, but he was the right build to require premium protein bars, and he still might be one of the six who were in room 513. I decided to sit through his lecture to get a read on him. What followed was one of the longest hours of my life.

The topic was maximizing masculinity, which apparently involves a lot of Greek letters. Alpha this and beta that. Chelovak expressed clear disdain for people who did not blaze their own path. His audience ate it up wholesale, obediently listening and taking notes.

The core message was sensible enough: Focus on self-improvement and work toward your goals. The problem is, once you've said that, you still had fifty-nine minutes to fill. Things didn't turn ugly until

Chelovak started talking about women. Despite his insistence that one should not focus on women, they kept coming up, though never as women and always as females. Women were presented as mercenaries, and interpersonal relationships were math problems, easily solved with the proper formula. A formula that included dollar signs.

"If I don't mute this, I'm going to puke," Elaine said into my earpiece.

"Please do. I wish I could."

Once the topic of romantic relationships was broached, the atmosphere changed. The room became humid as the audience voiced agreement. Chelovak's nonsense played well. The same routine had put butts in seats in the eighties and fifties. Probably did well in the 1850s and 1580s. The quest for manhood was an enduring topic. You'd always find guys who, inside, felt like boys and were desperate to be seen as men.

Chelovak spoke firmly and clearly, free of any accent. He'd picked his audience well. The crossover made sense. People who thought of themselves as failures in life were drawn to the lure of starting over in a new society, and Reynard's fandom was a place to reinvent themselves. They saw his world as an example of "the good old days," which, of course, had never existed.

The last fifteen minutes were reserved for questions. Every person called on was an obvious plant. Chelovak was hawking some kind of online subscriber community called the Lone Pack. For a fee, you could become part of a network of other alphas. I wasn't entirely convinced anyone in the room knew what the definition of *alpha* was.

The lecture ended suddenly with Chelovak telling everyone to "get after it," then marching out of the room to hasty applause sparked by audience plants. I was dying to get out of what had become a sauna created by a room full of musky guys on high-protein diets, but being up front was like sitting in row 35 on a plane. I detoured around the stage and exited into the back hallway.

Something was wrong with the exit door's pneumatics. The barest touch and it blasted open. The swinging slab narrowly missed Chelovak, who was on his phone, saying, "—front row."

Our eyes locked. There was recognition in his. He hung up his phone like he was trying to punch his thumb through the screen. His other hand twitched toward his weapon. I eased the door shut. He stared at me, trying to decide: fight or flight.

I shrugged. "You know, running away isn't very alpha."

Twenty feet behind Chelovak, a door slammed open so hard it bounced off the wall. The medieval ninja I'd already tangled with stormed through it, with another man on their heels. I recognized him right away, though I had only ever seen him on Bradley Corbett's screen:

Kurt Hooper, prime suspect number one.

"Watch the hall."

Hooper's voice was three octaves lower than what you'd expected from a body like his. He drew a broad blade from the small of his back. I'm not sure when a knife stopped being a knife and was considered a sword, but that thing was right on the line. Its intricate knuckle guard covered his hand.

"Bye now." Chelovak smiled. He threw a wave back at me as he and Hooper crossed paths.

The hallway was about double the standard size—wide enough for two service carts to pass at a squeeze. Hooper closed in, the hand with the knife in it palm up, as if he were presenting the blade to me. Behind him, medieval ninja drew their own knife.

"You guys wouldn't happen to have a spare dagger or something, would you? I'm feeling a little left out."

My chances weren't as bad as they first appeared. They could only come at me one at a time and the cramped quarters ruled out a second round of pepper spray. Hooper having a partner at his back was a win-win for me. Either they had to stay far enough away to allow Hooper to maneuver, or they hugged up on him, in hopes of getting into the action, which hampered his movement.

Hooper came in without hesitation, which was mistake number one. When you spent all your time armed, you lost respect for someone who wasn't. I lunged forward to meet him. He slashed toward my face. Rather than try to meet his blade, I shot an arm out past it and deflected the attack at his forearm. Our bracers clashed off each other, sending our arms apart.

I wasn't used to wearing arm guards. Hooper was. He used the momentum to fuel a low attack, targeting the outside of my knee. I stopped it by slamming a palm into his upper arm while sending out a backfist. He checked it while simultaneously sending a knife-knuckle punch at my hip. Hooper's hand was encased in metal. If the punch hit, I was going to be in a world of hurt. Being saddled with a limp would make me as good as chopped salad.

My solution was the Superman punch. I took to the air, throwing the target leg back while blasting a rear hand that caught Hooper dead center in the face. He reeled back, but I was too out of position to take advantage. We reset at the same time. I shook out my hands, breathing easy. Blood ran out of Hooper's nose. He let it flow. We were done feeling each other out. The next exchange would be decisive.

Doors opened both in front and behind us. Behind Hooper, a group of Special Guests from a panel that had run late filled the hallway, laughing. Over my shoulder, the hotel staff exited from the kitchens with ice-water carts.

Hooper sheathed his knife without looking. I tried not to show how much that impressed me. Behind him, the medieval ninja disappeared their own blade. I stared at them together.

"See you around."

Hooper wiped the blood off his face but kept quiet. By the time our oblivious interrupters had cleared the hallway, the two of them were gone.

You could have used my esophagus to sand the floor. Two fights, each of which had lasted two minutes, left me feeling like I'd hiked Death Valley. I went back to the mezzanine and helped myself to complimentary water loaded with enough limes to prevent scurvy. My thirst being quenched caused my empty stomach to cry out.

Pickings were slim at the lunch buffet. The cheese board had suffered carnage untold, but the salad bar was virtually untouched. I went for that, keeping clear of the greens, which didn't hold up in communal dining settings. None of the soups appealed. As much as I liked a nice soup, it got tiresome picking around the rice and noodles. Cornish hens were featured on the hot side. I grabbed one of them and a double helping of roasted Brussels sprouts.

The cafeteria being run by the hotel meant I was able to pay with forty American dollars for a midday meal. It was going to be a long weekend. I set the alarm on my phone right then and there so I would be up before breakfast was served.

In between bites and people watching, I consulted the program. The Revels looked to be an old-timey version of dinner theatre. They were a big deal, with limited seating. The VIP package provided by Will Norman guaranteed me a spot. He'd pulled out all the stops, but I wasn't naive enough to believe I was the only horse he'd bet on. And why wouldn't he? It's not like he had to put any money down.

Being in a public area gave the tails on me the chance to reset. Odds were, any eyes on me only stayed so while mine were diverted. Fortunately, I had cameras encircling my skull. Paging through the program, I spoke softly to Elaine.

"Anyone watching me?"

"Besides some thirsty gazes?"

"Blame Blake Dever. I look like a generic, attainable version of him, and these cons are known for being hookup havens."

"Someone in a black cloak is on your far right, ignoring their chocolate cake. Two college-aged girls in green are drinking iced coffees and pretending not to stare."

I abruptly stood up and stretched.

"They all looked away."

I bussed my dishes before heading toward the panel rooms. People who didn't clean up after themselves ranked right up there with folks who didn't rerack their weights. If we don't all do our part, society crumbles.

Back out in the lobby, the attendees buzzed with excitement, unaware murders were being attempted and committed all around them.

Elaine found something to say before I did. "I can't find anything online about Reynard's representation. No agent, manager, or lawyer. You would think whoever repped him would be shouting it from the rooftops."

"Reynard has used lawyers before. He had a paternity suit during *Never After*. Maybe he stayed with that attorney. From what I've learned, he stuck with people who did right by him."

"There might be a court record," Elaine postulated. "But if it was pre-internet, who knows? I've looked into Reynard before, just for fun. There isn't much."

"He might be actively bleaching his history. He wouldn't be the first person to revise his past on making it big."

"You know what they say: all writing is rewriting."

"Reynard had the beginnings of a cult going here. Legions of devoted followers, a system for ranking them up. He rewarded loyalty and results, played his people off each other." That thought sparked another. "I was assuming the Blackguard tunneled into Reynard's room on the sly, but what if they didn't? What if Reynard wanted them to have direct, secret access so he could send them off to do dirty work? If Reynard was making moves, now would be the time, while he had the cast and crew all together."

"But what kinds of moves? He was already in charge."

Corbett was the one to ask about that, but he was hugged up on Will Norman. I needed the next closest person to the top. The person who had been around longest.

"I need to talk to Sheila Polk."

Polk's next panel was an hour off, so I took the opportunity to try to check into my room. Elaine kept watch through the cameras hidden in my crown. Try as I might, I couldn't shake my tail. Either a woman with a moon theme or a figure in a black cloak kept in my shadow. I was going to have to do something. Over the next two days, sleep was unavoidable. I couldn't have a gaggle of murderer suspects knowing where I was resting my head.

I used the stairwell to set the snare, climbing to the third floor, then ducking next to the entry door. Less than ten seconds later, the door cracked, and a figure in a black cloak inched their head into the hall.

I snagged them by the hood and dragged them out. They vacated the cloak with a practiced whirl. I spun counter their direction, into a foot sweep. It connected hard, sending them so high in the air I had to wait for them to land.

My tail let out a groan as the wind was hammered out of their body. The pitch was higher than I liked in someone I was roughing up. A twinge of guilt seasoned with a dash of panic sprinkled through my nervous system. I put on my best poker face as I transitioned into knee-on-belly control.

"You're just a kid."

My shadow was somewhere between thirteen and fifteen. It's hard to tell with boys in that growth-spurt window. He had the solid leanness of a young athlete, and showed some training by trying to shrimp out from under my knee. But I had him in both size and experience. I surfed easily through his escape attempts, maintaining top position.

"While you're working on that, let's hear your life story."

A loose black mask covered his lower face, but his eyes were dark and sullen. The classic teenage gaze. He fought to keep his efforts silent. I didn't know what to threaten him with. I wasn't willing to hurt him and didn't have the acting chops to pretend I was. I tried to think, what was the teenage boy most afraid of?

Pinning him under my knee, I patted him down. He wasn't armed. His cell phone was in a convenient location. The screen was locked. I tugged down his mask and held it up to his face. Bingo. My first stop was his contacts.

Looking down at him, I asked, "How do you spell *mom* again?"

That got no reaction. I plowed ahead. It was important to display fortitude to the younger generation. "What, she doesn't care if you run around playing mazes and monsters?"

I thumbed through his text messages. Mom was near the top. Then came a cluster of group texts. Then one from a girl that let me know his name was Brenden. A week down was a text from Father Dearest.

"Are you a junior, Brenden? What should I call your dad?"

I showed Brenden the screen and hit the call button. He broke before the second ring.

"Don't. Please."

"Why not? Shouldn't your dad know his kid spends his weekends as an apprentice assassin?"

"He'll use it against my mom." The kid had sulky huffing down. "And I'm a squire."

"Your truculence is wearing thin, Brenden. Who put you on me? Cannon? Chelovak? Thelen?"

I listed my prime suspect third. That way, I could measure Brenden's reaction to the two wrong answers. Everyone deceives differently.

Some people look away, others bear down, convinced maintaining eye contact would read as veracity. When I used Thelen's name, Brenden looked away.

"Okay, I give up. You're one tough cookie, kid. Here's the deal: I watch you walk back down to the lobby from the stairs. Stay away, and your phone will be at the front desk by the end of the day. If I see you again, I set up a time to hand you and it over to your dad."

Brenden rolled up the second I turned him loose. "This is stealing. And assaulting a minor."

"Better call the cops then."

Brenden trudged his way down the stairs, pausing his angst long enough to hop the banister on the last turn. An unfamiliar twinge rolled through me. By the time I found out I had a kid, he was able to vote. Watching kids now, I couldn't help but feel cheated out of all the moments I had missed. After confirming Brenden didn't double back, I detoured to Elaine's room, making sure the kid's phone screen stayed unlocked.

Elaine saw me coming via my crown and was waiting with a cord in hand. Her door was only cracked for the two seconds it took for me to hand it over.

"Stealing from children. For shame, sir."

"Adversity builds character. Reynard's cult is crossing generational lines. I'm betting Brenden's mother is an Edgelord, and I'm further proposing his father has had enough of this crap."

"I'll look into it."

"The group texts too. Maybe he has a thread with his fellow squires."

"Or maybe this chippie in his DMs is leading him along. This isn't my first rodeo, Ken."

I managed to find my room without picking up another escort. It was a single with a bathroom to the right of the door and a closet to the left. No axe murderers were lurking in the corners, which was notable because there was an actual axe murderer at large. I had nothing to unpack. My street clothes were in Blake Dever's suite. Besides my wallet, keys, and phone, all I had to my name was Elaine's surveillance crown and Reynard's ring.

Elaine would have loved to get her hands on that ring. If it held any hidden secrets, for sure she would find them. But handing it over put a target on her. If you needed the ring to open the book, then whoever had the book would also be gunning for it. Said person would reason out that either the cops had it, Corbett had it, or I had it. They couldn't do anything about the cops, and Corbett was under Norman's wing, which left the target on me.

What I needed was a quiet moment to myself. Odds were sleep was out the window the next two days. Time-outs were the best I could do. It was cool in the room, but not cool enough. The thermostat bottomed out at sixty. The windows existed purely to provide a view. I clipped the curtains closed with a pants hanger. Everything with a light of any kind, even a power indicator, got unplugged. I sat in the provided chair, back straight, with my palms on my thighs. Say what you will about armor, but it excels at supporting posture.

Eyes closed, I regulated my breath. The trick to not thinking about anything was to focus on the mundane. The ambient odors, or the feel of the air on your skin. With no new stimulus, over time each sense turned off, one by one. Fatigue started to set in. Admittedly, a lot had happened today, and it wasn't even 5:00 pm. But something had occurred to sap the will out of me. To cause weariness.

It was the kid. Up until meeting Brenden, Reynard's baby cult had been an amusing development. A following in its first generation that might grow into something greater or fizzle out. Many movements had started the same way: a charismatic leader able to spread their vision. One so infectious people were willing to kill to realize it. Despite that, I hadn't taken Reynard's followers seriously. Brenden changed all that.

The Edgelords were the founding generation. Converts, if you will. Down deep, they knew they were weirdos. They possessed a self-awareness over their life decisions, and a measure of shame that came along with that choice. But children raised inside the system were different. Reynard's society was their sole reality. Their normal. Being an Edgelord was Brenden's world. If not for the threat that his dad, an outsider, might force him to leave the society, he would have rather died than talk. All his friends belonged to that world. Every formative experience would be entrenched in it. His first crush, his first kiss. His need for approval. Thelen, or someone like him, had stepped in as a father figure.

Being a squire was a real accomplishment. Becoming a knight, or whatever, was a goal akin to graduating. Then after that, maybe a member of the Blackguard. Something to strive for. An elite position among his peers.

And in the end, something worth killing for.

I had assumed Reynard had been murdered over either a personal beef or a financial opportunity. But now there was a third option: he'd been killed by a fanatic.

Or a heretic.

An hour later, I opened my eyes, refreshed and ready to vanquish evil. Also craving a giant coffee with what onlookers might suggest could be a lethal dose of cinnamon. Before I left, I made adjustments to the room. Cracked the drawers. Put a hair on top of the closet doors. Evenly spaced the rings in the shower curtain, and other small notable details.

As I was wrapping up, Elaine chimed in.

"I found Reynard's lawyer. A name, at least. And you aren't going to believe it."

"I can believe seven impossible things a day. We're somewhere around five. Fire away."

"Lancaster Goodday."

While the first name was new to me, the surname was not. "Unbelievable."

"Ken, before you talk to her, records show Lancaster passed away three years ago."

"I hear you."

She was in my phone under "Sixth Amendment." What a small world. Reynard and I had the same lawyer.

Mercie Goodday picked up on the first ring. "On a scale of one to ten, how much trouble are you in?"

"Funny you should mention scales. Reynard is my current client. And he's also dead. As in murdered. Want to talk about it?"

Mercie gulped. "Yes."

"I am going to take a wild guess and say you are currently at Chateau d'Loire."

"I am. What room are you in?"

"I think it's better I come to you."

Mercie gave me her room number. I said I'd be right there, after a stop for coffee, to which she declined my offer to bring her anything. The hotel had a mini café on the mezzanine, adjacent to the bar. A princess in fur trim stepped into line behind me. She was a reminder I had arrived at the age where you look at a young woman and realize they could be your kid.

"Hi. I'm Amethyst."

"I'm more of a tourmaline myself."

"Are you Ken Allen?"

I checked my area for black cloaks, green moons, and loaded crossbows. "It would be pointless to deny it."

Amethyst was ahead of the game. Every girl her age should have a polite neutral smile at her disposal.

"I am indeed Ken Allen. But if you need proof, you can google me."

"The top pictures were from like the nineties or something."

So, before her time. That world, it don't stop spinning. I dug out one of my business cards. "Does this appease?"

Amethyst leaned in to read it. "What's a gumshoe?"

I was second in line with places to be. "Stay on track, Amethyst. You didn't approach me for an autograph."

"Oh. Yeah." Amethyst glanced around, before leaning in to whisper: "Sheila wants to talk to you."

"What a coincidence," I whispered back. "Want anything?"

Along with the largest Americano they sold, I got Amethyst an iced something with extra espresso shots and two different kinds of syrup. It was probably irresponsible to give a teenager a hyper-caffeinated milkshake. Amethyst consulted her phone to make sure she relayed Sheila Polk's message accurately.

"Sheila has a panel at five. Could you meet her at the fifth-floor elevator at like four forty-five?"

That gave me less than an hour with Mercie Goodday. When it rained, it poured.

"Sure thing."

We took a selfie at Amethyst's request and she joined two similarly dressed friends who were hovering nearby. I decided the elevators were safer than the stairs, and took one to the fifth floor, where both Mercie Goodday and Sheila Polk were staying. It had also been the operating floor of the Blackguard. Reynard had kept his inner circle grouped up. When the doors opened at five, I stepped out of the elevator and whipped around. A figure in a black cloak looked at their shoes and a girl with a moon pendant focused hard on texting. I waved at them as the doors closed in their faces.

Once the elevator started moving, I went to the end of the hall and took a peek toward 513. The door was closed. Stern wasn't replying, but by now, she had to have conveyed my text up the chain. Cops were probably sitting inside, lying in wait in case a Blackguard member decided to risk it. At least they had quality snacks. Mercie Goodday was located around the corner from 513. I tapped on the door and checked both ways to ensure I was alone.

The door cracked with the chain in place.

"Give me some money," Mercie Goodday said through the gap.

"Why, does your door have a pay lock?"

"I want confidentiality in place or I'm not letting you in."

"Do you take gots?"

"It's pronounced gots."

"I've heard otherwise."

I dug a bill out of my wallet. "Do you have change for a twenty? You know how it is with ATMs."

Mercie snatched the twenty through the crack, closed the door, and reopened it enough to let me through. Once I was inside, she locked everything back up. I waited for her to talk first. It wasn't a long wait.

"When did it happen?"

"Reynard called me on the carpet this morning, before the con opened. I left for fifteen minutes, came back, and he was dead."

"He died here? In the hotel?"

I watched Mercie closely. She had maybe ten years on me, but we both looked young for our ages. Mercie had elven features with minimal makeup under straight blonde hair.

She was dressed like a privateer: a white shirt with billowy sleeves, wide belt, riding pants, and leather ankle boots. Her outfit looked like she'd forgotten the invite was for a costume party and scoured her house for last-minute options. A hunter-green serape was folded over the arm of the couch.

"Nice compromise."

Mercie ignored me while she thought. I took a seat on the sofa and popped the lid on my coffee.

"What did he want?"

"It's my turn to ask a question. Who is set to inherit Reynard's estate?"

"That's privileged information."

I got up from the couch. In an impressive display of agility, not a single drop of coffee was spilled. "Here's what you do: leave now. Call the hotel staff to help you with your bags so you aren't alone. The cops have blockaded the parking lot. You're great with cops. Way better than me. You'll probably end up UNO-reverse searching them. Good luck, Mercie."

I had the door unlatched and was working on the bolt when Mercie piped up.

"Wait."

I stopped to take a sip of my coffee but didn't turn around.

"I can't tell you who inherits, because I don't know. Reynard never told me. He only had questions as to what a valid last testament entailed." Mercie glanced at the office chair but stayed on her feet. Probably some lawyer thing. Keep on the same level as your opposition. "I didn't even want him as a client."

I waited her out. You had to do that with contrary types. She huffed and puffed while I pretended my house wasn't made of straw.

"My father suffered from dementia. Almost all his clients abandoned him, even though he could remember every detail about his long-time ones. Reynard was one of the few who stayed on. My father talked about Reynard like he was family."

"The paternity suit against Reynard is sealed. Do you know who brought it against him?"

"No one."

"Is this another privilege thing?"

"No. I don't know who the other party was. My father never said, would never have said. But from the way he spoke about it, Reynard is the one who brought the case."

I didn't know what to make of that. Reynard had implied the opposite was true. "You aren't dressed like one of his flunkies. Why are you here, Mercie?"

"That's privileged information."

"I've got a meeting in fifteen minutes. Can we skip assurances?"

Mercie went back into the tank. Frustrating as it was, I respected her moral stance. Hell, I shared it. Her reticence wasn't about me. It was about her, and where she drew her lines. My coffee was the perfect temperature. Cinnamon is pretty good for you. Anti-inflammatory, antioxidant. It helps insulin resistance and mental health. It also makes you feel warm things. There is a reason why they piped its scent throughout malls, back when there were malls. I resisted sharing all this with Mercie while she grappled with her conscience.

"I don't normally handle criminal cases. Or estates. You and Reynard were exceptions. Favors I performed for family and dear friends."

"I feel the same way about you."

Mercie snorted, which was as good as a guffaw for her. "My presence here, in essence, is to act as a glorified notary."

"So, Reynard was about to make something official. What was it?"

Mercie shook her head to indicate the question crossed her boundaries. "Are the police really outside?"

"And inside, keeping it quiet. Reynard isn't the only victim."

Mercie cleared her throat. As stoic as she was, it read like a panic attack. "You said the police were searching everyone who leaves the hotel. Did Reynard's killer take anything?"

"Maybe. Or maybe someone else who got there after the killer but before I did. Though that would have been a tight squeeze."

According to the wall clock, I had five minutes to get to Sheila Polk. "Keep an eye on your phone. I might have more questions for you not to answer."

Mercie escorted me to the door. "I don't always approve of my clients, but when I take a case, I see it through—"

"Same here."

"—but you aren't so bad, Ken."

"Back at ya."

I made it to the elevator doors with seconds to spare. A woman came from around the corner. Sheila Polk was dressed like the queen of hearts, with a white-and-gold cloak over a red silk gown. Her long hair was concealed under an ankle-length veil. In one hand, she had a rod, its topper shaped like a rose. She was flanked by a pair of guards in white-accented armor. Her smile was warm and mysterious. Beyond that, there was something triumphant in her posture.

Something that said: long live the queen.

10

"MR. ALLEN. SO GOOD TO SEE YOU AGAIN."

Sheila Polk's voice had changed. It was projected and clear, with an out-of-this-world accent, literally. She approached with measured steps, rose-topped rod in hand, like a bride on her way to the altar.

"Please, accompany us."

The *please* was nice. Monarchs should display proper manners. Polk's guards evacuated the elevator of its current passengers. In her defense, between her dress, me, and the guards, there wasn't room for anyone else. The elevator was a must. No way Polk could chance the stairs in a gown like that. The guards blocked for her to enter first, then went in before me. I put my back to the doors to watch Polk while we talked.

"We familiarized ourselves with your good deeds. Not your acting work," Polk clarified, "but your exploits afterwards. You have gained a reputation as a knight errant."

"Everyone makes mistakes."

Polk smiled magnanimously. "We have learned, on good authority, that you met with our Lord Reynard moments prior to his death."

Coming right out and saying it was a calculated move. Polk was telling me she was in the loop, without disclosing how she had gotten there.

"Well, it would have been hard to meet with him afterwards."

The doors opened behind me. I glanced back to see a white guard stationed outside, minding the hallway, before one of the guards in the elevator reached out to press the close door button.

"And Mr. Norman has already contacted you, regarding the *Tome of All Tales*."

Polk had a source. I didn't need three guesses to figure out who. "Corbett is a hopeless gossip. But who can blame him? Unemployment is stressful."

This time Polk gifted me with a laugh. "You really are quite the character. Put plainly, we will pay you double whatever Norman has offered you."

The doors opened again. Another white guard was waiting in the hallway. Again the guards inside closed the door, confirming all was well.

"Double is a lot."

"The Edgelords are not without resources."

"I don't accept gots as a form of payment."

"It's gots, actually. But we take your point. We will pay in whatever form you wish. Might I suggest precious metals?"

"Could you throw in a horse cart? Fifty million in bouillon would weigh a ton."

Sure, I was lying about what Norman had offered for the book, but every once in a while, a little white lie was justified. I needed to know what the Edgelords were working with. Without Reynard, were they a roaring lion or a paper tiger?

Polk stood motionless in thought before answering.

"Other rewards await the celebrated hero who would return the *Tome of All Tales* to its rightful owners. You would be honored as our savior. Granted titles."

"I don't like the sound of Baron von Allen. Is Duke available?"

Polk's jaw tightened as she resisted the urge to yell *Off with his head!* "The *Tome of All Tales* belongs to the society. For it to be in the hands of Will Norman, who has long been our founder's ultimate rival, is unthinkable."

This time when the doors opened, they opened on the ground floor. I backed out into two more white guards.

"I'll see what I can do, your royalness."

Polk nodded and exited the elevator. She had four guards on her, with at least two more on the floors above. Or one with a lot of hustle. Were the guards for pomp and circumstance, or was Polk legitimately concerned for her safety?

Polk's entourage parted the masses. I kept on their heels, surfing the wake. Polk could have taken the service hallway, but she wanted to be seen. This was her big moment. Her coming out. The crowd didn't simply part. They kneeled. The two guards from the previous floors caught up with us. Two more were waiting outside her panel room, making the white guard eight total, the same number as the Blackguard.

No way was I skipping her panel. I kept close enough to Polk to mind her train. The door guards kneeled as Polk passed through. I tossed them a nod. Approving their actions made it look like Polk wanted me there.

The white guards restricted access to the room. Being first in, I got a prime people-watching spot in one of the back corners. Each person allowed entry bore a rose, which they placed in a cast-iron ewer as they entered. The attendees' costumes were top notch. Any of them could have walked off the set. Though no one spoke, there was familiarity between them: nods of acknowledgment, hands offered or laid on each other's shoulders. All of them were used to wearing swords. Not a single one fumbled with their blade while sitting down.

Having dabbled in a few murder investigations, I took a special interest in the weapons. At this convention, there were two basic categories when it came to arms: fanciful and practical. The fanciful ones were beautiful: animal heads for pommels, winged crosspieces. The practical ones were plain. Their furniture was unornamented brass or steel. The guards were simple upswept curves. Nothing extra to get caught on drawing or that would impede technique. Their bone or shagreen hilts were sweat stained and smooth from wear. Their scabbards were discolored from the weather. The necks of said scabbards had further wear on the chokers from repeated drawing and sheathing at speed. The weapons also suited the environment, with shorter, thinner blades. And everyone wore a dagger. There were shields, but none of them was bigger than a dinner plate. These people had armed themselves for the environment, chosen their tools for a particular task.

While the VIPs varied in build, every one of them had thick wrists and Popeye forearms. Their costumes were practical, down to their footwear, which often had plated tops. When you've spent significant time around people swinging swords, you put some thought into protecting your toes.

While there were outliers, the vast majority were in their forties. Diehard fans who had been there from the beginning, along with a few rising stars.

Society people, Sheila Polk had called them. Folk whose nine-to-five was a secondary life. Their real life, their core identity, resided here, in the Lands Beyond.

Polk raised her hand, palm out, with such ceremony I fully expected light to emanate from it. The room instantly went quiet. Any warmth in Polk's face vanished, her demeanor shifting seasons from summer to winter. Then she started to sing.

I didn't recognize the words, but the tone matched a funeral dirge. Reynard really had been a full-service creator: a world, a belief system, a currency, and even its own language. Imagine inventing a language, and other people using it.

If Polk stuck to Lands Beyond-ese for the entire lecture, I was in trouble.

I jumped as Elaine translated into my earpiece. "The father has sacrificed. He may never have a son. His angel is given to bind the hells. He has become the land, and the land is him. It will flourish from his eternal lifeblood."

The room was dead silent. No way could I reply to Elaine without being heard, but Polk's allusions weren't lost on me. Her message was clear: Reynard had no blood heir. At least not a son. Which paved the way for her to step in.

When Polk finished, she lowered her hand and began to speak exclusively in Reynard's tongue. No wonder she hadn't kicked me out. This way, she got the best of both worlds: a demonstration of power without me being privy to its secrets. Fortunately, I had an angel on my shoulder.

"She's greeting the noble lords and ladies of the Lands Beyond." Elaine's delay reminded me of a meteorologist live on the scene. "Acknowledgement is grouped by color. She is also including their Aego. She's not doing everybody, just the head honchos. Less than ten percent of the room."

Each person Polk singled out rose and gave a salute, which involved bowing while tapping the back of their knuckles to their foreheads. As they did, those immediately around them hailed them, again in the language of the Lands Beyond. If I didn't feel in over my head before, I did now.

Once the introductions were completed, Polk paused for a deep breath. Then she spoke a single line, firm and clear. Elaine gasped in my ear.

"She just told everyone that Reynard is dead."

Polk went on a sentence at a time, letting each statement sink in before continuing.

"She states his death has been confirmed. She's—Jesus, Ken—she's saying he was killed and that the murderer is in the building."

A four-letter word escaped my lips before I could reel it back. Fortunately for me, other people were doing it too.

"She's spilling everything. She says the police have surrounded the hotel, and that now is the time for the true-hearted to prove their faithfulness."

The room erupted into a chorus, evenly divided between wails of grief and declarations of anger.

"Polk just told them the series bible is missing. That it is their duty to recover and deliver it to her, the next in the line of succession."

This would have been the time for Polk's authority to be questioned, but no challenge was tendered.

"She's good, Ken."

I had to agree. Polk was stirring the room to a boil, without it overflowing, by remaining rock solid.

"She's issuing orders. Everyone in red is to lock the building down. All entrances and exits. No one enters, no one leaves. Yellow will conduct the investigation and search. No one is to speak with the hotel staff or any outside authorities. She is declaring Chateau d'Loire Crucible territory."

Polk was taking the building hostage, instituting a siege of her own to counter the one the cops had placed around the building.

"Polk says only the lords are to know the situation. She's calling the rest of the guests 'subjects.' She says knowledge of the creator's death must be tightly controlled to prevent panic. Now, the rulers of the noble houses must report to her in turn."

Polk was a genius. By letting the power players in their little kingdom in on the situation, she had affirmed both their position and their loyalty. The first rule of public relations was to get ahead of the story. The question was, Who was she trying to get ahead of?

Polk called everyone in red to the front. The other hues rose and conferenced. I was too far away for Elaine to make out what Polk was saying when she started issuing more targeted orders. I took advantage of the chaos to slip around the perimeter of the room and get closer to her. I made it within ten feet before two of the white guards turned toward me. I put my hands up. Polk made a smoothing gesture and the swords stayed sheathed.

"I can't make her out, Ken. She's talking faster and more quietly. I'll record it for now, then go back and see what I can do. Speaking of recording, I'm also taking video. Pan around for me, to make sure we get as many faces as possible. The all-around cameras aren't great for centering images."

"As you wish," I risked.

Polk finished with the red team, who exited as a unit, and called up everyone in yellow next. Of the primary colors, they had the broadest demographics. Guys who qualified for the senior discounts stood shoulder to shoulder with young women who still had to show ID to get into clubs. Their instructions contained more loan words, like *electricity* and *internet*. Once they were discharged, it was just me, Polk, and the royal guards.

"What's going on here? All that sure didn't look good."

"The society takes their duties seriously, and this is a pivotal event." Polk kept her eyes steady on me. "You understand now, the devotion they have to the crown."

"You mean Reynard."

"Of course. The feast begins in an hour. We must prepare. Our offer stands, Mr. Allen. Return the *Tome of All Tales* to us, and you will receive the royal treatment."

I watched Polk go. She couldn't help but play it cute, but I caught her little jest. After all, the way Reynard had gone out was a prime example of what the royal treatment could entail, here at Chateau d'Loire.

———

I raced back to my room for some much needed privacy. After checking all the nooks and crannies to ensure I was alone, I started in with Elaine.

"If the Chateau has one secret passage, it probably has more. Any chance you can hunt down a floor plan, or even overhead images?"

"I'll see what I can do. How far do you think Sheila Polk is going to take this?"

I exhaled all the way from the pit of my stomach. "As far she needs to. She's declared herself queen, and the fate of the kingdom gets decided this weekend. We need to find out who her rivals are. I noticed there was no one in green in that room, so she isn't in cahoots with the Dame of the Moon."

"Or blue," Elaine added.

"Who sports blue again?"

"It's the Wythanes, the renegade house. They were exiled—"

"What actor?"

"Sven Hammersmith."

Who had the protein bar wrapper in his trash. The same type of bar present in the Blackguard operations rooms. "So Hammersmith has blue and black. Polk has red and white. But Polk isn't on the show. On the show, red and white are controlled by Dever, right?"

"Right."

"So far, Dever looks to be staying out of this. As far as the Dame of the Moon, who knows? She has spies in green everywhere, but they've just been watching from the sidelines."

All the moving parts were giving me a headache. The mini-fridge was stocked. Remembering the room was registered under

Will Norman, I helped myself to a seven-dollar bottle of water. Elaine piped up before I was finished.

"I'm going through the recording of Polk's instructions now. The red team was given instructions on how to monitor the doors. They are to log and search each guest before allowing them to leave. Also, they are to prevent anyone from entering the hotel and contact Polk immediately if anyone attempts to force their way in. That includes the police."

"She's playing chicken with the cops. They want to prevent the situation from escalating. Polk is risking a full-blown hostage situation on the gamble the authorities want to keep this quiet. But it's only a matter of time before it breaks on social media."

Elaine had the answer ready. "About that. The yellow team includes engineers and tech types. Polk ordered them to disable the alarms and firewall the routers to limit internet access. She's blocking all social media and email access."

I enjoyed a bag of cashews at Will Norman's expense. Speaking of Norman, he was still in the building, blissfully unaware a coup was taking place. Elaine took advantage of my full mouth.

"What do you think Reynard was planning that required his lawyer present?"

"If it was adjacent to what constituted a living will, maybe crowning his successor." My mind flashed back to the contents of Reynard's closet. "Reynard brought two baby crowns with him. One masculine, one feminine."

"Oh. Well, on the show, the king has one legitimate heir. But there are rumors that the king also sired an illegitimate child first. No one knows who it is, only that it was a girl. Which is fine, by the way. Women and men have the same rights in Reynard's world."

"I'm talking about the real world here, Elaine."

"I'm telling you: Reynard paralleled real-life events all the time. The big question is, Which child is older, the boy or the girl? The oldest child gets it all."

I set Elaine's crown on the bathroom countertop to dunk my head. The cold water helped. "So, Blake Dever is the prince on the show. How does his age line up with Reynard's paternity suit?"

It took Elaine seconds to work out the math. "Almost perfectly."

"And under this theory, Reynard had two kids near the same time. So, either twins, or one each with two different women. We need to find out who Blake Dever's mother was, and where she was when *Never After* was being filmed. That's when the paternity suit took place."

Elaine already had an answer. "Blake Dever is adopted."

"Let me guess, closed adoption."

"Yep. He's very vocal about never looking into it. His parents are his parents. He's gone off on reporters who have suggested otherwise in the past. It's one of the few things he's lost his composure over."

I took out my phone and texted Stern: *Did Dever ever talk about his birth father?*

Stern was quick on the draw. *Blake has nothing to do with this, Allen.*

Reynard was involved in a paternity suit, and if the shoe fits . . . *Dever is the right age. He ever mention how Reynard landed on him as prince?*

This time, Stern didn't even deem me worthy of a reply. I pivoted back to Elaine. "Any luck with that kid's phone?"

"Nothing earth-shattering. A squire is basically an intern. He was a little disappointed to be assigned to Archibald Thelen. His best friends both got assigned to John Cannon."

"His guards—that's why they were so undersized. They were kids." Washing my face didn't cut it. All the layers left my bathing suit areas eternally damp. "I need to find out if the gift shop sells undergarments. I didn't pack an overnight bag, and laundry service is going to be overwhelmed."

"Well, if you find the book, you'll never have to do laundry again. You can just throw out your shorts every night before bed. Sheila Polk didn't blink at the fifty-million-dollar price tag."

"Because she isn't planning to pay it. If I find the book, and she finds out, all the queen's horses and all the queen's men are coming for me."

I hit the gift shop right away, before the rush cleaned them out. There were no briefs, but I scored two pairs of swim trunks and a couple Chateau d'Loire souvenir shirts. You know the kind. "The Guy I was Hired to Protect Got Killed, and All I Got Was This Lousy T-Shirt." I picked up a toothbrush, deodorant, and other hygiene sundries, before raiding the snack section for items that hit my macros.

The total made me worried about making my mortgage payment before I discovered I could charge it to my room. Will Norman could handle the tab. Hell, his father could have bought the Chateau on a lark. Armed with that knowledge, I also picked up provisions for Elaine, managing to control my opinion of her dietary habits.

When I delivered them, I grabbed the box the crown had come in, which was also wired for video. Back in my room, I positioned the box facing the door to serve as a makeshift security camera.

My errands complete, I headed down to the feast.

It was in the third ballroom, which was reserved for special events and meals. All the tables and chairs reminded me that Chateau d'Loire had yet more rooms to be explored: the staff and storage areas.

The entrance was arrayed red-carpet style, with stanchions separating fans from the VIPs. Two guards bearing combination axe/spear deals flanked the door, one in red, the other blue. Invitation coins were being presented. I dug mine out of my VIP package, separating it from the one for tomorrow's scheduled ball and the other for Sunday's closing ceremonies, which included a full tea service. The dining arrangements were different from the standard six-at-a-round layout. Trestle tables ran the length of the room in four rows, with chairs along both sides. Nine out of ten seats were filled by the time I got there. Reynard's primary color system led to even stripes down the rows, as if the feast was being held atop a rainbow.

There was a fifth table at the head of the room, turned perpendicular, to present the guests of honor last supper-style to their fellow diners.

I consulted my ticket for a seat assignment and was pleasantly surprised to discover I was at the VIP table, albeit at the far end. Will Norman was already there, next to my empty seat, looking uncomfortable in his armor. I wondered whose presence Norman had axed for my benefit. Whoever it was, I was sleeping in their bed and sitting in their premium chair. Probably some squeeze he was looking to impress. Being on the corner, I was able to angle my chair to look down the length of the table.

The only other person seated was Bradley Corbett. He was on the far side of Norman, still in full costume. He looked everywhere but at me. If Norman or Polk had come to him with the same pitch they'd thrown at me, we'd gone from allies to opposition.

Blake Dever arrived on my heels. He was in armor with a white-and-red-quartered surcoat over it. His shoulders were emblazoned with winged lions, and a long sword was belted to his waist. He stopped for photos, politely waving. I tried to picture Reynard without the goatee. He and Dever didn't look much alike. Different hairline—Reynard had a widow's peak. Different cheekbones too. When comparing builds, you had to look at limb-to-torso ratio. A serious fitness routine could change about everything else. Dever was well proportioned, but I'd only ever seen Reynard seated, so I couldn't make a reliable comparison.

Dever finally broke free of his fans. He sat down three seats from Corbett and leaned over far enough to catch my eye. His lips twitched.

He wanted to talk to me, but not in front of either Norman or Corbett. I tapped a finger on my ear to acknowledge him. He nodded subtly back. If our signals got more complicated, he was going to start throwing sliders at me.

Sven Hammersmith came in next. He was in quartered blue and black, his armor embellished with winged serpents. He kept in character, maintaining a regal posture, with a long, thin-bladed sword in one hand and a helmet in the other. The helmet looked like something the Spartans wore, but with a crown molded on the brow. The back of his chair had a finial topping. Hammersmith placed his helmet on it and took his seat next to Blake Dever.

The Dame of the Moon entered next. Her seat was on the far side, completely opposite me. She was dressed the same as when we met. Every time I tried to steal a glance, the Dame was already staring at me. It reminded me of a Bruce Lee poster I had on my wall as a kid.

That left two chairs unaccounted for. One had to have been reserved for Reynard, making the other the seat of the queen.

Sheila Polk made her entrance last. Timing a dramatic arrival was easier in the modern age, when someone already present could shoot you a text. She took her time making her way down the center aisle, eight guards in white trailing behind in pairs. People rose as she passed, giving me an idea who was loyal to her, which was around half of the feast.

I nudged Norman. "How many of the people standing are cast or crew?"

"A lot." Norman shifted to get a better view. He was wide enough where I had to shift too. "Jesus, I had no idea so many of them had joined up."

"Whoever Reynard didn't appoint, he converted. It probably happened slowly. He had ten years. Plus, when you're on location, you're isolated. Not being part of a club can be tough to weather."

"Well, they're with Polk now."

Norman paled as much as his spray tan would allow. The people he'd assumed were loyal to him had jumped ship. If he had been counting on any of them to fork over the book, he could forget about it. My stock was going up.

Polk made her way around the table and took the queen's seat, with Reynard's empty throne on one side and Blake Dever on the other. When she sat, so did everyone else who was standing. The hotel staff came in through the service entrance and started laying down covered platters. Questioning murmurs rumbled through the room. The people not in the know were wondering where Reynard was, and why we were starting without him.

It took time to get all the platters in place. Some of them were big enough to require two people. In terms of utensils, I had a two-pronged fork and a carving knife, making it impossible for me to breach dining etiquette. Once the last platter had been laid, Sheila Polk rose from her seat, her half of the room rising with her. The remainder followed suit, displaying varying levels of confusion. Tempted as I was to remain sitting to make a statement, it was like being at a concert. I couldn't see jack from my chair.

Polk started in with the singing, again in Reynard's made-up language. Fortunately, my translator was on duty.

"She's saying grace," Elaine reported. "Addressing the sonless father, whose sacrifice fuels our bounty. His blood is the lifeblood of the land. We dine in his honor."

Polk was reiterating that Reynard had no heir. I looked to Dever for a reaction. He looked appropriately solemn. Did he speak enough Lands Beyond-ese to know what Polk was saying? He had to have picked up some over ten years. Norman was in the dark. He turned to Corbett for a translation and didn't love the results.

Polk touched her knuckles to her forehead, causing most of the room to copy the gesture. Two of the white guards pulled the cover off a huge platter in front of her. I half expected it to have a severed head inside. It was a relief when it turned out to be an entire roast pig, with an apple in its mouth and everything. Polk picked up the carving knife from Reynard's place setting and made a ceremonial cut. When she set the knife back down, the feast began in earnest.

Covers came off all the platters. Besides roast pig, there were dressed-out turkeys with the little hats on their legs and rib-laden slabs of some kind animal that wasn't beef. Root vegetables and round loaves accompanied the proteins, with tubs of butter alongside them. Wine and craft beer flowed. Conversation as well. Inquisitive murmuring filled the room. People were asking what had happened to Reynard.

I put off eating in favor of people watching. Food is a funny thing. When you slap it in front of people, they can't wait to dig in, no matter how hungry they were a minute ago. If you want to measure the quality of someone's character, watch when only half the table gets their dishes at the restaurant. The people who dig in without a second thought about those with empty plates are not to be trusted with lifeboats.

Norman was whispering something to Corbett. Probably offering him a corner office. He was running short on personnel.

"Quite the production with the whole pig," I said to him.

"Those are wild boar. The tusks give it away. And that's venison. The turkey is also wild game. You can tell by the color of the flesh." Will Norman offered an explanation at my quizzical expression. "My mother was a hunter. We used to go out every year."

"How'd she take it when you decided to follow in your father's footsteps?"

Norman laughed without mirth. "I think she saw it coming. I worshiped my dad growing up. She worked as an animal wrangler for a decade—that's how they met—but the minute she married my dad, she left for the ranch and didn't look back. This weekend was the first time she'd seen This Town in thirty years."

"She's here?"

"Was. I sent her home. You got her room."

At the tables, men and women ignored their place settings and drew daggers from their belts, taking apart the foul, swine, and venison as if it were second nature. Disassembling an entire animal is a skill. And like any skill, practice made perfect. If you were pondering a homestead lifestyle, butchering would be on the short list of must-have skills. As for the VIP table, the white guard made short work of the carving. In under a minute, the tableau looked like a cookbook cover.

While everyone served themselves, I scanned around for members of the Blackguard. The color-coded room made spotting them a smidge easier. They were at the head of the third table, directly across from where Reynard would have been sitting. All Blackguard members I had met were present, plus one woman. She had platinum-blonde hair, cut into an asymmetrical bob. I indicated her to Norman.

"Who is she?"

Norman turned away from a conference with Corbett.

"Tryne Koch. A European performance artist. Like everyone else, Reynard cast her. Europeans have fewer qualms about nude scenes."

"Say again?"

"You really don't watch the show, do you? There's as much sex on the screen as there is violence. Full frontal is practically required. It's made it a challenge to cast male parts."

"No surprise there."

It was a long-held secret that few male actors wanted to bear all on screen. Not meeting a certain audience expectation could be damaging to your career. It created an objective bias. Chances were, if a man was willing to go fully nude, he had nothing to be embarrassed about.

With Tryne Koch, all but one of the Blackguard were accounted for. There were seven official members: John Cannon, Mikail Chelovak, Archibald Thelen, Kurt Hooper, Tryne Koch were present.

Wallace Bowers was dead with an axe in his back. Number seven, Fernando Denoso, was on ice in room 513's bathtub.

I leaned over to get both Norman's and Corbett's attention. "Any idea who the eighth member of the Blackguard is?"

The question was left field enough to catch them off guard. Corbett recovered first. "Someone already on set. I'd know if there were any new arrivals."

Norman jumped in. "Reynard sat on the scripts until the last possible moment. It was like filming a soap opera. The audience doesn't realize how good the cast really is."

I looked to Norman. "You must have had to clear whoever it was. Get them insured, pay them, all that."

"Not if they were already playing another part."

"What about Blake Dever? Isn't there some fan theory he's the eighth member?"

"Hmm." Norman cut into his meat. "Could be."

"It would make the most sense," Corbett added. "In his role as the prince's rook, it's implied the character had a troubled past before his memories were wiped."

"What's a rook again?"

"He is the prince's double. He trades places with the prince in times of danger. It is his duty to die for the true prince."

"Like castling in chess."

"That was Mr. Reynard's inspiration, I believe. We will never know what his plans for Dever's characters were."

"Unless it's in the book."

Norman and Corbett had opposite reactions to that. Norman stuffed enough tenderloin in his mouth to constitute a choking hazard while Corbett pushed his plate away.

If the eighth member was Dever's build, that meant Tryne Koch had been my sparring partner in the hallway. Performance artist, my firm tushy. Reynard hadn't cast Koch because she skinny-dipped. He'd cast her because she was a highly trained assassin. The Blackguard had been his personal dirty-deeds unit. Koch earned her bones the same as the rest.

I studied the Blackguard, trying to get a hint of their social dynamic. Cannon and Chelovak were whispering back and forth but shut up whenever Hooper said anything. Neither Koch nor Thelen said a word. Thelen was busy eating. He used the back of his fork. Koch ignored her food in favor of scoping the room. Her eyes passed over mine like a disinterested lioness. While a good act, it was the wrong move. As the only new face at the head table, I should have been worth a gander.

A beefy guy in red-enameled chain mail stood up to give a toast. Elaine was there to fill me in.

"He's pledging his loyalty to Polk. Smells fishy to me."

"Bet he's a plant."

My wager was paid off immediately. Others rose in a wave to repeat the first toast. It became a contest over who could say it louder and prouder. Polk's enigmatic smile tilted another fifteen degrees. Between nods of acknowledgment, she ate ceremoniously, in small bites while maintaining a regal posture. A lot of eyes were on her. Now was not the time to have sauce running down your chin.

Norman tore at a turkey breast. "She's got them champing at the bit."

"She'll probably make whoever brings her the book grand marshal or something."

Dever maintained a stiff upper lip throughout the proceedings. While he didn't hail Polk, he didn't challenge her either. Was he staying out of it, or letting her dig her own grave in anticipation of a big reveal? If Dever was Reynard's long-lost son, how could he prove it?

Hammersmith pushed his food around as if none of this was his affair. If it was an act, it was a good one. When I got to her, the Dame of the Moon was looking at me again. How was she doing that?

She shaved venison off a haunch a thin slice at a time, ignoring her fork. I stood up with my plate and headed down the line. Sheila Polk looked right through me, a notch short of smug. Blake Dever started to say something, then remembered his company and put a sock in it. Hammersmith yawned. I stopped a step short of the Dame of the Moon and studied the venison.

"Where's the lean meat?"

"All venison is lean, as is the way with wild things." The Dame cut off a slab and set it on my plate. "Did the day transpire as expected?"

The meat was very good, rich, and unexpectedly tender. "Back during my reading, you keyed me in about the Chateau. How did you know about the hidden doors?"

"The midnight light reveals all to its chosen."

"You know, people might buy into this whole routine, but I think you're just going through a phase."

The Dame pinched off a smile. "You're very amusing, Ken."

Reynard had two crowns in his room: a masculine one and a feminine one. Maybe the feminine one was for Polk, but maybe not. I tried to see the Dame for who she was under the costuming, but it was tough. Take off the gown, the jewelry, and the full-face makeup, and she could have been anybody. The shape of her chin didn't do me much good, what with Reynard's goatee. And she didn't have his eyes.

"Reynard always had a reason for picking people. Some were right for the job. Others had proven their loyalty. You—I'm not sure why he chose you. But I'm going to find out."

"Good luck."

I headed back to my chair, detouring to snag a turkey leg. What I wouldn't have done for a salad course. I should have counted my lucky stars. Usually at things like this, it was carbs, carbs, carbs.

The hotel staff whisked away the platters and replaced them with more covered dishes. Coffee was served via a cart. The waiter wouldn't let me keep a carafe. An assortment of tarts, cookies, and miniature cakes were revealed. I checked my phone to make sure, but it wasn't my birthday, so I stuck with the coffee.

Norman shot up so fast I had to move to make room.

"It's been a great ten years, and we're just getting started. There are a lot of stories waiting to be told, and you people are the ones to tell it. All of you on the crew have had a hand in making this world. We're going to need you at Home Drive-In. Your skills, and your ideas. Here's to the beginning."

It was the best move Norman could have made. Polk could secure them a place in the society, but he could promise them real-world employment on projects outside *The Lands Beyond*.

Norman held up his goblet. Corbett half-heartedly followed, but only a smattering of attendees went along. Norman drained his cup and slammed it on the table. With the feast winding down, I took a wide-angle view of the room.

There were two kinds of drinking: drinking to celebrate and drinking to commiserate. As the guests sank into their cups, it became clear the latter was taking place. Conversation was somber with clustered outbursts of mirth. People were recounting stories, sharing their favorite tale.

Even if they didn't know Reynard was dead, they knew he wasn't present. Things had changed. The feast was a shadow wake for *The Lands Beyond* as they knew it.

Sheila Polk stood, which signaled for all others to stand as well. She said a few words, and people started to file out. Elaine caught me up.

"She dismissed them. Like a teacher giving permission to leave class."

Polk was asserting control, and the Edgelords were granting it to her. They existed inside a neo-feudalism. Without stratification, their organization didn't exist. And they wanted it to continue. They had fought to rise in the ranks, to gain status. If their society ended with

Reynard, all of that would vanish and force them to return to their mundane lives.

The series bible was the lynchpin. If Polk controlled the only existing text of Reynard's sacred words, now that their founder had passed into divinity, she was in essence the high priest.

I kept close to Norman and Corbett as we filed out. Blake Dever saw us leaving and rushed to join us. "What in the devil is happening?"

Corbett slipped away amid the egress. This case was becoming a juggling act. I put an arm around Dever's and Norman's shoulders like we were old pals and not co-conspirators. Out in the lobby, the after-party was beginning.

The mezzanine was packed. Beneath us, clusters formed in the lobby. People started breaking out mandolins. I angled so my back was to the wall to keep watch while I soaked in dueling covers of Wonderwall.

"Sheila Polk is taking over. She found out Reynard is dead. I thought maybe Corbett leaked it, but now I'm not so sure."

Norman huffed. "Corbett's with me. Count on it."

"Taking over?" Dever looked genuinely puzzled. I didn't buy it. On the slim chance he'd somehow dodged learning any of the Lands Beyond language, the context clues were overwhelming.

"The throne. Polk is dangerous. She's on her home turf, surrounded by literal fanatics." Dever nodded, thinking. If he was wrapped up in this, I had to keep him safe for Stern's sake. And my own. If anything happened to Dever, she'd kill me.

"Play nice with her, Dever. You don't want to upset the queen in her own castle. Your goal is to get out of here in one piece, capisce?"

"Yes. I understand."

I would have felt better if I could see if Dever's fingers were crossed or not.

Norman was starting to calculate. "Is she after the series bible?"

"It's more like an actual bible to them."

"That bitch. She's going to put me over a barrel if she gets it first."
Norman made a fist so hard his gauntlet creaked under the stress. His
face scrunched up like he'd kicked a post. "I'm doubling my offer."

I'm no math whiz, but this was an easy story problem. *If a television executive is willing to pay 20 million dollars, and a cult leader is willing to pay 50, how many lives is this book really worth?*

Three people were already dead. Three that I knew of, at least.
And night was yet to fall.

11

NORMAN WENT BACK TO HIS ROOM, striding like a man on a mission. In contrast, Dever was frozen in thought.

"Did the cops give you any grief?"

"I haven't heard from them since they searched my room. I assume that means I'm no longer a suspect." Dever ran his hand through his hair. "I wish Ava were here. She has a way of calming the atmosphere through reduction. Nothing seems to faze her."

I had to wonder if Dever knew Ava Stern at all. All she ever seemed was fazed around me.

The Blackguard exited the ballroom as a unit. Hooper and Koch went one way, the remaining four the other. Hooper and Koch were the ones to follow. They were the hitters. A crowd had started to form around me, on account of Blake Dever standing still for more than five seconds. I used it to slip away.

Hooper and Koch were already far down the hall, walking with purpose. They pulled their hoods up together. All the better for me.

Hoods were garbage for peripheral vision. Whenever I see someone jogging with a hood up and earbuds in, I want to stage an intervention.

There was enough traffic in the hallway to conceal my tail. I also made liberal use of the ferns as cover. Which were real by the way. That's how you know you're in a fancy joint.

Hooper and Koch hung a left at the end of the hallway, toward the hotel maintenance areas. I crouched down behind a particularly robust ficus and waited. Suspicious people looked behind them when they made turns. I peeked out as little as possible, once again missing all the bells and whistles Elaine and her father once provided, like little pencil cameras for clearing corners. The two of them were standing in front of a reinforced door. Koch crouched down in front of the knob as Hooper turned to check their backtrail. I ducked back behind the corner. Close call, but Hooper hadn't taken his hood down, so I felt okay.

I stood there with my back to the wall for three minutes, wondering how long it was going to take Koch to pop the lock. If she had a gadget for it, about two seconds. But gadgets weren't historically accurate, so she might have been using picks. Were picks historically accurate? Were there locks back then? Sometimes I regretted skipping college.

I toyed with the idea of pushing a fern around the corner for cover. Maybe Hooper would think the fern had always been there. Ferns were sneaky that way. I gave in and risked a peek. The hall was empty. I jogged to the door, fingers crossed it wasn't one of the self-locking kind. Turns out it was, but they had wedged a shim to keep it propped open. They also had left the lights on. The room was a narrow, longish maintenance area with a break nook. A kitchenette, lockers, and caged closets for staff supplies made up the bulk of the space. Another door was propped fully open at the far side of the room, providing a view of skeletal metal stairs going down.

I crossed the room and peeked over the rail. The stairs looped back on themselves in two half sets. The bottom ended in another door, this one unlocked. It opened with the forced air pressure of an industrial area.

The space was as large as the conference room above, most of it filled with commercial-grade mechanics. Giant furnaces and air circulators lined one wall. Rows of electric service panels lined the other. Fluorescent lighting ran the length of the ceiling. Warm, processed air whipped around me. Another closed door stood on the far wall.

I was halfway to it when a metallic slam sounded behind me. Tryne Koch was blocking the door I entered through. She rapped on it three times with the butt of a curved sword and the far door opened. Kurt Hooper came through it, a cutlass in one hand and his broad-bladed knife in the other.

They closed in from both sides in measured steps. Hooper did the talking. He sounded stuffy on account of my breaking his nose. "Where's the book?"

They stopped in unison, twelve feet apart with me in the middle. I was in real trouble. Last time, the two of them being forced into a queue had saved me. Now I was surrounded, with limited room to circle. Both were armed, which gave them reach, and both knew what they were doing. I had been given plenty of opportunity to get on board with the ancient weapons thing. But no, the guy who spent his days dressed as Jove Brand didn't want to feel ridiculous toting around a broadsword.

I turned my back to the furnace units to keep them in my eyeline. "What makes you think I have it?"

"Don't mess with us. If you gave it to Norman, he'd be on a helicopter by now. If Sheila had it, she'd let the world know."

There was contempt in Hooper's voice when he said "Sheila." The Blackguard wasn't working for Polk. The question was, Who were they working for? Getting killed in a sword fight was a surefire way to never find out.

"Okay, you got me. I'll take you to it."

"Nah, mate. You'll tell us and we'll send word. Either now, or after we've carved you up. Your choice."

Koch lowered the tip of her sword to indicate exactly where on my body she planned to start cutting. Getting her point across left her arm extended. It was now or never.

I snapped a kick into the flat of Koch's sword. She wasn't expecting it but managed to keep hold of her saber. Without putting my foot down, I transitioned straight into a crescent kick. Koch wasn't expecting that either. It caught her in the jaw, but the crescent is a garbage kick, reliant on the hip flexors. She reeled back but remained conscious.

Hooper lunged with a low cut. I dove into Koch to evade, grabbing her sword arm with both hands while trying a flying back kick. The kick missed, but so did Hooper's thrust.

Koch twisted away from my grip. Rather than fight it, I fueled it, spinning along and getting her between me and Hooper. While we waltzed, I hooked an arm under her elbow and dodged a headbutt. She saw the break coming but couldn't pull free without letting go of her sword, so that's what she did.

When Koch came out of her spin, she had the curved knife I'd seen before in her other hand. I ducked under a slash that would have opened my throat and booted her into Hooper. They bumped into each other, which bought me enough time to pick up her sword.

They took a step apart to give themselves room to work. At least I had both of them in front of me now. They were experts at European martial arts. I was the same with Eastern. While I had explored modern systems, like Brazilian jiujitsu, my bread and butter was wushu, the blanket term for Chinese martial arts. Wushu included short and long hand forms, gymnastics, and the cultivation of qi—internal energy.

It also included training with traditional weapons.

Growing up, I wasn't the best student. I never even graduated high school. But when it came to physical education, I was a sponge. If I saw a technique, even once, I could perform it. There were eighteen traditional weapons in wushu. I had mastered them all.

One of them was the dao, or Chinese broadsword. It was a required weapon in competition events. My technique with a dao had earned me fourth in nationals, which at the time was the highest ever for a non-native.

To get a feel for Koch's saber, I spun the weapon around my body, drawing figure eights in the air, twisting so the blade shielded me. The saber was weighted more toward the hilt, but around the same length of a dao, as it had been made for Koch, who was four inches shorter than me. While the flashy display had a purpose, I also wanted to inject a little doubt into the two of them. Chances were they knew Chinese weapon work as well as I did European forms. Facing the unknown might cause them to hesitate. The routine took maybe three seconds, ending in a guard pose. Hooper and Koch shared a glance, then shuffled in, slower this time. My chances were slim. The side who got the first cut in was going to win, and they had twice the opportunities.

Over Hooper and Koch's shoulders, I saw the far door open. A woman came through, dressed like an armored nun, her habit white rather than black. She wore a full-face mask, like comedy and tragedy but with no mouth.

Elaine inhaled sharply in my earpiece. "Oh my God, it's the Whisper."

The woman in white slammed the door shut behind her. Hooper and Koch glanced back at her, then did a double take that I might've found comical were I not facing death. The Whisper's robe was slit up the sides to her belt. She had a weapon strapped to each leg—metal batons fatter at one end, like miniature baseball bats.

Hooper, fighting to keep his eyes on me, gestured for Koch to intercept the newcomer. Koch didn't appear to love the proposition but acceded. I flicked the tip of my saber against Hooper's cutlass.

"Don't you just hate a fair fight?"

That woke Hooper up. He stood like a boxer, bobbing and weaving behind his blades, then cut out with his saber. When our blades met, he maintained that contact, riding along my sword, testing the pressure.

I'd never experienced that binding technique using a weapon but was familiar with it empty-handed. I kept tension against him as he thrust, withdrew, dropped, and rose, surfing along as he tried to beat my guard. Our arms extended and retracted, our feet swapped and circled, but our blades never parted.

My focus was total. I vaguely heard Koch and the Whisper's weapons clashing nearby. Our blades locked, Hooper made a move, stepping in hard to make a play with the knife in his off hand. I snagged his wrist and applied my hip.

Hooper's knife slid across my armor as he stumbled past me to slam into the stairwell door. Koch and the Whisper were fully behind me now. I spared a glance to make sure I wasn't about to get backstabbed. When I looked back, Hooper was already through the door and on his way up the stairs. He'd gotten more than he'd bargained for twice, which is two more times than preferable when sword fighting.

I let Hooper go. Catching one of them was better than maybe losing both. Plus, the Whisper had saved my bacon. It was poor form to leave her holding the bag, and I knew firsthand that Koch was a handful.

Turned out I shouldn't have bothered. The Whisper gave Koch the business, simultaneously attacking with one club while defending with the other. It was a clinic. She worked Koch from the outside in, tenderizing her forearms, elbows, and shoulders, until Koch had a hard time lifting her arms. After that, the Whisper battered Koch's legs until she was forced to take a knee.

With a flourish, the Whisper brought her club up, stopping an inch under Koch's chin. She applied pressure, forcing Koch to look up at her, then smashed a knee into Koch's temple that put her out.

"Thanks, you saved my skin."

The Whisper put a finger over where her lips would have been, under the mask.

"It's her whole thing, Ken," Elaine informed me. "The Whisper doesn't talk."

"Great. Well, let's hope Reynard didn't method cast."

The Whisper scooped Koch up from behind. She looked at me, then Koch's feet.

"Well, here's another first."

I grabbed Koch's lower half, and we walked her out the door the Whisper had appeared through. It was a big long-term storage space. Dry goods, boxed holiday decorations, and surplus furniture, all arranged haphazardly.

"Look, I need to question Koch. Got anything you want to ask her?"

The Whisper tilted her head at me like a schoolmarm looking down her glasses. I took her point. Koch wasn't the type to talk, and I wasn't the type to try and make her. We hauled Koch to the back wall, where a stack of boxes had been knocked over. The Whisper pressed on a block, and the wall opened to reveal a stairway leading up.

"Bootlegger tunnel, probably. How'd you find out about it? You ask around?"

The Whisper couldn't talk, but she could sigh. The stairs ended in cellar doors. We exited those, and I found myself in the back alley. We maneuvered Koch around the dumpsters and into the parking lot.

There was a BMW in a handicapped spot near the back entrance. The Whisper started to swing Koch's upper half. I joined her at the feet. We tossed Koch onto the hood of the car. The alarm started blaring. The Whisper ran back to the cellar doors with me on her heels.

We bolted the doors from the inside, then replaced the moving wall. I took another shot at conversation as we stacked the boxes back up.

"So, what's your story?"

The Whisper ignored me.

Back in the mechanical room, she found Koch's discarded cloak hidden in the drop ceiling. The Whisper threw it around her shoulders and headed out the stairs. We went out to the lobby together, where she disappeared into the festivities. I let her go. I had enough on my plate. Solving the mystery of the mute, bleached ninja-nun would have to wait.

Like it or not, Elaine couldn't wait to provide an origin story.

"That was the King's Whisper. Like this super badass secret agent. Not even the king knows her identity. The past Whisper trains her, then appoints her."

"She's on the show? Who plays her?"

"No one knows what character is under her mask. It was expected to be revealed in the final season."

"This again? Reynard sure liked his mystery guest stars. You said the show mirrors real life. So, you think this Whisper worked for Reynard in some capacity?"

"Probably."

"There have to be fan theories. Who's the most likely candidate?"

Elaine emitted a musical hum of false consideration. You know when someone is about to tell you they believe in aliens, or that we all live in a computer program? That's the tone she took.

"People think it's Lynn Chambers."

"The lead from *Never After*? That's way out there."

"The Whisper served the king before the prince. According to the lore, she would be around Chambers's age. Comparison screenshots show the Whisper is her height and build. And it would explain why she never talks. Fans would know her voice."

"Seems like a waste to coax Lynn Chambers out of retirement for a masked, nonspeaking role."

"Lynn Chambers was a big part of *Never After*'s success. The old-school fans worship her. The reveal would have been mind-blowing."

"Have to admit, that does sound like a Reynard move. This whole deal has entirely too many characters. At least we confirmed the Blackguard isn't working for Polk."

"How?"

"Hooper called her by her first name. Not Your Highness, or the queen, or even Ms. Polk, but Sheila."

Around that time, I realized I was walking around with a drawn sword. No one seemed to mind. I held it next to me as if it were on my belt and set course for the vendors. The shops were still thriving. It was plain good business to stay open when people were getting sauced enough to make fiscally irresponsible purchases.

A woman in her twenties with full sleeve tattoos and the muscle tone to pull them off had taken over at the booth. I set Koch's sword down in front of her.

"Got a prop from the show here. What do you say to a swap?"

It wasn't only that the saber was an unfamiliar weapon to me, thinner and longer than the dao. It was also that it did its work cutting and thrusting. I'd like to be able to defend myself without having to impale my attackers. I'd also like to not have to haul a trip hazard around. I hadn't put in the hours it took to make wearing a scabbard second nature. The Whisper had the right idea, using batons.

The woman picked up the saber, studying it from all angles. She tested its flex, then set it back down. "Is this hot?"

"I won it in a duel."

"Any paperwork? It's the real deal, that's clear enough, but you can get a lot more out of it properly authenticated."

"I'm curious to know how you can tell it's the real deal."

The woman waggled two fingers to wave me closer. She pointed to a stamp above the hilt. "That's a maker's mark. It's like a signature. Any smith worth their salt isn't faking that on a quality piece, and this is a quality piece."

"Why not?"

"They want credit for their own work, and it's also professional courtesy among smiths."

"Like plagiarism."

She nodded at my analogy. "So, what are you in the market for?"

"Do you have anything like a *jitte* or a *sai*?"

She turned to select a few obscure items from the armory, placing each on the velvet mat in front of me. The first was a short sword with a broad, upcurling guard and a basket handle.

"This is a parrying dagger. Classic when paired with a long sword."

Next was something much like the first, but single-edged, with deep notches at regular intervals along the back of the blade.

"This is a sword breaker. But the name is deceptive. Your opponent's blade gets caught in the notches. But since blades have flex, you exploit that to force a disarm."

Her selections were close, but no cigar. "Let me think about those while I have a look around."

I gave the booth a thorough once-over, skipped over all the positively deadly weapons, and closely examined the only possibly deadly ones. Even the maces—the clubs topped with balls, not the stuff you sprayed—could kill you. Blunt force trauma to the skull with a metal object was rolling the dice.

Forgotten at the far end was one such weapon. It was around two and a half feet in length, with a short handle and thin, flexible haft with a thumb-sized ball at the top. The ball had two faces carved into it: comedy and tragedy.

"What's this thing?"

Her tone was dismissive. "It's a jester's rod."

No wonder I liked it. "Could you take the hilt and guard off that dagger and put it in this instead?"

The woman required a deep breath to center herself. "I just work here, dude."

Elaine piped up in my earpiece. "I have tools in my room."

"What do you say, that dagger and this rod for this sword?"

The booth worker pretended to think it over, but she was coming out way ahead and we both knew it. There was no paperwork, but the maker's mark proved it as a legitimate prop from the show. There had to be screen captures of Koch holding it online. I borrowed a chamois used to polish the silver from the booth worker and wiped the saber thoroughly of any prints before handing it over.

"Want me to wrap these up for you?"

"Nah, I'll wear 'em out."

Before I left, I popped over to the video store and hemmed and hawed over which of the four *Never After* complete collections was the best for my needs. The booth must have been a family business, because a teenage kid was on duty to provide his opinion:

"The extra features are way better on the first collection. Later, when Reynard blew up, he had more control over what was included on the sets."

I had to agree with the kid. Reynard wouldn't be the first public figure to scrub his past on reaching the pinnacle. I got him to accept cash on the proposal a generous tip would be involved. My intention was to keep from using Reynard's made-up currency for as long as possible, ideally forever. Someone was tracking who used it: where, when, and how.

Ten minutes later, I was in Elaine's room. She hedged by explaining she didn't have a lot of tools with her, then produced a roll-out set you could use to launch a space shuttle. She began disassembling and threading while I got into the DVD set. By the time I had the cellophane off, I realized my fatal flaw.

"Hotels don't have DVD players."

"You know, I own that whole series digitally."

"I'm more interested in the behind-the-scenes stuff."

Elaine opened one of her armrests. "Give me the disc. I'll cast it to the television. Enjoy."

Ten seconds in, I was already wishing I could pause it. Elaine opened the armrest again. "You'll have to sit by me."

I rolled the office chair over, the two of us parallel playing. The behind-the-scenes footage was a little more than an hour. The first time through, I focused on the foreground and what the documentarians were trying to show us.

Never After was a low-budget underdog production. Well, as underdog as a major network drama could be in the early nineties. Their situation created a familial unity. The cast and crew mingled freely. They called each other by their first names. You couldn't get them down. Laughter was the default reaction to an unforeseen issue. Everyone was young, optimistic, and thrilled to be working at all. This was the age of puppets and prosthetics. The puppeteers joked around, pretending the puppets were enjoying a cup of Joe and sneaking cigarettes between takes. The horses were real, however. You couldn't have a fairy tale without real horses. Their wrangler was a young woman, fit and wild. Horse girls were a breed all their own. You'd always play second fiddle to their first and greatest love.

Reynard was around my age back then, blond instead of white and rocking a ponytail. He was trim back then as well, emanating both vim and vigor as he wove through production, talking closely with everyone, player or production. Despite his later reputation as a control freak, back in those days he was open to input. Everyone sat in a drum circle, discussing character arcs and story. Plot points were adopted or discarded based on special effects innovations or limitations. It was a dream scenario for a fresh-faced creative in the business for all the right reasons.

The bulk of the documentary's time was split between Reynard and Lynn Chambers, *Never After's* ephemeral star. Chambers looked like a teenager, but in This Town, where people made careers out of playing teenagers, that didn't mean much. She was so pale she glowed, with dark curly hair threaded with silver strands. It did whatever she wanted it to, swaying and settling as if it were a tail. She possessed a melancholy quality that persisted when the cameras weren't rolling, as if she knew a tragic fate awaited her. Faint smiles were but a momentary break in the ennui. Reynard took that as a challenge, fighting to brighten her gloaming.

Chambers was a real talent, able to simultaneously project fragility and strength. Her looks and affect fit the grunge era to a tee. *Never After* should have catapulted her into the spotlight. Instead, Chambers vanished from the face of the earth.

As with most behind-the-scenes footage, the documentary dove into the special effects. Lo and behold, a familiar face showed up.

Ray Ford.

"Your father worked on *Never After*?"

Elaine didn't look away from her task. "That's why everything holds up."

"I'm surprised they could afford him."

"He was chasing my mom back then. She worked on the costumes. It was her dream job."

I skipped around to find anything to do with costuming. There were a few minutes devoted. Elaine's mom was dark skinned, with a short, art deco haircut and engaging features. She talked about the blending of traditional expectations and modern styling, so the viewer could identify each character's mythic roots. Her excitement was contagious.

Elaine set down her tools. "Could you mute that, please?"

"I'm sorry, Elaine. I'm such a bonehead."

"It's okay. I'm glad there are things like this out there. Some days, I'm very glad."

I fast-forwarded past Elaine's mom and watched the rest of the footage, then skipped back to the start. Elaine's father had worked on set. He could probably provide valuable insight. But he'd cut me out of his life. If my first attempt at rebuilding the bridge with Ray Ford involved his daughter being in any kind of danger, it was doomed from the start.

After brewing a mediocre pot of complimentary coffee, I watched the footage a second time. This time, I muted the sound and studied everything going on in the background. Every time a new face popped up, I paused to study it. People can change appearances entirely over the space of thirty years.

Archibald Thelen for example, was sporting blond hair with frosted tips and a soul patch. But his accountant mannerisms were still present. Thelen played gofer, providing coffee and running messages for Reynard. When he wasn't tasked with anything, he scanned around like an owl looking for rodents.

Sheila Polk was easy to spot with her impossibly long hair. What she was doing on set, I had no idea. She didn't appear to play any role, either in front of or behind the camera, nor was she credited. Reynard ignored her completely, though she fawned over him from a distance. The only cast or crew member who interacted with her was Lynn Chambers. Polk acted like her assistant, except Chambers never asked for anything. Polk brought her tea, snacks, and applied or removed a jacket from Chambers's shoulders as she saw fit. Chambers only reluctantly thanked her, as if she were trying to discourage Polk.

The smell of ozone and solder filled the air as Elaine got serious with fusing my newly acquired weapons together. I leaned in to study the footage. It was a mental trick. Leaning in told your brain it was time to focus.

A man walked into frame from the far side of the camera. The angle showed only a view from the back. He had thick black hair and was wearing a wide-shouldered tailored suit, a fad I was not sorry to see go. Though the suit made sense on him. He was a mountain of a human being. He turned into profile back toward the camera for less than a second, then was gone.

"No way."

I rolled it back a frame at a time. The more I looked, the more I was sure of it. The massive build, the strong features.

"That's Will Norman's father, William senior."

"Hmm?" Elaine turned toward the screen for the first time.

"The billionaire who owns Home Drive-In. What was he doing on the set of *Never After?* It was a network show."

I looked the show up on IMDb. No Norman was listed in *Never After*'s credits.

"What does this mean?" Elaine asked.

"I have no idea. Except that Norman's father and Reynard knew each other way back when. Before Will Norman was even born."

HAVING EXHAUSTED THE FOOTAGE, I USED Elaine's enhanced internet to dig up everything I could find about Sheila Polk and Will Norman's father. Polk was tougher. She wasn't in the industry and hadn't done anything of note prior to being a founding member of the Edgelords. She had no social media presence that didn't involve the society. All I could find was a single sentence, stating she grew up in the Pacific Northwest on an agricultural commune. There was no mention of parents or siblings or a career before jumping on Reynard's bandwagon.

Will Norman's father was the opposite. There was too much to comb through. The elder Norman went by Bill. He'd founded a cable company in the Midwest, then swallowed up his competitors. In need of content, he'd invested in premium services like Home Drive-In, along with, shall we say, more adult-oriented channels. The success of those led to the creation of pay-per-view. In the early stages of the internet, he'd pivoted to providing online service while also acquiring telecom companies, to corner the high-speed market. From there, things really snowballed.

Bill was three for three: tall, dark, and handsome. Perpetually tan with thick, dark hair and a permanent smile. Very tall. Six and a half feet, maybe, with long limbs and huge hands. In one picture, he's cradling baby Will in his palm like a doll.

They were inseparable. Though the Normans didn't maintain an online presence, being in the public eye meant getting periodically photographed by one clickbait site or another. You could use Bill Sr. for scale as Will Norman grew into adulthood. Will took more after his mother, thin and fair. Though Bill Sr. never showed much muscle tone, Junior hit the weights early. By the time he was in high school, he had a six-pack and bicep veins.

If you arrayed the photos chronologically, you were also left with a timeline of the work Will Jr. had done. His nose had been first and had gone through at least three iterations. Hairline had been next, then brow. After that, a chin implant, complete with cleft, and cheekbones. He also turned up the volume with weights, packing on muscle, and stayed bronzed year-round. He never got within six inches of his father's height, but was a foot wider. With all the changes, he had become a different person. Now he looked more like his father than his mother.

I wondered what it was like, wanting so badly to be like your father that you'd change everything about yourself. My recently discovered kid had the same problem growing up. His mother had neglected to tell him the man who raised him wasn't his biological father. Neglected to tell me as well. It led to the kid growing up with issues he was still trying to solve, and never might. I was doing what I could to help, but in the end, the man who brings you up is your father, no matter who provided the genetic material.

"Okay, the metal should be cool enough for you to give it a whirl," Elaine said as she turned her chair to present my new scepter. She had removed the basket hand protection and upturned guard from the dagger, with some alterations to both, and attached them to the jester rod's flexible metal shaft topped with the little ball.

"I twisted the quillons so they'd hold on to anything they caught better, and removed some of the basket for a quicker draw and more range of motion. The new furniture is threaded on. Be sure to tighten it after use."

"I can't believe you did this all right here."

"Well, I didn't have to worry about triggering the fire suppression. Reynard's people already shut it down."

I made a little space and tried it out. The shaft was light and slightly whippy. I wouldn't want to be on the receiving end of the ball topper. But I also wasn't worried about decapitating anyone by accident.

"This is going to be a lifesaver. Literally. Thank you, Elaine."

"Oh, you. It's fun, having the band back together."

I tilted my new cudgel, examining it from every angle. "How's your dad?"

"In China. After everything that happened last fall, work dried up here. He's working on some street racing movie. Building the cars."

Ray had been framed for several fatal accidents during the shooting of superhero films. Clearing his name cost our friendship.

"Getting back to his roots. Think I should reach out when he returns?"

Elaine exhaled in thought. "Maybe a card."

"Roger that."

"So, what now?"

"Time's a wasting. The bar is still open. That's where the real convention takes place at things like this."

"Okay. Take off your belt."

I handed it over. Elaine added a flexible metal clamp on the right side. "That should hold your new scepter. Just give it a tug. Way faster than having to draw it out of a sheath."

I strapped my belt back on and clamped the scepter into place. It was secure, but being much shorter than a sword and not having a scabbard, it didn't get tangled up when I moved around. I practiced pulling it a few times, getting used to the same-side draw. It felt faster than a cross-body one. It was also harder to block.

"I like it."

"It's how the Romans did it. Great for when you have a shorter weapon and are in close quarters. Same-side drawing is also friendlier when using a shield."

"Why would I need a shield?"

"How the hell should I know?"

We shared a laugh. I donned my crown, its four cameras coming to life on Elaine's screen.

"Wish me luck."

"You don't need luck. You have me."

<hr />

The mezzanine was packed when I arrived. I went to the balcony corner so I could also look down into the lobby. Spirits were high. Laughter rolled through in waves. People acted out their favorite scenes, shouted what I assumed were famous quotes. Stringed instruments dueled from opposite sides of the space. Everything was in place for an epic celebration.

But the moment was off. Something didn't ring true.

I wove through the crowd, taking in the revelers. Their costumes were good. Their styling on point. In the bar area, I was able to pick out some crew members, huddled in tight clusters, reminiscing.

But no one stood out. I didn't know the entire cast on sight, but at events like this, even the lowest billers drew crowds like a lodestone. They became stars around which fans orbited.

"Elaine, are any of these people on the show?"

"No one so far."

I went down to the lobby level and completed the circuit. Not one familiar face. No big cast members. But more troubling was the absence of the high-ranking Edgelords. Not a single person who had been invited to Sheila Polk's pseudo coronation was in sight.

"Where is everybody?" Elaine whispered into my ear.

I took the stairs up a level and lapped the second floor. The few convention goers I saw were stumbling back to their rooms. Same with the third floor. And the fourth. On the fifth, I heard distant, soft knocks. Caught glimpses of people moving in pairs or trios, with purpose, to a door where they were promptly admitted.

The sixth floor was locked down. People in red guarded from the corners, overlapping their views. The seventh floor would be off-limits to all but the major VIPs and cops.

Anyone in the know about Reynard's death had withdrawn to quarters to plot and plan. In the public areas, the oblivious convention goers caroused, living their dream of existing in the Lands Beyond. But in the rooms above, resolve was hardening. Loyalties were being laid. Blades were being sharpened.

Sheila Polk, the red queen, had marshaled her forces. On the other side, the unknown would-be monarch behind the Blackguard opposed her. A battle was coming.

The long night was upon Chateau d'Loire. When the sun rose, so would the body count.

Both sides were going to be scouring the hotel for the series bible, and I was high on the list of possible holders. I went up to my room, passing it and doubling back to make sure I wasn't being followed. Inside, I performed an inspection. All the drawers were now fully closed. The hair on top of the closet door had fallen off. The shower curtain had been moved. It wasn't the staff—the room had been cleaned that morning before check-in.

Someone had been in here, searching.

I left immediately, pausing only to grab my new acquisitions.

"Elaine, I hate to impose, but someone found my room. I need a place to crash. I don't snore. I think."

"You don't. Come on up."

I made double sure I wasn't being tailed. It didn't inspire much confidence, as I had already been sure I wasn't previously followed back to my now-rifled room. Elaine confirmed, via the crown's cameras, no one was stalking me on the way to hers.

The chain and bolt went into place as soon as I stepped through. I was dragging the desk over to block the door when Elaine stopped me.

"I brought wedges."

She provided two adjustable metal deals that looked like book-ends. I worked them into the door next to the bolt and hinges. Anyone who wanted to get in would have to demolish the door. To an outsider, it might seem an extreme measure, but Elaine had spent several years of her life nestled in a secure compound on account of an extremely dangerous ex-boyfriend, who was as good at tech stuff as she was while also being built like Hercules. And he'd been willing to kill to get what he wanted. Attending this convention was a big step for her. One she wasn't taking without a safety net.

Confident we were now as safe as you could get under the cir-cumstances, I took the time to unwrap myself. Now I knew why knights needed an extra set of hands. Elaine's room sported a walk-in shower. Judging by the array of products, her skin and hair routine was extensive and expensive. I opted for the complimentary soap and shampoo provided by the hotel. For me, there was no such thing as too much water pressure. Chateau d'Loire failed on that account, due to the mandatory water conservation mechanisms present in all California faucets and fixtures. I persevered. Suffering came with the territory. My newly acquired Chateau d'Loire T-shirt and swim trunks would have to do for pajamas.

Elaine went into the bathroom next. I didn't ask her if she needed help because she didn't. I snagged two pillows and the extra blanket from the closet. In terms of floors I had slept on, I give Chateau d'Loire a seven out of ten. The carpet was deodorized and there weren't any bugs, but it was light on the padding.

Elaine was in the bathroom for maybe an hour. She came out in a sleep cap with a built-in blindfold and a robe made from the same stuff they use in weighted blankets. She got into bed and threw the down comforter at me.

With the comforter repurposed into a mattress, I was comfy and cozy, but Mr. Sandman refused to bring me a dream. I'd just gotten back into town after spending eight weeks communing with nature. It wasn't the bedding that was the problem. There are all sorts of techniques for falling asleep: breath control, procedural body relaxation, counting sheep. None of them worked for me now. I did my best to think about nothing, but instead I pondered what was worth killing for.

Boiling it down to love or money was overly simplistic. Love always implied love for a person, but that wasn't always the case. Soldiers fought for love of their country. Activists died for love of a cause. Zealots killed over their religious beliefs. People would do anything for the thing they treasured most.

Even if it was a world that didn't exist.

If we are honest with ourselves, each of us creates our own world. We revise reality to suit us, to make it into a place we can accept. We simplify situations, reduce others into two-dimensional beings, and flat-out ignore what we can't force into our worldview. Who was I to judge someone who decided to walk away from this world and into another? For good or ill, Reynard had created a land worth living in. He'd provided a structure where someone could rise in the ranks, gaining respect and importance. From what I gathered, the

Lands Beyond was a simpler place. Sure, people plotted, stole, and killed, but they didn't exist in tremendous debt. They didn't worry about retirement. Their world was one of inexhaustible bounty, of endless possibility. And everyone was playing by the same rules. Merit mattered. Killing in the name of your king was something to be celebrated. The rewards were worth it, and not just the material ones. You gained the respect and admiration of your peers. Slay one dragon and you were forever the dragon slayer.

I drifted off with visions of Reynard's Technicolor factions dancing in my head. They clashed in the open field, champions exchanging cuts and parries in an endless tennis match where love meant death.

There was a soft tapping at the door. I jumped to my feet, cudgel in hand. Elaine sat up and lifted her eye mask. I put a finger over my lips and went to the door to check the peephole.

The hallway was empty.

The tapping came again. Whoever was knocking was standing next to the door, out of line of sight of the peephole. I waited them out. They tapped one last time, then the bolt turned on its own. The wood groaned under the increasing pressure, but the door didn't budge.

The room phone rang. It was loud. I was tempted to ignore it, but if I didn't pick up, they might assume the room was empty and try to break in. I motioned for Elaine to answer.

"Hello?"

"Sorry to bother you. This is the front desk. There is a report of a package outside your door. We wanted to inform you, in the event it is stolen."

"Thanks, but I'm not expecting anything."

Elaine set the receiver down. I went back to the peephole. Four figures passed by, weapons out, all of them in black.

The Blackguard was resorting to a door-to-door search for the series bible. They'd planted someone at the front desk for when people called down to complain. If they had the front desk, they had access to the room keys and registrations. You could call the cops after suffering a room invasion, but nothing was likely to be stolen. The Blackguard just wanted the book. And when you did call the cops, in this case, they'd tell you to pack up and leave. It was in their best interest to quietly evacuate as many guests from Chateau d'Loire as possible.

The hero in me wanted to throw open the door, take them on before someone got hurt. But four to one was impossible odds. If the Whisper hadn't shown up to bail me out, two of the Blackguard would have been enough to end me. Hopefully, people knew better than to put up a fight.

I went to Elaine's bedside and spoke softly. "They're getting desperate. This place is a powder keg. You need to consider bailing."

"Back at ya, big guy."

She had a point. What was keeping me here? Sure, the money would be nice, if I was dumb enough to believe either Polk or Norman would actually pay it. But I already had my dream job and wasn't looking to retire anytime soon. Heck, the way things were going, I'd be lucky to retire at all.

There was some guilt over Reynard getting offed on my watch, but it wasn't like he'd hired me to bodyguard him. And I'd been on the job shorter than your average smoke break when he was killed. You couldn't really blame me for mucking up, and that was coming from a guy who blamed himself early and often.

At any time, I could walk out the doors, submit myself to a search, and be free and clear. So why stay?

I could tell myself it was duty, or the pursuit of justice, or the need to finish what I started. All those things were present, in different measures. But the truth was, this was what I'd signed up for. If I wanted safe and stable, I'd go back to telling actors to brace their cores and not hyperextend their joints. I'd never admit it to anyone else, but I was having a hell of a time. I forced myself to lie down and spent three hours in low-power mode, not quite asleep and not quite awake. I let my consciousness drift in hopes it would come up with something to work with.

Who had killed Reynard? Not Polk or anyone loyal to her. If it was one of Polk's people, they would have grabbed the book. Polk was just making her move in the power vacuum. Not the Blackguard, or they wouldn't be looking for the book now. They knew the book's value. They wouldn't have left it behind.

Someone else had offed Reynard. Someone who hadn't planned to. Either they took the book with them, or another someone showed up right after to snatch it up. Which put a lot of traffic in that suite during a very short time frame.

All the deaths after were fallout. Reynard dies; the Blackguard discovers it via their secret passage. Whoever is running them hatches a plan to score the book, but two of them don't want to go along with it: Bowers and Denoso, the guy in the bathtub. One gets an axe, the other gets put on ice.

But then, how does the murderer get into and out of Reynard's room without using the repurposed dumbwaiter? I was back where I started.

My eyes popped open. Natural light was bullying its way into the room from under the curtain. I vaulted to my feet so hard I went airborne. Elaine sat up and raised her eye mask.

"What?"

"You're alive and I'm alive. Great way to start the day. Want anything from the breakfast buffet?"

She lay back down. "I'll text you."

My morning routine was quick. That's male privilege for you. I worked my way back into my outfit, strapped on my scepter, and donned my crown. After removing the jams from the door, I listened carefully before peeking out to ensure my passage went undetected. Elaine was safer during the day, when everyone was awake and foot traffic abounded. Still, I suggested she replace the wedges behind me.

The Blackguard hadn't gotten in last night. Her room was earmarked to be rolled.

It was a little before seven in the morning. The breakfast buffet was fresh and gloriously untouched, but I had other entrees on my mind. The omelet guy came out of the elevator with his crepe-crafting counterpart. Being so fresh-faced and squared off this early suggested ex-military. He raised his eyebrows in recognition. I restrained myself and let him come to me.

"Need any help setting up?"

"We'll just be a minute."

He handled my nudging with the grace of a saint. I did my best not to drool. Once he got the menu set out and flame going, he acknowledged me as if I had just appeared. I managed not to propose as I put in my order.

"Dealer's choice."

He made a nod while I attempted to determine the polite amount of time one waited before broaching an informant. Elaine texted me down an order I would have kicked back if I was her father. I informed her there was a crepe station and she revised to the classic banana Nutella combination.

"Today's the day. Keep an eye out for health nuts."

The omelet guy flipped without need of a spatula. "This have anything to do with us being paid double overtime to stay over last night?"

"The less you know about it the better off you are. But if anyone wants a peek in your cart, let them have at it."

The guy dropped a picture-perfect Spanish omelet on my plate with a shrug. "It's the hotel's cart anyway. It's not like I bring it from home."

I scarfed down my omelet. Normally I force myself to take twenty minutes to eat, but every second counted.

I grabbed Elaine's crepes and absconded with the plate and a silverware setting, then stopped by the cafe to coffee up and fill Elaine's iced chai order. She followed my arrival on the cameras and had the door ready. I cleared space on her desk for her plate and cup.

When I turned to leave, she held up a finger for me to wait for her to wash down her sugar bread with some sugar water. How could she eat like that and not need a nap after?

"Why does the omelet guy matter?"

"I want to know who was meeting with Hammersmith and why. Someone is up against Polk, running the Blackguard from the shadows. It could be the guy behind the protein bars."

"An omelet isn't a lot to go off of, evidence-wise."

"Tell me about it."

"What's the agenda?"

"Check the convention programming for any can't-miss events. Get face time with anyone worth it who will let me within talking distance. Follow up on all these loose threads. But if my limited experience counts for anything, something will happen to throw all this off the rails."

Elaine was done with her breakfast by the time I worked up the courage to bring the next topic up.

"You consider maybe getting out of here?"

She went into the bathroom, taking off her hair cap on the way. Putting the wall between us maybe helped. "I was on lockdown for five years. Going home now would be admitting defeat."

"These are special circumstances, Elaine. People are getting murdered, and with me on everyone's radar, you're only one degree separated from it."

Her voice took on that distant quality women got when they were futzing with their hair.

"Maybe I'll go to Disneyland. No one dies there, right?"

"People do, it's just that they have all these tunnels to move them around secretly. I knew a girl who spent a couple of years working as a mermaid. She said the place was like a spider's web. There's at least three ways out of every location." I slapped my forehead. "I'm a real dummy. I have to go."

"What's going on?"

"Stay tuned. You'll see. And if you're staying, wedge this door shut."

Blake Dever was scheduled for a Saturday-morning panel titled Prince and Pauper: Playing Both Sides. It was no surprise the powers that be would want a big name to kick off Saturday. You needed to give people a reason to set their alarms after a wild Friday night. The shock was that Dever had agreed to do it. As a top biller, he should have the swing to set a more favorable schedule. Either Dever was a real team player, or Reynard had leverage.

Stern was my back channel to Dever. She hadn't answered any of my texts after being pulled out of the game. I hoped she hadn't gone and done something stupid, like gotten herself locked up. Knucklehead moves were my purview. I kept my message vague, in case her phone had been seized.

Need something from your boy toy.

If I didn't have a VIP pass, I would have never gotten into Dever's panel. As it was, I caught plenty of dirty looks being able to skip the queue. The front rows filled up first. However, the end of the first row provided a terrible view of Dever's seat. I snagged it and turned to take in the audience. It looked like a community college brochure. Dever was a ratings dream: He appealed to every demographic. The Venn diagram of Dever's sex appeal was basically a thick-lined circle.

One key category was missing: power players. None of the usual suspects were present. No one in black or white. Dever wasn't being guarded or stalked. Stern would have been vindicated. She had been so sure her main squeeze wasn't a suspect.

Dever arrived through the service hallway a full minute early to thunderous applause. A convention assistant begging to be noticed beat him to the water carafe. A second contender managed Dever's chair for him. He endured the pampering with grace. His muscular neck was likely on account of continuously nodding thanks.

At 10:00 am on the dot, Dever greeted the audience, muttering *hello* with stunned amusement. Rapport was instant. Charisma—you either had it or you didn't. Dever's felt natural and unrefined. You liked him in spite of his God-given gifts, as if he were a normal bloke struck by a lightning bolt that made him handsome and famous.

Dever gave a short talk, often pausing for laughter. He chuckled along with everyone, as if still terribly amused by an anecdote he'd repeated a hundred times. The content discussed was his initial casting: How Reynard had seen him in an obscure stage production of *Robin Hood and His Merrie Men* and somehow remembered him for a lead role several years later. Dever also postulated he had won the part because he looked like a young Reynard, and what writer didn't cast himself in the main part?

After that, Dever opened to questions. They came in three varieties: confirming or denying rumored behind-the-scenes occurrences, extremely specific inquiries that proved the asker was a true fan, and lore-related queries more suited for a superfan than a cast member. Dever adroitly dodged the first category, delved deep on the second, and called on the audience to answer the third. If the guy ever wanted to run for office, he was a shoo-in.

Citing the need to be considerate to the next panel, he wrapped things up. In response to the wave of dismay, one of the convention assistants gave an unnecessary reminder when Dever would be appearing at a booth to sign autographs, and that the main event—the main cast panel—would take place that night before Saturday's feast.

The other assistant furiously waved me in as if I had missed some cue. Guess I didn't have to work out a way to get next to Dever.

He wanted face time with me. I tapped my chest to confirm I had correctly interpreted her gesticulating, which was enough to send the assistant into conniptions. She ushered me into the back hall, profusely apologizing to Dever about my ignorance in improvised sign language. Dever laid a hand on the assistant's shoulder to comfort her.

"It's no trouble. My friend suffers from hand blindness."

"Yeah, don't ask me how many fingers I'm holding up."

The assistant bounced looks between us until Dever gifted her with a chuckle that said he was laughing with her. She trailed him all the way to the kitchen, where she could follow no more.

"Ava relayed your message."

"Did she call me Allen?"

"Not with any level of endearment. How may I be of aid?"

I led Dever into the storage room with the linens and carts. "I need access to your suite."

"I'm afraid you won't fit into my haversack."

"I have a better idea."

"Do tell."

"Let's get you out of those clothes."

13

"THIS WON'T WORK."

Dever said it by way of argument, as reassuring as it came out. I tried not to take it personally.

"We're the same height. Same build, with the same hair color and cut. I just have to move fast and avoid eye contact."

"What if you're stopped?"

I unbuckled the straps on my armor. "Then I'll have to rely on this impeccable English accent."

"Dear Lord, are you making fun of me?"

"Imitation is the sincerest form of flattery. Now drop your trousers."

Dever unbuckled his sword belt. "I shall close my eyes and think of Ava."

I had Dever with his pants down. If ever there was a time to go at him, it was now.

"Reynard ever have you out at his cabin? The one in Maine."

"Hmm? No. Afraid I've only ever been to Southern California and New York, for Broadway."

"That story about how he cast you true? He really see you in some play years before the show?"

"That's what he claimed." Dever stopped to consider. "Though we didn't speak at the time. I had no idea he was present. But I saw no reason to challenge his tale."

I measured the distance before the next question. If Dever was going to take a swing at me, now would have been the time. "Ever look into who your biological father is?"

Dever's head snapped toward me. "I beg your pardon?"

"Reynard was involved in a paternity suit around the time you were born. Though public belief is the suit was filed against Reynard, it may have been the opposite: Reynard had been trying to prove a child was his. Do you know if Reynard filed a suit against your parents?"

Dever blinked a lot, trying to process what I was saying. "That's utterly ridiculous."

"You said it yourself on your panel: Reynard cast a younger version of himself as the prince. The two of you are the same build, or would be if Reynard had ever worked out, and have the same coloration. Do you know who your biological father is?"

"No. And I don't wish to know. My mothers are my parents."

"Reynard mirrored real-life events on the show. Casting you as the prince while you were secretly his real-life heir would have been right up his alley."

Dever ran his hands through his hair to self-soothe as he worked through my theory. "I would like to tell you to go to hell, but in truth, Reynard was forever trying to recruit me into the Edgelords. He leveraged every angle. Obligation—that I owed him for my casting. Bribery—a higher salary, more of a merchandising share. Threats, though I took those as empty. He could kill me off in the final episodes, but not before then, not without unthreading his entire tapestry. And

even if he did, my career had been launched beyond any scuttling."
Dever paused a moment, as if torn. It wasn't a long moment. Dramatic
pauses were considered self-indulgent on episodic television. "His last
attempt was resorting to blackmail."

Dever mussed his hair in anguish. Every one of them fell right
back into place.

"This is a safe space, Dever."

"I hate to speak ill of the dead."

"You're an actor. Act like Reynard's still alive."

It was Dever's turn to grab my gaze. "Ava must not know."

The bastard had me. My ability to keep secrets was the cornerstone
of my second act as a private investigator. If I leaked Dever's secret,
my new career was sunk.

"Let's hear it, Dever."

"Please understand Ava and I had just started talking. We hadn't
yet consummated our relationship."

"Dever, are you from a long line of gardeners or something?"

"Beg pardon?"

"Enough with the hedging. Spit it out."

"I'd only known Ava for a few weeks prior to leaving to film last
season. There was a scene that required an intimacy coordinator. She
brought a stand-in with her for demonstration purposes. I succumbed
to temptation."

It was a tale as old as time. If you ran a poll, I'd be willing to bet
people stepped out on their partners most often in the beginning, before
the foundation had settled. Everyone had their vice. Dever didn't
use drugs, didn't drink, didn't even cheat on his diet. His weakness
was sex. Not a problem, when you're a regular schlub. A just-say-no
attitude isn't required when no one is offering. But everywhere Dever
went, women were throwing themselves at him.

He went for the smile and hair muss again. "Even the finest
swordsman has difficulty defending against two opponents."

I could have socked him one right then and there. Stern would never forgive him. She was tough as nails, that wasn't a front. But her armor was there for a reason.

No one wanted to hear in the beginning, when someone was supposed to be swept off their feet, they were a free-floating entity. But to Ava Stern, it wouldn't matter if it was day one or day ten thousand. I knew her type.

If someone wasn't all in, they could shove off.

"A honeypot, I think it's called," Dever went on. "Reynard tried to leverage me. I refused. He claimed there was a tape. I refused to be coerced. There was a reason for my reputation, I told him. Going public with the footage may have aided rather than damaged my career."

"But no tape emerged."

Dever nodded. "Reynard had woven his tale from whole cloth, a thing he did so well."

"How did Reynard react when you called his bluff?"

"I thought he would rage, but it was quite the opposite. He seemed pleased at my demonstration of backbone. My impression was that an act of defiance was a rare occurrence."

"Like a proud parent."

"This can't be true. Reynard could not have been my father."

Our garment exchange was complete, though I retained my crown and cudgel when Dever tried to pass me his sword.

"Keep it, you might need it. Behind closed doors, the knives are out."

"I want you to know that what occurred is the great regret of my life."

"Rest easy, Dever. I'm not out to break hearts."

"You are a prince among men, Ken Allen."

"Keep your compliments. I'm not doing it for you."

The smile went away, and for the first time I saw the real Blake Dever. There was a cold spark, under the pomp and circumstance.

"As you will. Now to our current task. What would you have me do?"

"The elevator guards are going to get a close look at me. I need you to distance them."

"I can recall several racy limericks that may suffice."

Dever patted me on the shoulder and left the storage room for the elevators. Thirty seconds later, he led the guards past my door. I ran for the elevators and pulled out my set of hotel keys. The elevator key was a stubby round deal. I had to use it to access both the cab and the controls to reach the penthouse level. It took time. I glimpsed the guards coming back around the corner through an inches-wide space as the doors closed.

On the penthouse level, cops were stationed outside Reynard's door. I turned my face away and made for Dever's suite. They'd be expecting him to be coming back after his panel.

The key heads matched their door motif. The lock was tricky. It didn't go straight in. I could feel eyes on my back. It was okay, I told myself. Dever would have also struggled. It's not like he lived there.

I stepped inside and closed the door behind me without turning around, leaving the security chain dangling. If I left a different way than I came in, I wanted Dever to be able to get back inside.

I fixed the layout of the penthouse suites in my head. Reynard's was to the right of Dever's. Between the two throne rooms was Dever's kitchen and Reynard's bedroom. The hidden dumbwaiter had been in Reynard's room. Maybe Reynard had chosen his room specifically because he had known about that passage. The thing about searching for secrets is that you tend to stop when you find one. But there wasn't a limit on the number of secret passages a room could have.

I went into Dever's kitchen and started poking around. On the wet wall, there was upper and lower cabinetry like any normal kitchen. But there, in the corner, sat a floor-to-ceiling standing closet. A broom closet doesn't get much use in a hotel with a cleaning staff. Which made such a cabinet a weird choice. Inside, it was empty, except for the shelf. Pulling on it didn't work but pushing it in did. The back of the closet swung open, revealing a passage that ran parallel to the wet wall.

I realized why the door was designed for the shelf to be pushed in—so you could close the cabinet door behind you and reload the switch. I did so and stepped into the passage. It ran the length of the maintenance closet adjacent the long wall, ending in another door. I had my guesses as to where it led and got ready to catch falling objects.

The back of Reynard's bedroom closet swung open. The cops had cleared it out. Yesterday, I had dismissed the closet as a possibility because the killer would have no way to replace any fallen items behind them when they left. Which was the case—this particular passage hadn't been used. But if Dever had a secret door in his kitchen, Reynard might have one too.

The trick was getting to the kitchenette. It required passing through the throne room, which was a crime scene. Which meant first leaving the closet, not knowing what was on the other side of the door.

"Elaine, please tell me what's in this room."

Ever so slowly, I cracked the closet door. I took off the crown and turned it sideways, angling it as much as I could to take in the room.

"There's a cop asleep on the bed, and the bathroom door is closed."

I stepped out of the closet, leaving the door cracked, and went to the bedroom door. The throne room stood empty. Reynard's body was gone. I crossed over to the kitchenette, which was also empty. Where the heck were all the cops?

The metallic sounds of an antique key being worked into a vintage lock made me jump. Someone was coming into the suite. I closed the kitchenette door behind me, then went right for the standing cabinet.

The cops were using it as a coat closet. Only there was no closet bar, so they just dumped everything in a pile. All the coats, scarves, and beanies were new, purchased for the unexpected winter. When the door swung into the secret passage, the coats came along. Muffled voices from the throne room got louder as they approached. I stepped into the cabinet and plowed through the coats, closing the door behind me.

The voices hit the kitchen. If they opened the closet door it was all over for me. From the hidden passage, I started shoveling coats back into the cabinet, careful not to toss too hard and pop the door open from the inside. The coats kept tumbling back onto me. From the far side of the door, two cops were discussing the disaster this investigation had become. The top brass was playing the situation all wrong. Heads were going to roll, short straws were drawn, and other relevant metaphors were invoked. I prayed to the universe no one needed their coat.

Then someone said, "I'm out of here."

It was shift change.

I shoved the secret door closed as much as it would go. It wouldn't latch. I braced myself against the wall as the cabinet door opened from the kitchen side.

The cop on the other side of the secret door started digging for his coat, complaining about what a bunch of slobs everyone else was, as if he wasn't part of the problem.

The unseen cop started throwing the coats out. I could feel the weight coming off the door. I eased up pressure so the back of the closet wouldn't make a noise as it secured. He found his coat and stormed off, the door still open. I waited until the kitchen was quiet to latch the secret door. At that time, I also quit holding my breath.

I made my way down the hidden hallway. Dever's kitchen had connected to Reynard's bedroom. If my sense of direction was correct, Reynard's kitchen should connect to Hammersmith's bedroom.

I kept my voice low. "Elaine, I've misplaced my program. What's Hammersmith's schedule look like?"

"He's got a signing after lunch, then the big panel followed by the Saturday feast."

Which left an hour to kill. I made myself as comfortable as one could in a secret passage. I should have picked up one of those hooded cloaks. You walked around wrapped in a blanket. "Hope he takes Fairchild with him. Mind giving me a wake-up call?"

"All set."

I sat with my back to the wall and drifted off. I didn't sleep, just let my consciousness wander. A little non-thinking could do a world of good. It was dark and quiet and still in the passage. I visualized the penthouse level of Chateau d'Loire from above, opening like a lotus flower. The four suites, and the four spaces between. Who could visit who, with no one knowing. Had Reynard chosen which suites Dever, Hammersmith, and the Dame of the Moon were given?

"Up and at 'em, big guy."

After a quick stretch, I popped Hammersmith's bedroom closet, parting a curtain of garments. This was a gamble, but thus far, everywhere Hammersmith went, Fairchild followed. I took a breath to center myself and came out of the closet. There was nothing new in Hammersmith's bed or bathroom. The only change in the throne room was the camera equipment having been stowed away. Either Stern had been right and the whole filming situation had been to establish an alibi, or the events that had transpired put a damper on their romantic weekend.

The kitchen was the same, but for the empty champagne bottles. Maybe something worth celebrating had happened, or maybe they just liked champagne. The standing closet was where all the others had been. I started to get that gut feeling. The butterflies that heralded an adrenaline rush flapped to life. A Blackguard's protein bar wrapper had been in the kitchen can. Whoever had met with Hammersmith had been in this room. It hadn't occurred to me earlier, but why not just stuff the wrapper in one of your many tactical pockets? Unless, of course, you were looking for an excuse to get access to the kitchen.

The standing cabinet was bare. A broom was leaning against the wall next to it. My butterflies intensified. The broom should have been in the closet, but in their haste, someone had forgotten to replace it. I'd missed that last time.

I pulled the shelf and stepped inside, closing the door behind me.

The series bible was there, on the floor, within arm's length of the hidden door.

I carefully reached for it. It was only an inanimate object, but I experienced an irrational sense of danger, as if I were trying to handle a rattlesnake. It was for sure the series bible. I'd only seen it the once, but it was a hard object to copy.

The book was heavy. Ten pounds maybe. It was built like a safe, completely enveloped in a metal case with a locking hasp.

"Is this thing booby-trapped, you think?"

"I'd have to get a closer look at it." Elaine could barely contain herself. "But offhand, I would say yes. Acid vial maybe. Or a small incendiary."

"Sounds tricky."

"I could do it."

"But you can do anything."

"It's not that hard. Anyone with some technical skills could do it."

Something about what Elaine said tickled my memory, but it was hard with the series bible in my hand. I had the book and I had the ring. Twenty million dollars, if Will Norman was to be trusted. Carrying it around was dumb, but leaving it behind was equally boneheaded. Someone put it here, which meant at least one person knew where it was. And if anyone else learned or already knew about the passages, they could stumble across it. I tucked it inside my gambeson, which was the best I could do for now.

With the cops back at their post, my only way out was going forward. If my mental map was correct, the Dame of the Moon's bedroom was at the other end of the passage. As much as I believed a woman should be allowed her mysteries, exceptions had to be made when multiple murders were involved. I got a rundown on her itinerary from Elaine.

"She's scheduled for a morning tea. Ooh, she's teaching how to read leaves." Elaine paused. "I want to go."

The desire was heavy in her voice. All my protective instincts kicked in, but so did my sympathetic ones. Her first time out of her hobbit hole in years and now she was under house arrest.

"You know what? You should."

"Really?"

"Stay in view of people. Keep with the crowd. If someone tries to get you to go off with them, raise hell."

"Or use the flamethrower in my chair."

It was fifty-fifty Elaine was kidding. The gadgets she and her father once made for me were beyond state of the art. If someone came at Elaine with a sword, I wouldn't be surprised if she whipped out a lightsaber.

I eased the back of the Dame's closet open. It was packed with garments elaborate enough to house all those mysteries discussed prior. I used the same trick with the camera crown as before to use Elaine to scout the room.

"It's a mess, but it's empty."

Elaine wasn't kidding. There were a lot of clothes. Closer to a week's worth than a weekend's. It skeeved me out, going through the Dame's things, but that was the job. She hadn't wanted the place searched. Either it was on principle, or she had a reason. The Dame had fully unpacked. The drawers were full. She liked to read vintage fantasy novels, with airbrushed covers featuring teased hair and dragons. She'd brought half a dozen. How she thought she'd get through them during what had to be a packed schedule was beyond me.

The bathroom was likewise stocked. High-end skin products, at least five bottles for hair care. She did have a lot of hair. Come to think of it, so did Sheila Polk. Long hair was popular in the fantasy community. I'd had a ponytail once, in the nineties. It looked horrible and I had no idea how to take care of my not-so-luscious locks. Growing your hair had a kind of momentum. Thankfully, the Calabrias forced me to cut it to play Jove Brand. The additional grief I would have suffered had I kept it was incalculable.

There were two toothbrushes in the holder. Unless the Dame had different ones for morning and night, I had stumbled across what we detectives called a clue. Lots of clothes for ladies, none for men. Same for toiletries.

There were several gnarly hair monsters in the shower. You couldn't have hair like the Dame without some shedding. But some of it might belong to her secret partner. It was too wet for me to make out its hue. I used a wad of toilet paper to scoop it all up.

Searching the throne room took no time at all: the Dame had staged it for her private readings—there wasn't much clutter. I was sure to check the bookshelves. Even a high-school dropout such as myself had read *The Purloined Letter*.

The kitchenette held no real surprises. The Dame had brought all her own food and really liked farmer's cheese. There was no alcohol but many varieties of loose tea, along with homemade jams and honey. Those paired well with the three different kinds of bread present.

Having wrapped up with the Dame's suite, it was time to head back to Dever's. The Dame's cabinet was bare. I slipped through into the secret hallway adjacent the second maintenance closet and into Dever's bedroom closet, where a messenger bag was hanging. I cleared it out and tucked the book into it. There was a hair dryer in his bathroom. Not the one that came with the room, but a high-end stylist deal that had to be Stern's for sure. I made a note to rib her about it and dug out the clump of hair from the Dame of the Moon's shower.

I laid the hair out on a towel and got to work with the dryer. Here I was sure I was onto something, but all the hair was black. I tossed the dry clump toward the trash. It was in the air when I caught what I had missed. I snatched it up and looked closer. Two of the hairs were completely white. I hadn't seen them against the white towel. They weren't the Dame's. White hairs would have stood out against her outfit. According to my watch, I had fifteen minutes to get back to the Dame's suite before her panel was over. I made my way back into her kitchenette and put the pot on to boil.

The tea was ready when I heard someone come into the suite. I was all set up for the dramatic entrance, but they went into the bedroom. I followed them. I cracked the door first to make sure I wasn't walking in on a sensitive moment.

The room's occupant didn't hear me come in. She was sitting in the chair, using the natural light through the window to read one of the paperbacks. Thirty years had barely put a dent in her. Stripes of white, instead of strands, were the only sign of time's passing. Her expression was still melancholic. Distant. Some people affect a character. It's when they don't know they are being watched that the true self shows through.

The woman in the chair was a haunted person. Some people were. They carried a heartbreaking darkness, passed from mother to daughter, father to son.

I cleared my throat as I stepped into the room. She looked up from her book, a cursed girl cast into a role of the evil queen.

Lynn Chambers, alive and in the flesh.

LYNN CHAMBERS ACCEPTED MY GENEROUS OFFER of her refreshments. She blew on the tea before taking a sip and waited for me to lead.

"I'm Ken Allen, detective at large. You can look me up."

"My daughter already told me all about you. You've quite the reputation."

Chambers didn't bother to deny it. The Dame of the Moon was her daughter. They had the same complexion, the same hair, the same unknowable eyes. I tried the tea. Licorice root, slippery elm, and rose hips. Naturally sweet and good for the vocal cords.

"When it comes to what you've heard about me, only believe half of the good stuff and none of the bad."

Chambers nodded. "I'm well aware how the media likes to exaggerate."

"The story sells better than the truth." I took another sip and decided to rip off the Band-Aid. "Tell me about the paternity suit."

"I wasn't behind that suit. Not that it would have mattered. Rex had a condition: genetic chimerism. It fascinated him: having two different sets of genetic material, like some mythological creature. That's why chimeric animals are a staple in *The Lands Beyond*. With the technology back then, it would render the results of any blood test inconclusive."

Chambers seemed to think what everyone else did: that someone had brought the suit against Reynard. But according to Mercie Goodday, Reynard himself had been the one who filed the suit. And he hadn't filed it against Blake Dever's parents or Lynn Chambers.

"Wait. When did Reynard find out he had a daughter?"

"Between the first and second seasons of *The Lands Beyond*."

"Must have boiled his parsnips when she showed up at his door."

"Lila felt compelled to meet him." The ghost of a smile played on Lynn Chambers's face. "There's a unique agony a mother experiences, deciding when to tell their child who their father is. I'll always wonder if I waited too long or not long enough."

"People have a right to know where they come from." I failed to keep the edge out of my tone. Having a mystery father was a sore spot.

Chambers stared at me with a small measure of affection. "Lila said the two of you had commonalties. She likes you, which is rare."

"I'm surprised Reynard brought her into the fold."

Chambers's laugh had depth. Comedy and tragedy. "Lila didn't give him much choice. She's my daughter, but she's also his. She inherited his willingness to coerce to get what she wants."

"Does that put Lila in the market for a crown?"

"Why don't you ask me that, Mr. Allen?"

Lila Chambers, née Reynard, a.k.a. the Dame of the Moon, was in the doorway, clutching her tiara in a balled fist. She looked better without the crown, but she'd inherited a widow's peak from Reynard. The crown covered up that seed of similarity. Any other like features were obscured by her makeup and costuming.

I got up and offered her my chair. "Thought about it. Decided I prefer nonrhetorical answers."

Lila stayed right where she was, blocking the exit. The laws of physics bounced right off her. I had to be half a foot taller, but we stood eye to eye. Her voice had lost all its mystery but none of its authority.

"Try me."

"Okay. Did you kill Reynard?"

I'd been practicing one fighting art or another going on thirty-five years. Every instinct screamed at me to defend myself. But sometimes you deserve what's coming.

Lila slapped me hard on the jaw. She knew what she was doing. Her hand was cupped and she connected with the ridge. It rattled me and stung like hell. I let it sting. Rubbing it was unmanly.

"So that's a no."

Which meant she'd learned Reynard, the father of her dreams, had been murdered from me during our first visit, and hadn't given the smallest sign. "You suspected he was in danger."

"When he sent Alexi to me, I knew he was worried."

Hiring Alexi for the show had been a smoke screen. Reynard knew there were traitors in the midst, so he sought out the toughest, most loyal free agent in the world and assigned him to protect Lila. He'd chosen wisely. His taste in detectives, however, was up for debate.

"Reynard had two crowns in his room, one masculine and one feminine. If the feminine one was for Lila, who is the other one for?"

Chambers dwelled on the steam rising from her cup. "I have no idea."

"Assuming the paternity suit was legit, who else was Reynard snuggled up to when *Never After* was filming?"

Lynn Chambers sipped her tea. "Who wasn't he? Rex always enjoyed female attention. The stable mistress, the costume designer—"

"What about Sheila Polk?"

When Chambers set down her cup, it rattled. "No. Sheila can't have children."

It was an intimate detail. I thought back to the behind-the-scenes footage, the way Polk doted on Chambers. The fact that she was uncredited but still tolerated on set.

"Sheila Polk is your sister."

Lynn Chambers cocked her head in frank reappraisal. I never got tired of that look, when people realized I had two sticks to rub together.

I turned to Lila. "Does Sheila Polk know who you are?"

"No. No one knows where I come from."

"You'd think the two of you sharing this room might provide a clue."

"I wear a mask when I'm out." Lynn Chambers futzed with her dishes. She was a stress cleaner, which beat being a stress drinker by a mile. "I haven't seen Sheila in thirty years. It was come with me or stay with Rex. She chose Rex."

"What are you doing here?"

"All cast members are required to attend."

"You're on the show? As who?"

Elaine was in my ear. "Say you're the Whisper, say you're the Whisper."

"I play the Whisper, the king's secret confidant."

I winced at Elaine's exclamation in my ear. "Thanks for saving my bacon earlier."

"I'm sorry?"

"In the basement. Hooper and Koch would have carved me up."

Lynn Chambers looked at me like I was speaking another language. Whoever had been in the Whisper's costume earlier, it hadn't been Lynn Chambers.

"Did Reynard make you bring your costume?"

"Yes, he did."

"Where is it?"

Chambers walked me to the closet and unzipped the costume from a tailor bag. The other Whisper, her outfit was close, but it wasn't an exact match.

"Why keep it a secret?"

"I appeared as a favor to Rex. He begged me. Assured me that I would never have to say a single line or attend a single event. I agreed on those terms and Rex cleared me with Will Norman."

"When Mom told me she was going on the show, I knew right away why."

"Because of your gift."

Lila scoffed. "It was all over your face, Mom. I knew then and there, Reynard was my father. And if Will Norman had the power to get you on the show while keeping your name secret, he could do the same for me."

"If you've never done on event, what are you doing here?

"Rex . . . he said he was worried that he didn't have much time left. Asked me to attend as a final favor to him. There was something in his voice. He sounded like the old Rex."

Lila wasn't impressed. "I told her not to come. He wanted her here, for some little game he was playing. Reynard loved his drama."

Lynn Chambers brushed crumbs off the desk into her hand. "You didn't hear him, Lila."

"Because he spoke with you alone, which is what manipulators do. They isolate you. He was going to use you for some twist. Some reveal."

"I don't believe that. He was never cruel to me. It was as if he knew the end was near. You heard Ken. He foresaw his own death. He knew things the way you know things."

"I don't know things, Mom. I make educated guesses."

Lynn Chambers ran out of things to clean in the immediate vicinity and got up in search of a mess. "I'm sorry, honey, but you got it from both ends. It's what drew Rex and I together. To make you. It was fate."

It was time to steer the conversation from the esoteric to the practical. "What if he was going to announce his heirs, complete with lineage? That's a hell of a reveal. The Dame of the Moon is my daughter and heir. Here's her mother, the long-lost Lynn Chambers, back from thirty years in exile to confirm it. He had a crown ready for Lila."

The Dame's eyes could have frozen lava. "I would have thrown it back in his face."

"That's a lot of money to turn down."

"With a string tied to every dollar. I'm not like him. I don't relish playing puppeteer."

Lila seemed genuine in her claim that she was not like her father. Then again, she had a battalion of moon-themed spies lurking around every corner. However, accusing her of following in Reynard's foot-steps was a recipe for disaster, so I let it go.

"What about the series bible?"

"I don't have it."

"Would you want it?"

"For kindling. Nothing would please me more than to destroy his legacy."

That I believed. But then again, Lila was a hell of an actress.

"Your aunt wants it and she wants it bad. So does Will Norman. And someone else. Whoever is behind the Blackguard." I turned to Lynn Chambers. "Is Archibald Thelen the mastermind type?"

A corner of Lynn Chambers's mouth turned up. "Archie wouldn't tie his shoes without Rex's permission. That's what Reggie loved about him. Archie lived to serve."

The freedom in being a follower. You were relieved of all the pressure of decision-making and did what you were told. The respon-sibility of your actions lay with your master. Service was its own reward.

"What about Will Norman's father, any idea why he was on the set of *Never After?*"

Lynn Chambers shook her head. "I'm sorry, I don't know who that is."

"He owns Home Drive-In," Lila said. "Strange, him being there."

I agreed. "Coincidences tend not to be coincidental in this business."

Other than to bask in my discovery of Lynn Chambers, there wasn't much reason left to linger.

"Things are heating up. The convention is over in twenty-four hours. Come checkout on Sunday, the building is going to clear out. Anyone after the series bible has to find it before then. Where's Alexi?"

"Waiting by the door into the suite."

"Keep him close. When Sheila Polk or whoever gets desperate, they are going to kick down this door looking for the series bible." I turned to Lynn Chambers. "Your sister, what would she do if she found you here?"

Lynn Chambers sighed. "Sheila has a temper. When we were kids, she took a magnifying glass to my dolls. My first kiss was in our childhood treehouse, with a boy Sheila fancied. Shortly after, the treehouse burned down."

A temper was a dangerous trait in a monarch. Walking out the door wasn't an option. Polk's guards would unmask her at the entrance, and any superfan would recognize Lynn Chambers. I was taking a risk, giving away my secrets, but if something happened to either of them when I could have helped them, I would never forgive myself.

"All right, follow the bouncing detective."

I showed them the entrances to both secret passages. "The bedroom exit leads to Dever's suite. The other one leads into Hammersmith's. But hiding out in the passage might be the better option."

Both Chamberses took my suggestion stoically.

"Okay, back into the fray I go."

"Why not stay here, with us?" Lila asked.

"This isn't over yet. I still have a job to do."

"You don't owe Reynard anything."

Lynn Chambers broke in. "Lila, let it go."

"Why do you even care about all this, Ken?"

All I could do was shrug. "I am what I am."

Lila huffed. Her mother touched her arm. "He's the real thing, Lila. A knight in shining armor."

I was far more comfortable with being roasted over being renowned. "Not with all this tarnish. Now, court jester . . ."

I headed out to have a talk with Alexi, who beamed on seeing me.

"Take care of them, big guy. And watch out, these people know their way around a sword."

Alexi smiled and shook his fist. Happy looked good on him. "No problem, Ken."

I used their bedroom passage to head back into Dever's suite, completing the circuit. After confirming I was alone, I placed a call to Mercie Goodday. She picked up like she was staring at her phone waiting on me.

"Go ahead."

"I know about the two secret ladies, with a capital L. Name one so I know you do too."

"Lynn. Your turn."

"Lila. They claim Reynard didn't discuss inheritance with them, and neither of them appears to want to wear a crown."

"I'm listening."

"There have been multiple murders, with more on the way. Now, I'm all for adhering to your morals, but keep in mind it's your morals versus more murders."

Mercie went quiet for so long I checked my phone to make sure the call was still connected.

"All right. Enjoy the rest of your weekend, Mercie."

"Wait."

I waited.

While I did, I explored Blake Dever's pantry. Dever wouldn't begrudge me helping myself. The fridge held nothing but frittata. I tossed a piece in the microwave.

"Ken?"

"Yeah. Chewing, sorry."

"There is one basic legal principle you need to keep in mind."

"Go on."

"Possession is nine-tenths of the law."

"Okay?"

"One more time. Possession is nine-tenths of the law. Do you understand?"

I didn't, then I did. It took me a minute to catch my breath. "Sorry. Got it."

"Good luck, Ken."

"You too. See you around."

My legs went light at the revelation. I had to sit down. At least I knew who was inheriting R.R. Reynard's kingdom.

Me.

15

TO NORMAN, THE SERIES BIBLE WAS required to finish the show. Completing Reynard's vision was the only way to satisfy the audience. The sets were built, the contracts signed. A hundred million dollars, maybe more, was already spent. And the show's legacy was at stake. The ongoing DVD sales, streaming subscriptions, merchandising, and spin-offs. If the series stumbled at the finish line, all of it would go up in smoke.

To Sheila Polk and the rest of Reynard's followers, the series bible was akin to a holy document. It contained all the secrets. The sacred mysteries. And there was only one copy. Whoever controlled it possessed the word of their founding father. They decided what content to share. And who would know if they embellished a little?

But the series bible was more than that. Reynard, in his infinite humor, had turned it into the key to his kingdom. Possession was nine-tenths of the law, Mercie had said. Whoever had the series bible in their hands became Reynard's heir.

And at the moment, that was me.

The question was, Did anyone else know? Reynard played his cards close, but he did enjoy poking the bear. Maybe someone had figured it out, or at least suspected. As it was, the situation was a powder keg. If this got out, Chateau d'Loire was going to explode into chaos.

What to do? I could have marched out the door, handed it over to the cops. The series bible was technically evidence, though I doubted it contained anything that would help reveal Reynard's killer. If he had known who was out to kill him, then he wouldn't have needed to hire me.

I could take it to Mercie, have her officially declare me the heir. That's why Reynard had requested her presence. She was here to certify the victor, to whom went all the spoils.

If I didn't want to be king, I could play kingmaker. Present the book over to the monarch of my choice. Put an end to this before anyone else died. But the book was the best leverage I had to out the killer. And maybe nip Reynard's baby cult in the bud before it grew into a beast beyond reckoning.

But first, I had to satisfy my curiosity. Before going any further, I took off the crown. Elaine wasn't getting a free peek this time. Anyone who saw the contents of this book had a permanent target on them. I laid the book, in its safelike protective case, on Dever's table, then dug out Reynard's ring and slipped it on. I thought back to Reynard opening the book. The way he had held it, how he had passed his hand over the top.

It took me three tries to find the correct cadence, the right pattern. The hasp popped open. I took a breath and opened the cover. Inside was an actual book. Not a laptop or anything like that. The first page was nothing special. I flipped to the second, then the third.

What was on those pages was drama at its finest: it made me want to laugh and made me want to cry. I closed the book and checked the hasp was locked three times. Reynard had left behind quite the legacy. Anyone who saw what was in here would have everything they needed to take Sheila Polk or Will Norman for every penny they had. If people thought the series bible was worth killing over before, wait until they got a look inside.

Elaine's voice in my ear made me jump. "Ken, you've made the news again."

I locked up the book and re-donned Elaine's circlet. "Tell me it's finally about my famous beanless chili recipe."

"Check your phone."

The screenshots showed an article from *This Town Tattler*.

BY JOVE, KEN ALLEN CANOODLES COP
Exclusive Scoop by Chuck Charles

Ken Allen, once a failed actor, now a novelty detective, has been caught swapping spit with State Special Investigator Ava Stern, his assigned babysitter. It appears Stern took her duties as seriously, as the photos will show. This is nothing new for Allen, who has long been a rumored boy toy for many A-list celebrities, in his former life as a concierge "personal trainer."

While this holds few consequences for Allen, Special Investigator Ava Stern is sure to be called on the carpet by her superiors. This reporter also suggests she take a full STD panel.

I was more interested in the photos than the purple prose. In the grand tradition of clickbait, they started with the most scandalous picture first. Stern, in a black cloak, was facing the camera with a wry smile on her face, like she just got done calling me a jerk. Then in the second picture, she was laying one on me. Big-time. Really digging in. You only saw the back of me, blond hair and all. I had one hand in her hair, one hand on her butt.

You never see my face in those two photos, but my mug is clearly visible in the ones underneath that show me alone, in the same outfit, taken earlier in the day. When you look back at the other pictures, it has to be me. Same clothes, same build, same blond hair.

Except it wasn't me. It was Blake Dever.

We had swapped clothes only hours prior. So while I was off solving mysteries, Dever had gone and hooked up with Stern, who had snuck back into Chateau d'Loire at some point. The cop manning the section of dragnet she slipped through was about to get into serious hot water.

But not as hot as Stern. Forget supposedly making out with me, someone she had investigated in the past. She had defied orders and gotten back in the thick of things. Being the good friend I was, I decided she should know sooner rather than later. I texted her the screenshots, adding: *Looks like our secret is out.*

Chuck Charles, the "journalist" behind the hit piece, had had it out for me since last fall, when I forcibly removed him from the golden goose he'd been feeding off of. He probably spent every last penny he had buying those pictures. That was the thing about This Town: rise or fall, your enemies never went away.

Stern replied fast. *Got it, thanks. Any actual updates?*

Playing it cool in the face of career suicide was on brand for Stern. She was already in it up to her neck. If she also knew about the book and she didn't take it off me, she'd be six feet under. I decided to do us both a favor and not tell her.

Oh, you know how it goes.

Stern wasn't about to give up so easy. Another text hit my phone. *Where are you, Allen?*

In your boyfriend's suite. Which was bad, because, if you asked Dever, it was the last place he knew I was. *All these rooms look the same. Also, in case you're wondering, I'm not currently hiring. This is a one-man show.*

Time to go, before Dever brought Stern up here. I used the passage from Dever's suite through the Dame's, apologizing along the way to Lynn and Lila, and back to Hammersmith's. His mandatory appearances were satisfied and he wasn't one to dawdle among the little people. As much as I wanted to stash the book, there was no good place to do so. I headed into Hammersmith's throne room and took a seat in the big boy chair.

What was it with thrones? Being on display wasn't for me. Every time you passed gas, there were witnesses. Then again, I guess no one was going to call you out. That was real power: making a stink free of consequences.

Hammersmith came in arm in arm with Fairchild. Both were dressed in blue, their armor accented to look as if covered with a layer of frost. Both were armed. Hammersmith being eligible for a Denny's discount didn't lower his threat level. He'd been using a sword on screen for five decades. And rumor had it he only ever lost because the script said so. Fairchild was an unknown. He didn't seem like much, but I'd known guys who looked like actuaries able to choke out body builders.

"Hope you don't mind me letting myself in."

Hammersmith refused to be flapped. "Please, make yourself at home."

"I'll make this quick. Who from the Blackguard was here Friday morning?"

"I've no idea what you're talking about."

Hammersmith was a good actor. There was nothing on his face. Fairchild, however, reacted as if he'd walked into an invisible wall.

"I know it was a while ago, and a lot has happened since yesterday morning, so I'll refresh your memory. It was right after Reynard was killed. Someone came strolling out of your bedroom closet with news. They were real broken up. Needed a drink of water. From your kitchen."

Hammersmith needed a ten count to formulate a response. "But our home movies show we were alone."

"Forget that lame attempt at an alibi. You're wearing a watch in the footage. The time on it doesn't match the time stamp on the video."

Fairchild looked from me to Hammersmith like he was watching a tennis match. Hammersmith's eyes widened a fraction.

"Pretend we know what you are talking about. What do we get in exchange for divulging this information?"

"You get cleared as an accessory after the fact. Whoever your visitor was, they were loyal to Reynard. They didn't kill him."

"However do you know that?"

"Because your guest had the book and needed a place to stash it. If they were loyal to someone else, then that person would have the book instead."

Fairchild couldn't help but glance toward the kitchen, but Hammersmith kept his cool.

"Man, you two must have torn up the place up looking for it. After the rest of the Blackguard killed your visitor, I mean." I flipped the flap on the messenger bag to give them a peek at the series bible. "But you didn't look hard enough."

They started to inch closer. Hammersmith did a better job, alternating feet from side to side, pretending to consider.

"I was surprised you got wrapped up in all this, Hammersmith. You didn't need the show. You had your own career. And you didn't seem to be enchanted with Reynard's new society." They were too close for comfort now. I stood up and gestured to Fairchild with my cudgel. "The things we do for love."

The two of them unsheathed their blades together. The layout helped me with once again being outnumbered. The fake firebowl between us provided an obstacle, and the conversation pit meant I had the high ground. They were lovers, and they were fighters, but they had never fought together. They came in too tight, almost side by side, protective of each other. I knew Hammersmith was smitten with Fairchild. He'd gotten wrapped up in all this madness for his beau's sake. Now I knew Fairchild felt the same way.

They had reach on me with the long, thin-bladed swords. Crowding them turned that advantage into a disadvantage. Fairchild tried a high cut I wasn't familiar with. It started above his head and arced diagonally toward my neck. The arc of it made Hammersmith withdraw. I shoved Fairchild's forearm upward to send it off course. At the same time, I whipped the cudgel toward his knee, snapping my wrist to maximize the springiness of the shaft.

Fairchild wasn't wearing knee protection. The sound of his kneecap snapping was crisp and clear. A sympathetic shiver ran through me, but it was hard to get too broken up over a guy who recently tried to decapitate me. And knee replacements were getting better every day. I didn't linger.

The cudgel rebounded, fueling the next strike. Fairchild's guard was down. I had a clear shot at his head. But my new weapon was more effective than I estimated. A knock on the head might prove fatal. I cracked his elbow instead, and he dropped his sword.

"Stop!" Hammersmith lowered his blade, his face crestfallen. "Please. Stop hitting him."

I checked my next swing but kept Fairchild between me and Hammersmith. "I'm not the one swinging to kill."

Hammersmith dropped his sword and rushed to treat Fairchild. "This affair has gotten entirely away from us."

"You have the power to end it. Call off the Blackguard. Hand over whoever killed the ones who wouldn't go along with this coup attempt."

Hammersmith's reaction was pure confusion. "However would I do that?"

"The two of you run the Blackguard. Or Fairchild does, through you."

Hammersmith barked laughter. "We are but pawns in this game."

It had been a good guess, but the wrong one. Neither Hammersmith nor Fairchild were playing king from the shadows. "But the Blackguard was here Friday morning."

"Yes, it was as you said. Denoso appeared in our bedroom out of nowhere. It was quite the shock. He was greatly disturbed and went into the kitchen to gather himself, as you surmised. Kurt Hooper arrived right after him."

So Denoso grabbed the series bible when he discovered Reynard was dead and ran to stash it. The rest of the Blackguard assumed Denoso still had it on him when they killed him. They must have blown a gasket when they searched his body and came up empty.

This had been a big swing and a miss. I still didn't know who killed Reynard. Hooper had both the technical skills to sabotage Reynard's cabin and the martial skills to do him in close quarters. He also had a beef with Reynard. But Denoso had been with him, and Denoso's loyalty to Reynard had gotten him killed. He would have defended Reynard, or at least avenged him, had he been present when Reynard was killed.

No, Hooper and Denoso had arrived in the aftermath, and Denoso had grabbed the series bible and run to stash it.

I was back where this all started. Who had killed Reynard? Since no one came up the elevator in the time I left and returned to find him dead, it had to be someone who knew about the secret passages. And what made Hammersmith so important to rate a room next to Reynard, if he wasn't running the Blackguard? Unless it wasn't Hammersmith who was important. I kneeled next to Fairchild.

"Who are you to Reynard? What's your job?"

Hammersmith answered for Fairchild. "He is a chronicler."

"He chronicles with a camera?"

"A picture is worth a thousand words."

"Is that how you knew about Blake Dever and Agent Stern? You spy for Reynard?"

Fairchild managed a weak nod.

"Where's your footage stored?"

Hammersmith left the room and returned with a laptop. "It's all here."

"Nothing on the cloud?"

"Oh no. Reynard would not allow that."

"What's the password?"

Hammersmith told me. I couldn't use the kitchen passage without letting them know it existed. I said an awkward good-bye and left via the actual door. I looked both ways before crossing the junction. No cops in sight. The real pickle was how to get off this floor. I needed Dever for that.

Back in his suite, I sat down at the kitchenette table and cracked Fairchild's laptop, navigating to the same folder Fairchild had back when he showed me the bogus alibi footage. A search for Dever came up short.

"Elaine, what's Dever's characters' names?"

"Thane Mallory and Perrish Graystone."

The footage of Dever's tryst was under Graystone. The five seconds I spent skipping through it to confirm it was legit were enough to turn my stomach. My finger hovered over the delete key. What would be the best for Stern? Would I want to know?

The two of them came into the suite, happily bantering. I slammed the laptop shut and met them in the throne room, eager to get out of Dever's shoes.

"Mission Freaky Friday is complete. You can have your clothes back."

Stern went for her gum before realizing she was already working on a piece. "Report in, Allen."

"Or what, you'll arrest me?"

She was steamed but didn't press. Dever stripped without a shade of embarrassment. I'd be damned if I was going to back down. He liked boxer briefs too. His body had a few more creases in it than mine did. I told myself it was because I liked to stay hydrated.

Stern didn't demur.

She was covered head to toe in the hooded cloak. It wasn't much of a disguise. For sure, her fellow officers had been instructed to wrangle her in if they saw her, but I doubted they would scale the blue wall and do so.

When we were back in our clothes, Dever piped up.

"I put a call in to my parents."

"And?"

"Reynard is assuredly not my father. He was here, filming *Never After* whilst I was being conceived somewhere near the Isle of Lewis."

Dever wasn't Reynard's love child. The timeline and their physical similarity lined up, but in the end, he was a red herring. Down to Reynard literally dressing him in red. But if it wasn't Dever, who else fit the bill?

Stern told Dever she would see him downstairs. They kissed, which signaled my breaking point in the staring contest. Stern didn't say a word to me until we were in the elevator.

"What's that you got in Blake's bag, Allen?"

I became very interested in the control panel. I was a bad actor, which meant also being a terrible liar. If Stern got a clean gander at my face I was cooked.

"Dummy prop." Opening with a redundant statement was a stellar start to my fib. "Figure I might use it to get a confession. Like *The Maltese Falcon*."

"Bad analogy." Stern's voice was toneless. "Everybody thought the Falcon was real. Which meant it might as well have been real. The ironic twist was more for the audience."

"Yeah," I said, to say something. The elevator was taking forever. The building was only seven stories high, for cripes sake. "What are we going to do about this tabloid article?"

The elevator doors opened into the service hallway. Stern leaned on me immediately. I got the hint and buried my face in her cloak, an arm around her. She laughed, a little giddy, as we stepped out of the elevator past the guards. She was really carrying me here. Once upon a time, I'd told her she had what it took to make it on stage. She'd about taken my head off in response, so I didn't speak my truth on that topic again.

The second we were out of sight of the guards, she pulled away.

"We aren't going to do anything, Allen. This hit piece is a win-win for me."

"What? How so?"

"It keeps Blake a secret and makes being assigned to your cases a conflict of interest. If I manage to keep my job, I'm off Ken Allen detail. I can get back to working real cases."

Being between panels, the back hallway was sparsely trafficked. I did my best to manage the indignity. "That's not fair. Me being framed for murder was a real case, and my second case ended up being your case in the end. And for the record, you wanted in on this one."

Stern smiled like she didn't hear a word I said. "Sweet, sweet freedom."

Despite her protests, Stern stayed glued to me when we hit the lobby. "So where are we off to now?"

"What do you mean by 'we,' kemosabe?"

"This again, Allen?"

"Look, you're a cop, and everyone knows it—because of my high-profile solves you keep getting credited for. You're cramping my style."

"Didn't know you liked your grapes sour, Allen."

Stern's phone went off.

"Thought I put this on silent. Hold on, Allen."

Whatever the alert was, she didn't like it. "I have to go. Keep in touch. You're taking an awful big risk with this fake book trick."

"The convention ends in eighteen hours. It's either hit it out of the park or go down swinging."

She let me go, which was a mild shock. I doubled back into the kitchen and asked around for the omelet guy by telling everyone who would listen I owed him a hundred bucks. He and his crepe-making accomplice produced themselves fifteen minutes later, both of them looking like they just had their eyes dilated. I patiently reminded them through the fog who I was and what our arrangement had been.

"Oh yeah."

The omelet guy reeled his fingers until the crepe woman realized he was asking for her phone. They had gone above and beyond, with her taking poorly framed photos of each person that placed a suspiciously healthy omelet order. There were a dozen people I didn't recognize, then Will Norman with a six-egg-white, one-yolk, lean-ham, spinach deal that was crying out for some seasoning. I might be a health nut, but I'm not dead.

I paid the man and was avoiding a hug when the crepe woman piped up.

"You wanted me to remind you of something."

"Yeah." Omelet guy thought hard. After ten Mississippis he added, "It had to do with a baking pan."

There was only one healthy egg product that involved a baking pan I could think of. "Was it a frittata?"

Omelet guy snapped his fingers and pointed at me. "That's it. We made a frittata for the guy in the suite."

"Blake Dever?"

The omelet guy shrugged. "It was for a guy in a suite."

I returned his hug and went toward the special guest room. Walking around with the book was dumb, but I couldn't think of a place

I trusted enough to stash it. Sheila Polk and her mysterious rival were turning the hotel over. Elaine wouldn't be able to help herself. She'd break into the book. I couldn't have anyone but me seeing what was inside.

I weighed my next move on the dumbness scale and decided it balanced out between genius and idiocy. I texted Will Norman:

Need to meet up. Big news.

He didn't text me back, but my phone rang from an unknown number less than a minute later.

"I'm happy with my current phone plan, thank you."

"Ken? It's Will Norman."

"What's with the new number?"

"I'm having issues with my cell. What's up?"

"I found the book."

Norman's line went quiet for a moment.

When he came back, he was short of breath like he'd been jumping up and down and cheering. "That's great. I knew you could do it. Can you come to me?"

"Sure. First, let me get you my routing number. Twenty million, right?"

The line went quiet again. "I wish it was that easy. We have to draw up a contract at the studio, have our people go over it. And you'll want to find a way to hide the money, or the IRS will fleece you."

"I guess you're right. I mean, there's no real hurry to get the book to you. I'll just lay low, maybe try to sneak out. You have any ideas?"

The pause was slighter this time. I could hear Norman's calloused hand close over the receiver. Lifting weights took its toll. "Sit tight in your room. We'll figure it out."

"Sure thing. I'll stop and chat with Mercie Goodday and hunker down."

"Don't do that."

Not *Who is Mercie Goodday?* But *Don't do that.*

"Why not?" I did my best to keep my voice taunt-free.

"You know lawyers. You're essentially committing a crime. She would be obligated to report you."

"Ten-four." I hung up with Norman but kept my phone next to my ear so as not to appear like I was talking to myself. "Elaine, are you there?"

"Yep."

"Is that box the crown came in still live streaming from my room?"

"Sure is."

"Keep an eye on it. If I am right about this, you're in for a show."

"I'll put it through to your phone."

I made myself scarce the best way I could come up with on short notice: by hiding in a bathroom stall. As an added side effect, it served as a potent appetite suppressant. Elaine routed the live stream to my device.

Watching a phone screen on the can—such was the glamorous life of a private detective.

While I was hunkered down, I pondered the issue of hiding the book. There just wasn't anywhere I was comfortable with. It occurred to me that the ring, however, was easier to conceal, and this was the perfect place to shed the necessary garments.

I'd been in the stall all of five minutes when my loaner hotel room got the full shock and awe treatment: four Blackguard members, hooded up, rushed in, weapons drawn. Once they cleared the room, they hunkered down to wait for me. They had acted on a moment's notice, ordered by someone who had them on speed dial, someone whose commands they didn't question.

Will Norman was the black king.

Elaine shared some choice words before asking how I knew.

"The omelet guy. Norman had to adjust to fit his macros. I should have known from the feast. He put down like two pounds of lean meat. But I was too busy looking around instead of right next to me."

"So he was lying about needing the book only to finish the show."

"Yes and no. He's not lying about wanting to finish the show, but I'm betting he also wants the book for other reasons. Like he knows about it being Reynard's will. The Normans and Reynard had something going on. I'd bet my official detective decoder ring on it."

"What makes you so sure?"

"Reynard got a meeting with Norman after ghosting the industry for twenty years. At that meeting, he convinced Norman to fork over fifty million dollars while also allowing him unprecedented creator's rights and control. A generation prior, Will Norman's father visited the set of *Never After*. He and Reynard knew each other. But when Reynard went to pitch *The Lands Beyond*, he went to the son instead, who claims they never met prior to that first meeting. Why not go straight to the top?"

"Maybe Reynard did, and the elder Norman pawned him off on his kid."

"But wouldn't Will Norman include that detail when discussing the show? That he saw something that his father didn't? It pushes the prodigy angle. No, something's up. I can feel it."

"Okay, so what now?"

"Now I give Norman what he wants."

16

THE BIG EVENT OF THE DAY was the fencing tournament. Guess they had to settle. Ballrooms were crap for jousting. I stopped by to take it in. It was a ghost town. The big names—Hammersmith, Dever, and Cannon—had all canceled. They had more pressing matters, like trying to kill me. Polk's VIPs, who comprised the rest of the fighters of note, had also withdrawn to lock the hotel down and perform a book search.

All that was left were fans. Their disappointment was palpable.

The stand-out bracket was the under-eighteen category. Despite their age, they were fast, skilled, and motivated. As a child martial artist myself, I felt a kinship with them. Learning a skill from a young age is a different beast than coming to it as an adult. Your mind is a sponge. Your body more resilient. Not only do you recover quickly, but your physique develops based on the specific demands you put on it. And you will never be braver. Child gymnasts display a lack of fear a fighter pilot would envy.

Your self-worth is tied to the pursuit. It balances on the approval or disapproval of your instructors. If you have absent parents, that approval means the world. Positive or negative, their reinforcement fuels your inner fire. Believe me, I know.

Above all, time is on your side. It isn't only the lack of adult responsibilities and stresses. When you are younger, time moves more slowly. An hour feels like forever. You can never imagine one day being a teenager, driving a car. The clock is still on your side.

I watched the kids spar, their focus pure, their weapons an extension of self. The nostalgia was overwhelming. At that moment, if someone had a knife for my back, I would have been finished.

This was what Polk and Norman were fighting over. Not the franchise or the merchandising. That was just money. This was the real treasure. The wealth was in the followers. To a monarch, their devoted subjects were everything. They would form a web of influence. Provide support to their fellow followers. Give everything, even their lives. They would be fruitful and multiply, adding to your ranks. When it came to rulership, the power was in your people.

Bradley Corbett appeared in my eyeline, breaking my musing. He was still in the playing card getup. New boss, same job.

"You need to bring the book to Mr. Norman before Sheila discovers you have it."

"What are you doing, Corbett? You were only ankle deep. When this thing blows up, Norman is going to drag you down with him."

"Are you talking about the police? Do you really believe Mr. Norman's father would allow him to be arrested?"

We made eye contact. Corbett's went wide and he looked away. He'd said something he hadn't meant to.

"Norman's father knows what's going on? How long has he known?"

Corbett decided now was a good time to study the carpet pattern. I've seen three-year-olds with marker all over their face do a more convincing job looking innocent. Norman's father being in the loop made a lot more sense than Stern having the swing to shut the building down. He probably had the governor on speed dial. Of course, if things turned bad, Stern would make a great scapegoat.

"Naughty, naughty Corbett. Does Will Norman know you went over his head?"

Corbett huffed. "How are you any different? You're just as much a mercenary as I am, holding the *Tome of All Tales* ransom."

"You kidding me? I'm the only person in the scramble still working for Reynard."

"He can't help you anymore. And Sheila Polk is nothing without the tome. Mr. Norman, however, has a foot in two worlds."

"What's that supposed to mean?"

Corbett's shade shifted into chartreuse. "Nothing."

"Reynard was in meetings all day. Who was on Reynard's schedule before me?"

"The Dame of the Moon. But I wasn't privy to that exchange."

"How about after?"

"Mr. Norman, but he didn't meet with him. The elevator guards can confirm that."

"What about Polk?"

"He didn't meet with her. Not that morning . . ."

"But she was in his room the night before?"

"Yes."

Had to hand it to Reynard. The man wanted to have his cake and eat it too. He was trying to mend fences with Lynn Chambers while her sister was warming his bed. Had Polk known Reynard was dead all along?

If Polk had learned anything about Reynard's estate, it would have behooved her to get rid of him before he could tell any potential competitors. As much as Reynard loved his secrets, no man was immune to pillow talk.

"When I first met with Reynard, he said a woman friend had been using his cabin. That it burned down while she took a walk. That was Polk he was talking about?"

"Yes."

"Archibald Thelen, was it his job to sweep Reynard's property for threats?"

"Yes."

"On a scale of one to ten, how much trouble did Archie get in, missing the sabotage that almost got Polk killed?"

"Mr. Reynard told Mr. Thelen that he would be dealt with once the season began. But soon after, Thelen uncovered the sabotage to Mr. Reynard's trailer and all was forgotten."

Corbett was getting antsy. He shifted weight from one foot to the other like he was standing on hot coals.

"You want my advice, Corbett? Walk out the front door. Right now. Things are going to go from bad to worse, and it's going to happen soon."

"And go where? *The Lands Beyond* is my whole world."

I didn't have the heart to tell Corbett that world was about to come crashing down around him.

The tension in the special guest area was too thick for a knife to cut through. Fortunately, there were larger blades available. I walked the aisles as if I didn't have the thing everyone was looking for on me. Archibald Thelen was holding down the Blackguard booth with the aid of three squires.

One of them was Brenden, the kid I caught tailing me on Friday. He avoided eye contact. No one could sulkily ignore your existence the way a teenager could. There were some things I was thankful to have missed.

Thelen marked my arrival with the enthusiasm of a DMV worker fifteen minutes before close.

"Corbett says you screwed up vetting Reynard's cabin. Almost got Sheila Polk killed."

"We performed a full inspection. All systems were intact prior to Ms. Polk's arrival."

"Good thing you uncovered the tampering with Reynard's trailer in Scotland. Really redeemed yourself there."

Thelen didn't reply, but one of his eyes twitched.

"You ought to learn to control yourself. Maybe take an anger management course. Tell your boss I want to talk to him in person."

Thelen's tone was akin to yawning. "Mr. Reynard is indisposed."

"Stop the charade. You know I am talking about Norman. He screwed up, sending you guys to my room. We face-to-face within an hour or I take the book to Sheila Polk."

Thelen bored into me, trying to determine if I was bluffing. Thankfully, I didn't have to put on an act. I stared back, wishing I had some gum to casually blow a bubble.

Not wanting to admit to anything, he said, "You have been heard."

I walked away with a grin. Who doesn't love being validated?

With an hour or so left before the Saturday feast, I made my way back out to the lobby and posted up near the doors in case things got hairy. I was warming up the wall when Norman called from the unknown number.

"Hey, are you in your room? I can drop by before dinner."

"Quit it with the song and dance. You and I both know who is in my room and who isn't. Sending your goons to take care of me really hurts my feelings, Norman."

The line went muffled again, this time for almost a minute. Who was Norman talking to? "Where are you right now?"

I looked around. A pair of adolescents in black cloaks were staring down at me from the mezzanine.

I said, "You know where I am," and hung up.

Norman showed up five minutes later. He was in neutral colors, looking more like Robin Hood than the Sheriff of Nottingham. His perfect, surgically altered features were the personification of a ransom note.

He was armed with the same sword. His broad shoulders and thick wrists suggested he might know how to use it.

"Where is the book?"

I stepped into whispering range. Close enough to see the rims on Norman's contacts. "In the bag."

"Show it to me."

"Nuh-uh."

Norman turned away. "Then we have nothing to discuss."

"How about you being the eighth member of the Blackguard?"

That got Norman facing me. "That's ridiculous."

"Every time I tell you something, the men in black react. I checked the screen captures. You match the build. You aren't a member of Reynard's society, but your arms suggest you know your way around a sword. When it came time to film, your presence on set would never be questioned. And you could clear yourself, no problem."

Norman's jaw clamped down. His knuckles turned white around his sword grip.

"Must have hit hard, Denoso stashing the book before the rest of the Blackguard offed him. He sure didn't want you getting your hands on it. That's the thing about using hotheads. They have their lane, but it's a one-way street."

Norman was so tense he was vibrating, but he didn't crack.

"I've seen what's in the book."

Norman's eyes flicked around in calculation. "I don't believe you."

"Reynard opened it in front of me. I copied him and abracadabra."

"How far did you get?"

The question told me Norman didn't know what was in the book.

Maybe no one did. If I had been Reynard, I sure as hell wouldn't have shared its contents.

"Cover to cover."

"I can pay you, but it's going to take time."

"Where are you going to get it? You don't have your own money. And if you use studio money, then Home Drive-In owns the book, not you. Guess you could call your dad, but then you're admitting you can't handle the business. You know what I think? I think you always planned to take it off me, if I turned it up. Dead or alive."

"I didn't. Please believe that, Ken. This got way out of control. I never wanted anyone to die." It was hard to read Norman's face. His forehead, the corners of his eyes and mouth, they didn't wrinkle right. "I'll have the funds once I get the book to Mercie. Don't take it to Sheila Polk. She doesn't have whatever she promised you either."

"I don't want money, Norman. I want the killers. They turn themselves over to the cops, and you get the book."

Again with the expression of angst. The question was whether it was internal strife or external pressure. I felt mildly guilty, lying to him. No way was I giving him the book. What I wanted to know was how much control he had over his people. I had my theories, why they might be loyal to him, the corporate suit, over Polk, the society favorite.

"I'll need to talk to them." Norman took a deep breath. "It will have to be after the feast."

"After you."

We walked toward the ballroom together, picking up members of the Blackguard as we went. There were a hundred witnesses in the lobby and hallway. I kept close to Norman and counted on the crowd to keep me from getting Julius Caesar'd.

The feast was arrayed the same as the day before. Blake Dever, Sven Hammersmith, and the Dame were already present. I took my spot at the end of the VIP table, next to Norman. He spoke without looking at me.

"There's a lot you don't understand."

"Yeah. Calculus. How airplanes stay up. Why people don't realize that CGI is just watching cartoons."

"No, I—"

Bradley Corbett scooted his chair in. Norman clammed up before Corbett could overhear us. Once everyone else was seated, Sheila Polk made her grand entrance, escorted by her guards-in-white. This time, they stuck with her, kneeling before the table. She raised her hand for what I assumed would be a repeat of the Lands Beyond version of saying grace.

A tension settled over the room. Something was off. Where were the covered platters? You had to have food to bless. Polk spun toward me and thrust a finger.

"Seize the bastard usurper! Seize Ken Allen!"

A hundred swords were drawn together. I kicked away from the table and pulled my cudgel. Next to me, Norman held his blade in both hands. Polk had pulled a fast one, bringing her guards to the big table. It put the Blackguard on the far side of both me and Polk.

Norman could have let them have me, but that also meant giving up the book. We went back-to-back. Dever was still in shock. One of the white guards shouldered him out of the way to get to us. Two others closed in on my side while a third jumped onto the table to get to me. The one on the table got there first, chopping down at my head from above like he was splitting a log.

I batted his sword aside with the cudgel and snagged him by the ankle, pulling hard. It couldn't have gone any better. He fell backward, his head slamming into the edge of the table. I kept the cudgel moving, sweeping it in an arc to cover my flank. There was a metallic ting as I deflected an unseen thrust.

The table was the only cover to be found. I rolled over the surface, coming to my feet next to Blake Dever. He'd woken up enough to draw his sword. He spun and knocked the guard who'd shoved him aside on the head with his pommel. The guy dropped like a bag of rocks.

There was no one left between me and Sheila Polk. Her eyes went wide at the realization. As I reached out for her, one of her guards dropped his sword and dove over the table at me. I shoved him down into my knee. He ducked enough where I got mostly helmet. It smarted something fierce. I adjusted, and the second knee caught him flush.

The feast erupted into chaos. Norman, Dever, and I were way outnumbered, but there were too many swords against us. They all got in each other's way. If it occurred to them to drop the hardware and dogpile, we'd be done. Hammersmith, completely ignored, shoved his way toward Fairchild. Polk squeezed past him and escaped around the table, into her supporters. Corbett vanished like he'd graduated from magic school. The Dame of the Moon was also nowhere to be found, which I was thankful for. I had my hands full trying to save my own skin. No way were we getting out the way we came in. The only other exit was through the back hallway. I turned to tell Norman. I had guessed right. He knew how to fight. He bound blades with a white guard, hit a nice little trip, and slammed the flat of his sword into the guard's helmet.

"Kitchen!"

Norman nodded. Dever got the bright idea to flip the table on its side. I lent a hand, and over it went, putting a half wall between us and the masses. Dever and I were side by side as we came around the end of the table, with Norman bringing up the rear. Being a step ahead of Dever, I was first around the corner.

A society veteran in red thrust at my shoulder. I met the stab halfway, snapping my cudgel into his blade. The sword sprang off course. I used the momentum to send a backhanded blow into my attacker's jaw. His legs wobbled. I put a thrust kick into his chest, shoving him into the attackers queued up behind him. It gave me the space to burst through the doors into the hallway.

Two of Polk's people were in the hallway, but so was the Whisper
—the one who took down Tryne Koch, not Lynn Chambers. One guard
was already down, and the other was getting tenderized. The guard
tried to repel her onslaught, but he was doing about as well as a singles
player up against doubles. The Whisper drummed him down before
either I or Dever could get involved and waved us toward the kitchens.

"Where are we going?" Dever asked.

I drew up the layout of Chateau d'Loire in my mind. "Polk's
people are guarding the exits. We hit the penthouse level. Our best bet
is to hide behind the cops."

The remainder of the service hallway was clear. In the kitchen,
the cooks were preparing the feast, but there were no servers around.
When I turned the corner, the guards were absent from their post by
the elevator doors. I glanced down at the cooks' footwear. They were
wearing old-timey boots, the kind without laces.

I looked toward Dever to say something and sent a forehand into
a sous-chef's jaw. The knife he was concealing clattered to the ground
as the rest of the staff sprang into action.

There were three of us and a dozen of them, in a room full of boiling things and fire.

"Elevators."

Dever and the Whisper joined me, withdrawing into the short hallway. We'd lost Norman somewhere. The guilt I had over abandoning
him was short-lived. Norman had his own personal guard, and he'd
only defended me to keep the book out of Polk's hands in the first
place. Being the only one of us with a set of keys, I was forced to
let Dever and the Whisper hold them off. The little circular key was
easy to find. I turned it and slammed the up button. The elevator cab
must have been at the top, because the doors didn't immediately open.
Three was a crowd in the hallway. My cudgel was too short to get at the
murderous kitchen staff from the back line. I played defense instead,
batting away any cuts that slipped Dever and the Whisper's defensive

net. Behind me, the elevator chimed its arrival. I threw a full-force spinning back kick as the doors slid open. If the cab was empty, I was going to look pretty silly. It wasn't. My foot passed through the narrow opening to connect solidly with an armored torso. I continued with the same leg, keeping it chambered and putting a sliding side kick into my would-be ambusher's face. He went out immediately, slamming against the back wall. I grabbed him with an under-over before he fell. Moving a limp body off the ground was a Herculean task. I applied my hip and tossed them out of the cab.

"Going up!"

The Whisper backed her way into the elevator, but Dever didn't move.

"They'll never let the doors close," he said, throwing us a depreciating grin. "Don't worry. Polk wouldn't dare kill the headliner."

The Whisper tried to join Dever, but I grabbed her in a bear hug, pinning her arms so she couldn't brain me. The doors shut. I waited until we started ascending to turn her loose.

"I'm going to need you to liaise with the cops. And Dever is right. They won't hurt him."

The Whisper shrugged me off to fume, pounding the wall with the butt of her baton.

"You don't have to keep up the act. That costume can't hide your fighting style. Your baton work is pure Krav Maga."

The Whisper stared up at the ceiling and groaned.

"I missed you. Did you miss me?"

Special Investigator Stern's voice was muffled but unmistakable. "Can it, Allen. I came back for Blake. Not that he deserves it."

The venom in Stern's voice got my attention. I was dying to see her face. "Trouble in paradise?"

"I'm not in a sharing mood."

"Well, it's a good thing you're here. I got on your fellow officers' bad side pretty quick."

"Join the club. I'm barred from the premises."

"Don't worry. I've almost got this wrapped up. Just a few loose threads and they'll be pinning another medal on you."

"Joy of joys. And you're kidding yourself. I'll be lucky to catch traffic duty after this."

"Not if we get the solve. You're getting scapegoated. Will Norman and his father are behind the lockdown. Corbett blew the whistle the second he had a chance."

Stern considered that. "Norman must really want to finish the show, if he's willing to sword fight over it. You wouldn't think he needs the scratch. Maybe he's looking forward to being in the saddle for once."

Her words lit my brain up like a Christmas tree. "Elaine, can you check and see who the animal handler was on *Never After*?"

Stern cocked her head. "You have Elaine Ford on the line? No wonder you seem so smart."

"Maurine Henson."

"Now look up who she married and tell me it's Will Norman's father."

"Oh my God, it is."

Stern jumped in. "So what does that mean?"

"That Maurine Henson traded up, big time, thirty years ago."

The elevator door hit the top. Both of us got ready, but the hall was empty. We crossed the space quickly and in a hurry to Reynard's door, where I applied the key.

I went through first, hands high. "Don't shoot, I give up."

Sheila Polk was on the throne, flanked by guards brandishing pistols.

"Your surrender is accepted, Mr. Allen."

17

POLK OCCUPIED REYNARD'S THRONE with perfect posture, palms hovering. The chair could have been a stool for all the work its back and arms were doing. There were six guards in the room, all seasoned society members. Two of them were armed with identical handguns, taken from the elevator guards. Both gunmen held their pistols properly and adhered to trigger discipline.

"You might be on a throne, but you're off your rocker, Polk. There's no going back from taking cops hostage."

Polk's laugh was pure musical theater. "We are not responsible for our overzealous subjects, who will be lauded for their good works."

Stern looked at me but didn't say anything. Polk was basking in the privilege of every monarch who had recently discovered mono-loguing.

"We will be protected. Ask yourself why the police threw this ludicrous gauntlet around Chateau d'Loire. Why so few law officers arrived. What we know will ensure our safety."

Polk's expression was pure self-satisfaction. Whatever she claimed to know, she felt it was worth amnesty.

"Now, Mr. Allen. The book, if you please."

The gunmen were fifteen feet away and I was no longer protected by a bulletproof blazer. Stern, similarly, was not in her day-to-day lawperson garb. Polk's people had already demonstrated they were willing to kill for her about twenty times over, swinging swords around. I dug into the messenger bag as I walked toward Polk and the pistols.

"Here you go. But it won't do you any good. It's locked and booby-trapped."

"Stop right there, Mr. Allen."

Polk wasn't about to let me too close. Darn it. I held up the book, encased in its metal sheath. "Should I throw it at you? It might leave a mark."

Polk didn't budge. "Set it before us and back away."

I took a knee, as if I were about to pledge fealty. How I was going to get out of this one, I had no idea. All I could think of was to buy time. "I can't help but notice you don't have that wheelbarrow of gold bars you promised."

"Had you acted nobly and brought the book to us unforced, then such rewards would have been yours."

My options weren't looking good. I could frisbee the book at one of the gunmen and get shot by the other, or frisbee it at Sheila Polk and get shot by them both.

Losing the book didn't mean it was over. Polk still couldn't get it open without the ring.

"Now, retreat to your friend. Whom I will deal with soon enough."

Polk looked back at the Whisper. From the edge in her tone, she wasn't expecting to find Stern under that mask. Which was good for us. No way whoever she thought was under there was as dangerous as Stern. The gunmen stayed where they were, while one of the white guards retrieved the book and presented it to Polk. Polk accepted the book and confirmed it was locked.

Polk stared at me. She knew about the ring and that Reynard didn't have it on him. She was dying to ask about it, but if she did in front of everyone, they might connect its significance. Being the only one able to open the book guaranteed her power.

I looked back expectantly, failing to control my closemouthed grin. It took Polk some time to compose a tactic that wouldn't involve tipping her people that Reynard's ring and the book were connected. I used that period to dream up and abandon harebrained schemes.

"You have despoiled our founder, who gave all to realize our kingdom on Earth. If you looted one thing from his remains, then why not another?" Polk said all this without blinking. "Seize him."

Two of the white guards moved in, each of them taking one of my arms. The gunmen stayed where they were. I'd experienced a few tropes of the trade but hadn't been looking forward to encountering this one. Chances were, I was about to be tortured. I hoped they didn't start with my toes and work their way up.

I was deciding which hardboiled quip to deploy first once they started taking the tongs to me when the doors burst open. The Blackguard breeched like a well-oiled machine. Half of them came in through the bedroom via the secret passage, the other half through the entrance door. They were all masked up, but being a trainer had given me a keen eye for body types. Hooper and Cannon were on the bedroom side, Chelovak and Thelen on the entrance side. All were armed with triangular shields and throwing hatchets.

I was in everyone's crosshairs. One gunman dropped into a stance and started firing toward the door. The other suffered decision paralysis, turning a full three-sixty and trying to decide who to shoot first.

Bullets ricocheted off shields. Three out of the four throwing axes found their mark: two in the shooter and one in his brain-frozen companion. The chaos caused the men managing my arms to slack off. I hooked one behind the elbow, clasped my hands together, and drove my arms upward like I was starting a golf swing. The guy with the trapped elbow yiped as his shoulder popped. Once you tore a rotator cuff it would never be the same. I tossed my other restrainer into him and broke free.

Polk's guards got into the game. They drew their swords at the same time as the Blackguard. I spun out after completing the throw and used the momentum to aerial clear of the melee in classic wushu fashion. The flank afforded me a good view of the proceedings. The white guards were game, but they were surrounded and had protecting Polk to think about.

Will Norman came in through the main entrance, standing across from Polk like they were on opposite sides of a chess board. Bradley Corbett kept behind Norman's bulk, peeking out from one side, then the other.

Me, I didn't have a dog in this fight. There was only one person I counted as an ally in the entire room. My focus was on finding her and going from there. I had no success until I looked down.

Stern was on the far side of the room, dragging herself toward a corner. Her blood stood out, red against white cloth. What happened next remains fuzzy. A chemical surge ran through my body, like lightning set on fire. In that moment, if I had thought to try, I probably could have blasted into orbit.

John Cannon dropped a white guard with a thrust into his armpit. He'd lost his shield once the guns were out of the picture. Shields didn't suit his idiom. He saw me coming and twisted as he dropped, issuing an intricate low cut designed to geld me.

I batted it aside and bowled him over with a flying knee. The way to beat an artist was to brawl with them. Using both hands, I forced the shaft of my cudgel against his throat. His eyes went wide. He didn't know how to respond. They didn't cover mounted chokes in fencing class. His sword was no good this close. He decided to drop it and try to bench press the bar off his neck. I doubled down as all four of our hands got in on the struggle.

Cannon was strong, but I had gravity with me. The cudgel bore down on his windpipe. Panic kicked in. He turned on his side to escape the pressure, and that was that. I spun into an armlock and snapped it without thinking. The cry Cannon emitted was worthy of a lead vocalist. Good thing he was a singer, because his harp-playing days were on hold.

Mikhail Chelovak turned at the sound, saw my face, and decided to give me berth. Thelen was next to him. His eyes passed over me with all the interest of a man checking freeway signage. I was not the stop he was looking for. We left each other alone, putting one last Blackguard member between me and Stern.

Kurt Hooper had a blade in each hand, both of them splashed with red. All his dreams had come true. The fantasy battles which had long occupied his daydreams were finally realized. He turned to face me, clapping his saber and knife together in anticipation.

I moved first, flicking out a backhand feint. Hooper bought it, ducking under, which made it worse on him when I teed off on his groin. The right way to Rochambeau wasn't to go for the classic field goal-style kick, but rather to arc up straight from the ground with a round kick, bypassing the thigh at an angle. Hooper was wearing a cup, but my shin was also armored, so the kick still smarted something fierce. I knew from prior experience. You couldn't spar for three decades without catching a few. Getting a groin shot with a cup on felt like were you trapped inside a drum during a spirited performance of *Stomp!*

Hooper tried to back off and reset but I kept on him, putting a little more steam into the backhand opener this time. He deflected it with his knife while cutting out with his saber. At the same time, I launched into a front leg kick combination: kick-tap-kick. The first swept his instep to upset his balance and the second crashed into his jaw.

I shouldn't have hit him again, but truth be told, I didn't consciously decide to. My forehand shot caught him square in the teeth. Already unconscious, Hooper didn't notice. He went down hard, still grasping his blades. As much as I should have been worried about braining the guy, all I could think about was Stern.

Stern had gotten herself propped against the wall and was applying pressure to the area above her left hip. I stepped over Hooper and bent down to check on her. She sounded more annoyed than concerned.

"Stupid ricochet. It didn't get anything important, it's just making a mess."

Stern was playing it off, but I knew better. She wouldn't take herself out of the game for trivial reasons. She'd crawled out of the fray rather than go for one of the loose guns. It took two tries for me to reply. I had to clear my throat to make room for air. "Yeah, that's not coming out."

I bent deep and took her in my arms, all those dead lifts finally paying off. Will Norman caught my eyes, didn't like what he saw in them, and let me pass. I left the suite and set course toward the elevator.

"What are you doing, Allen?"

"Taking you out of here."

"If you leave, you aren't getting back in."

"Forget these jokers. Let them kill themselves over Reynard's book. They deserve everything that's in it."

"Put me down. I'm going to be fine."

I loosed a doubtful grunt. We were at the crossroads, literally. The elevator was within reach. It's not what I wanted, but I carefully lowered Stern to the ground. She removed her mask to better examine her wound. The bleeding had slowed down.

"The ricochet took a lot of the pepper off that round, but it looks like you're on your own, Allen. Funny how it keeps working out that way."

"Imagine how big your next medal is going to be, now that you've been wounded in the line of duty."

Stern studied the carpet. "Someone sent me video of Blake screwing around. I lost everything this weekend. I need this to be worth it."

How had Stern seen the footage? The laptop was still in my bag. No one else had seen it. Except . . .

Elaine's voice broke into my earpiece. "She deserved to know."

The camera crown. It was always recording. Elaine had made the decision for me.

There wasn't much left for me to do for her but hold Stern's hand, and she didn't need that. I couldn't unlock from her eyes.

"We've got a royal mess to untangle here."

This time when she shook her head, there was a measure of amusement mixed in with her exasperation. "You're the real deal, Allen. As much as I hate to admit it."

Heat rushed into my face. "You too."

The Dame of the Moon had nailed me at the start. I wasn't willing to risk myself when it really counted. I didn't go for what I wanted most, not since missing the one big swing and turning my life into a punch line. I'd let failure beat me down, make me afraid of even trying. It took being framed for murder to wake me up. Since then, I'd turned things around enough so that looking into the mirror didn't make my heart sink.

The same was true when it came to love. At the same time I'd sealed my fate bombing as Jove Brand, I'd gotten involved in an affair with a married woman that had fatal repercussions. The whole deal had made me risk averse when it came to matters of the heart. It taught me I couldn't trust myself. That I didn't know how to pick them to start with.

I knew what I wanted more than anything, but my body seized up at the thought of going for it. No force on earth could have moved me.

Thankfully, Stern didn't suffer from the same condition. She grabbed me by the collar and pulled me in. Our lips met full force and locked like they were magnetized. There was no awkwardness to that first kiss. It was as if we had been doing it our whole lives. And it was everything I ever hoped a kiss would be. Fit for the climax in movies. The music swelled. Time ceased to exist.

Stern shoved me away. It took some effort. Our mouths didn't want to be apart. She stared at me as if I was the one who had done something shocking. She talked first. I was too busy trying to stop panting.

"For luck."

"Yeah. I. Uh. Time to fight evil. You know. How it goes, I mean."

"Get out of here, Allen, before I die of embarrassment."

"Ten-four."

Polk streaked by, clutching the series bible. She was moving so fast it left me wondering if she wore roller skates under her dress. It was a straight shot to the Dame of the Moon's suite. Polk pounded on the door until someone opened it, then disappeared inside. Reynard's suite door was wide open. The last of Polk's guards were struggling to hold the Blackguard off to cover their queen's escape.

Stern leaned on me as we hobbled toward the Dame's suite. All of a sudden, I was weak in the knees. I managed to only trip over my own feet twice. The Blackguard didn't have keys. They'd have to find another way into the Dame of the Moon's suite. I, however, did have a key. In retrospect, I should have knocked and announced myself prior to barging in. The instant I cracked the door, I was pulled through, launched skyward, and slammed into the ground at a force approaching terminal velocity.

"Sorry, Ken."

Alexi Mirovich pulled me to my feet. I held on to him for dear life while my lungs refilled. Lacking the wind for a quip, I waved a hand like it was no big deal, I often went skydiving without a parachute.

Sheila Polk, Lynn Chambers, and the Dame of the Moon, a.k.a. Lila Chambers, were conferencing around the tarot table. I didn't catch most of it because my ears were still ringing, but from the body language, Polk was making her case as to why they shouldn't just turn her over and stay out of it. It would be a hard sell, seeing as Polk had turned her back on them thirty years ago, in favor of Reynard.

Stern used the wall for support while she secured the entrance. I gestured for Alexi to take her place. By the time the Blackguard started kicking down the door, I was bipedal again, albeit with the stability of a newborn fawn. I stood on the knob side. Alexi was more than capable of doing the heavy lifting.

It took three kicks for the door to crack. When it swung open, Alexi conducted a repeat performance, except this time with no brakes. Thelen's legs slammed into the ceiling, then down he went, spiked into the ground like Alexi was trying to win one of those carnival strongman games with the mallet. Thelen would have died, had Alexi wanted to kill him. The pistol he was holding sailed toward the Dame's throne. Stern hobbled over after it.

Will Norman was next in line. He recovered well to the sudden appearance of a Russian mixed martial arts champion, lunging a thrust at Alexi's back. I stepped out from behind the door, snagged Norman at the elbow and threw a knee into his solar plexus. It banged off his armor. If I lived through this, I'd have a welt for a month. I put a foot out and jerked Norman into the room.

Norman stumbled into Alexi, which was the same as stumbling into quicksand with opposable thumbs. I was freed up to battle Corbett, who was still mostly in the hallway. He split attention between turning and running and throwing a shot my way. Had he fully committed to marksmanship, it would have been bye-bye Ken Allen. I shoved his gun arm toward the ceiling and drove a right hand into his liver. There was no space for armor in Corbett's playing card-inspired ensemble. The punch took a few seconds to register. Liver punches always did. Then Corbett melted like ice cream.

I took the gun off him and made it safe, clearing the magazine and ejecting the round in the chamber. Corbett tried tugging his Jack's rod out of his belt as I pulled him to his feet. I batted his hand away and tossed it aside.

"Cut it out, Corbett."

Corbett pulled a move I never saw coming. He just slumped. Became dead weight, as if he were a toddler throwing a tantrum. I dragged him six feet before the situation got too embarrassing for the both of us.

Whatever Alexi did to Norman, it worked. Norman backed away from him with his hands up. Alexi had Thelen over one shoulder. I pointed to the pile of Corbett.

"Help me with this?"

Alexi grinned and yanked Corbett into the air, his toes barely touching the ground. I shoved the door back into place as best I could. All the suspects were assembled: Will Norman, network executive and heir to billions; Bradly Corbett, right-hand man and last to see Reynard alive; Archibald Thelen, Norman's left-hand man with secret access to Reynard's suite; Lila Chambers, Reynard's unacknowledged daughter and heir to the throne; Lynn Chambers, Reynard's former lover back from exile; and Sheila Polk, who usurped both her sister and Reynard at first opportunity. Stern limped over and took a seat on an armoire in the hallway, where she could keep an eye on everyone, pistol in hand.

This was it, my time to shine. If only I knew who had done what.

"Let's start at where I entered the story. Reynard was sure someone was trying to kill him. Positive there had been two attempts on his life, both via sabotages to his residences. He hired me to determine who the culprit was. Since Reynard isn't here to receive the results of my investigation, I'll tell his heir. Because his heir is in this very room, indeed."

I watched carefully then, who looked at who, and who looked at no one at all. Things were starting to fall into place. I pointed at Polk. "And it was you, alone at his cabin when it burned down."

Polk got back into character, chin high. "That's correct."

Archibald Thelen was starting to stir. I addressed him. "You checked the cabin beforehand and found nothing amiss. You ever make a mistake like that before?"

Thelen shook his head as much as his strained neck would allow.

"Then, when you performed the check on Reynard's trailer in Scotland, you uncovered signs of sabotage."

Thelen gave no response.

"Or did you?"

Still no response.

"See, the sabotage thing hung me up. I was stuck trying to figure who could have both had the access and ability to burn down Reynard's cabin and gotten to him Friday morning. But the truth was, his actual killer had not made prior attempts on his life. Reynard had hired me under a misconception. You see, no one had been trying to kill him."

Polk and Thelen were the only ones who didn't look surprised. Bradley Corbett, hype man to the end, did me the favor of exclaiming in the negative.

"What happened instead is simple enough: two people close to Reynard, desperately trying to get rid of the other." I looked at Sheila Polk. "You turned to the same tactic you've used since childhood, and burnt down the cabin yourself to put Thelen on the chopping block. And it worked—cast a pall on Thelen. How had he missed the sabotage? Could he be trusted?"

I kneeled down to check Thelen's pupils. They were dilating, which was a good sign.

"You couldn't have that, could you Thelen? You'd been around as long as Polk, since *Never After*. No way you were getting pushed out. So you fabricated that sabotage to Reynard's trailer in Scotland. Reinforced to Reynard that if not for your tireless efforts, he would have died. Polk couldn't out you as faking it, because then she'd have to admit to her own shenanigans."

Thelen rested a hand on his forehead.

"Is that a yes?"

"Yes."

"Thank you. Stay awake, Thelen. You might have a concussion." I gestured between Thelen and Polk. "What neither of you imagined was that, in his paranoia, Reynard would turn to a third person. Facing death made him obsessed with his legacy. You see, royalty passes down through blood, and Reynard had sired an heir thirty years prior. An heir he thought would meet him with open arms. Instead, they murdered him."

The Dame of the Moon's eyes were like daggers. "How dare you. I didn't kill Reynard. I didn't want this stupid crown."

"No, you didn't want to sit on the throne. And neither did his killer, for that matter. But Reynard offered it to you anyway, didn't he, Lila?"

"Yes."

"And he handed you the murder weapon. Put the crown in your hands. Let you try it out."

"It was like he was testing me." Lila's sullenness returned. "I don't much care for being tested."

"He wanted to make sure the path of succession would be clear. He was trying to gauge if you would challenge his chosen heir. Because as his firstborn, you might have a legitimate claim."

The entire room fell quiet, all of them confused except for one. Lynn Chambers broke the silence. "Firstborn? But Lila wasn't a twin."

"No, she wasn't. Nonetheless, there was another child. After all, Reynard had two crowns in his closet. One for a girl, and one for a boy. Back during *Never After*, Reynard chased women other than just you on the set. And I think he caught one of them."

18

WILL NORMAN STARTED TOWARD THE DOOR. "I've heard about enough of this."

Alexi snagged Norman by the sword belt. "I have not. Go on, Ken!"

"There was a paternity suit after *Never After* wrapped. The details were kept private, but everyone assumed it was filed *against* Reynard. But that wasn't the case. The suit had been filed by Reynard, trying to prove a child was his." I turned to Lynn Chambers. "But the suit wasn't aimed at you."

"No, I never denied Lila's parentage."

"So, the suit involved a second child. But Reynard lost the case. The results were a false negative, due to his genetic chimerism. Isn't that right, Will?"

Will Norman's face was unreadable, partially a side effect of all the work he had done, partially because he was fighting to keep it that way. "How should I know?"

"Because Reynard filed the suit against your mother. She was the stable master on *Never After*. Bill Senior is on the special-features footage, visiting her on set."

"Let this go. Now." Norman steamed like contents under pressure. "Before you get into trouble you can't get out of."

It wasn't only a moral thing, that I refused to be threatened. It was that there was nothing you could threaten me with. As for material assets, I barely made the mortgage on my condo, which also served as my office. Retirement was a distant dream. I had a kid, but family money on his mother's side set him up for life. The only things I really treasured were the things I had lived through, and you couldn't take those from me.

"It explains why you green-lit *The Lands Beyond* in the first place: Reynard forced you to. Ten years ago, when he came calling at Home Drive-In, he told you. Said he was your biological father, not the billionaire who raised you. That he couldn't prove it back then, but that DNA testing had come a long way."

Sheila Polk laughed like she had a mirror-mirror on her wall. I turned to her. "And you knew, didn't you? Back at the feast, you said, 'Seize the bastard usurper, seize Ken Allen.' The first sentence wasn't referring to me. It was referring to Norman, who was next to me."

Polk preened. "I walked in on Reynard and that woman in the stables during *Never After.* Reynard would never admit Will was his son, but he had that smile when I broached the topic. He said, more than once, that Will Norman was a prince among men."

I let the legitimate empathy I felt for Norman leak into my voice. "Reynard blackmailed you. Threatened to tell the world, unless you funded the show. Leveraged unheard-of rights and control."

Norman turned to leave. "I've endured enough of this nonsense."

It would have taken being under gunpoint to keep him there. But I had something better. I had an Alexi Mirovich. A glance from me, and

Alexi reeled Norman back in with nary a pause. The room was filled with people, but they faded into the background. It was just me and Norman.

"So, yesterday morning, after I left, Reynard met with you."

Norman perked up. "If that were true, there would be a record of me using the elevator. The guards on duty would have seen me."

"You came up the dumbwaiter, like the rest of the Blackguard. You're the secret eighth member."

"That's—that's . . ."

"Save it. You know how to use a sword when you have no reason to. You could be on set, but your absence also wouldn't be noticed, since you aren't part of production. You can keep your own casting a secret, like you did with Lynn and Lila Chambers."

Norman started shaking his head and didn't stop.

"I know it wasn't your choice. Reynard forced you into it. He used his leverage to turn up the pressure, season after season, year after year, until you finally broke. It all came to a head this weekend."

I made the mistake of looking around. Everyone was looking back at me.

I instantly broke into a cold sweat. It was hard to imagine that some people enjoyed being the center of attention.

"Reynard had a big plan for the weekend. He was going to name you, Will Norman, his heir."

Norman's head shaking reached a full one eighty. His face started to turn red. "Shut up, shut up!"

"All these years, holding you over a barrel. Years of threats and humiliation, and with the finish line in sight, he was going to out you anyway. Reveal there had been a secret prince all along. Publicly declare you his son."

Norman was dying to reply. His lips parted, then closed as he swallowed his words.

"He offered you the crown. He put it right in your hands."

Norman's voice cracked. "The son of a bitch."

"He thought you would be pleased. It was all over his face. Looking down at you from the throne. Lording over you."

"And I—"

Norman caught himself.

"You begged him. Pleaded with him not to. But he wouldn't listen. He even made you bring your mother."

"Why would he—?"

"Because Reynard wanted confirmation from the mothers of his children. It's why he asked Lynn Chambers to attend, because he was going to out Lila as well. That room you lent me: at the feast *you* told me it was your mother's. My seat at the banquet, that was hers too. But why? The animal wrangler on *Never After* doesn't rate a seat at the big table. The royal consort, however, that's a different story. When he put the crown in your hands, that's when you realized why he forced you to bring your mother along."

Norman was a tough cookie. He started to cry, tears streaming down as his face twitched, but he kept it locked down.

"So you showed him what he could do with that crown. Where he could shove it." This gig could be brutal. Sometimes you had to say something harsh. An untruth with enough impact to break a person. "You killed your own father."

"He wasn't my father!"

"Sure, he was. Every time you looked in the mirror, you saw Reynard's face. No matter how many times you went under the knife, Reynard was always staring back at you. All the plastic surgery in the world can't change that deep down, you're just like him."

"I'm not! I don't screw with people to get my rocks off."

"And you stood up to him. Gave him what he had coming."

"Damn right." Norman stopped at hearing the words come out of his own mouth. He cleared his throat. "You—you can't prove that."

"Sure I can. Take off his gloves, Alexi."

Norman struggled to no avail.

Alexi removed Norman's gauntlets as fast as he would have shed gloves from his own hands. Both Norman's hands were bandaged. The bandages were bloody, aggravated by swordplay. The cuts must have been deep.

"Your wounds will match the pattern on the crown. You killed Reynard. Then you left the way you came, down the dumbwaiter, and sent your mom home."

"Why didn't I just leave then?"

"Because when the haze cleared, you remembered the series bible. You had to have it."

Corbett finally chimed in. "But if Mr. Norman hated the show, why would he want to finish it?"

"He doesn't care about the show. He cares about what Reynard wrote down about him in that book. But thanks for speaking up, because this is where you come in."

"What?"

"Maybe you were in the room when Norman did the deed, maybe you came in after. That doesn't matter. You saw the series bible right away. Your heart raced. But you couldn't keep it. You were sure to be searched. Maybe arrested. You called the Blackguard up to retrieve it while you went down to meet me. Then, when we arrived on the scene together, you were sure to ask if the book was missing, so I knew you didn't have it."

Corbett looked legitimately confused. He was one of the best I had ever seen. Everything he did was genuine. You believed he was really going to faint or puke. The guy could even change color at will, like a chameleon. He could have won an Oscar, back in the day when actors were allowed to be ugly.

"Was it your idea to send them to Hammersmith's suite? I think it was. You knew about the secret passage from when Reynard called upon Fairchild to film. You needed to create some suspects. Norman was covered, sure, and you could perform your way out of anything. But a killer was required."

Corbett issued a nervous laugh. "Ken, you're being crazy."

"Gaslighting is beneath an artist such as yourself, Corbett. So Denoso grabs the book. You'd prefer Hooper, but it was fifty-fifty, and you lost the coin flip. Denoso is loyal to Polk, or just hates your guts, who knows? He stashes the book while implicating Hammersmith, then Hooper and the rest kill him before confirming he still has it."

Corbett laughed. "That's giving me a lot of credit, Ken."

"Sure is. I mean, you've been running the Blackguard all along. It was you who ordered Bowers and Denoso killed."

This time, Corbett's color change was involuntary. "What?"

"You had me believing it was Norman for a while there. But the Blackguard had no reason to be loyal to him. He's the eighth member, against his will. He never wanted anything to do with the Edgelords. You cozied up to Norman right away. You were next to him every time I called. He kept covering up the phone to talk to you. You used the information to issue orders to the Blackguard while making it look like Norman was in command. Heck, you might have run it even before Reynard was dead. It would explain how they got on board right away."

"Prove it."

"I don't have to. Norman will pin everything he can on you to save himself. Or his father will. We'll see how loyal the Blackguard stays to you when the charges start rolling in. Personally, I'd take my chances with the cops." I pointed at Sheila Polk. "Her side might have been afraid of the Normans, but you're another matter. And with most the Blackguard off the board, you're out in the cold. Now, let's talk about the book."

Corbett's eyes flicked toward the series bible. Sheila Polk caught his glance and clutched the book to her chest. I untied my shoe and slipped off my sock as smoothly as someone could, hopping on one foot. Reynard's ring was where I hid it, around my second toe. "I thought long and hard about what would be fair here. In the end, I think everyone needs to see what you've been killing each other over."

I slipped Reynard's ring on and gestured for Polk to hand over the book. She hesitated, but in time, curiosity won out. It didn't hurt that, if I was telling the truth, both Norman and Corbett were facing serious charges, leaving Polk as the last wannabe monarch standing.

Despite Polk cradling the series bible like it was her baby, the case was still cold to the touch. I repeated the sleight of hand with the ring over the hasp, and it popped open. The actual book wasn't built unto the case. I withdrew it, pulling it free of a mechanism that reminded me of a storm door's pneumatics—Reynard's little booby trap.

Polk, Corbett, Norman, and the Dame of the Moon couldn't help but shuffle toward me, drawn by the gravity of the moment. I held the book up with one hand, as if I were a crossing guard, and opened the cover. That left a free hand to turn the pages. I didn't want them to miss a single one.

The first page was blank, like a lot of books and notebooks. An insulator, so nothing important got damaged.

The second page had ten words handwritten on it:

My Life Is My Art, My Art Is My Life.

The third page was blank. And the fourth. And the fifth.

The book was thick. Maybe three hundred pages, almost all of them white as pure driven snow. Around page ten there was a little doodle. Nothing special. Reynard wasn't an artist. Every dozen pages or so there was something like that. A scribble, from Reynard pretending to write while being watched.

But that was it. No secrets. No stories. No ideas. Not even a stray musing. The series bible was a big fat nothing.

Their reactions ran the gamut. Norman exhaled, everything in him relaxing. Corbett stared in shock, his mouth moving yet no sound coming out. Sheila Polk wailed, deep and mournful, at the revelation.

The Dame of the Moon laughed, clear and hard enough to break glass. Lynn Chambers, the only one not to step forward, shook her head, as if recalling what a rascal Reynard had always been.

"You knew?" I asked her.

"Oh, no. But I remember *Never After*. We flew by the seat of our pants. It was a collaboration. Everyone contributed. Rex, he controlled the chaos. That man loved to create, but he really hated to work."

Reynard had become a character unto himself. The bigger the show became, the more certain everyone was of his genius. Of his vision. He leaned in, committed to the ruse. Convinced everyone that he knew what he was doing. That the ground under their feet was firm. That their future was set in stone.

When the opposite was true.

The world that they all loved—crew, actors, and fans alike—the people and places that spoke to them, in the end, didn't exist. They never did. Reynard wasn't a prophet. He wasn't a divine conduit, transcribing a message from another realm. Nor was he a genius, weaving a web of intricate design from start to finish.

Reynard was assembling a puzzle without a box or borders. He was adrift on the waves, trusting land was over the horizon. Most of the time, he just borrowed from his real life. Mined the people around him for ideas.

In the end, the guy was making it all up.

His heirs, voluntary or not, were inheriting a house of cards. Killing each other over a booby prize. *The Lands Beyond* started and ended with him.

Polk collapsed. Her thousand-yard stare was broken only by regular blinking, like she was sending a biological SOS. She couldn't bear Reynard a child. The only piece of him she could ever keep didn't exist after all.

Corbett rubbed his temples, recalculating. The result was respect. "The old man really was something. I'll give him that."

Norman was on a rollercoaster. The relief was replaced by the realization of what he'd done. When he spoke, it was to himself. "I have to call my father."

The Dame of the Moon had to sit down. Tears of laugher gave way to sobs. Lynn Chambers moved to console her.

And once again, I had gone and ruined everyone's future.

———

Stern called in the cavalry. No one tried to run. There was nowhere to run. For a murderer, Norman didn't look too worried. Then again, you don't see a lot of billionaires doing hard time.

Polk wandered back into reality. All traces of the queen were gone from her tone and posture. She spoke so softly, I had to crouch next to her.

"What was going to happen?"

I thought she was asking about Reynard's plans. "Not sure. Anoint Norman and keep flying by the seat of his pants. If it ain't broke, don't fix it."

"No, in Crucible. The ending. What was the ending?"

"Oh, you mean on the show." Polk hadn't processed that her question had no answer. "If I had to guess, Reynard would have revealed Will Norman as the secret Blackguard member. Killed off Dever's character. Dever had been a misdirect in real life, so chances are, his characters were a misdirect on the show as well."

Polk nodded and started to breathe. "What then?"

"Then Reynard crowns his real-life heir king on the show, making his kid ruler of both realms."

Polk looked up at me, a new light in her eyes. "Really?"

"Sure. Reynard said as much. My life is my art, my art is my life."

Polk's gaze fell. "It is all for naught. Soon everyone will know the tome is blank."

What to do? Should I take down Reynard's cult, or let them march on? His world wasn't all bad. It meant something to a lot of people. Gave them purpose. A sense of worth. In the end, it wasn't my call to make.

I handed the series bible to the Dame of the Moon.

"Here. You're the oldest child. Hand it over to the police if you want. If not, you're good at disappearing things."

Lila's eyes went wide. "Don't do this to me."

I slipped off the ring and pressed it into her palm. "And that's precisely why you're the one who should have it. Heavy is the head that wears the crown, Lila."

Epilogue

SO HOW DID IT ALL TURN OUT?

Sadly, the real world works much the same as fantasy, by the golden rule—he who has the gold makes the rules. Will Norman's dad came riding to his son's rescue. That's something Reynard didn't get. Blood might be thicker than water, but blood is more than what runs through your veins.

Your parents aren't just who you share DNA with. They are the people who were there, day in and day out. The people who sat by your bedside and bounced you on their knee. Who nursed you when you were sick. Who read you stories at night and endured you from toddler to teenager. He should have asked Blake Dever. Dever didn't have to go looking for where he came from.

He already knew.

Hooper, Dekker, and Thelen took the fall for their comrades' murders. Then Hooper shocked the world by confessing to Reynard's murder, claiming he didn't like the direction his character was going.

Hooper might even get out one day. He had the best legal team a billionaire could afford.

Corbett went to work for Norman at the network, in close collaboration with Sheila Polk, the three of them claiming to be piecing together Reynard's magnum opus posthumously while tirelessly searching for the series bible, which was still out there, somewhere.

Was I mad?

I said it before, and I'll say it again: Who am I to decide? To me, justice lies in the wishes of the victim. Would Reynard have wanted his chosen heir to rot in prison? Would he have wanted his legacy destroyed by the truth? The man traded in fiction. He lived and died by its sword. Hell, if he got to pick how to go, he might have chosen the way it happened.

Given the choice, I'll take the story over the truth any day. Stories have to make sense.

Once again, Ava Stern was the hero of the day. Had things turned bad, who knows what would have happened? But as it was, Reynard's killer was found and a major crisis averted. Blake Dever was overseas working on a new Robin Hood series for the BBC and Stern was back to busting bad guys. As far as the world knew, she and Dever had never been an item. She and Ken Allen, now that was up in the air, according to the tabloids.

One more thing. If you're wondering what happened in my love life, after that fateful day at Chateau d'Loire, I'm sorry to say that Ken Allen does not kiss and tell.

Now, if you'll excuse me, I have a date to keep.

Acknowledgments

LIKE MANY OTHERS, I CUT MY teeth behind a dungeon master's screen. If it wasn't for the people who showed up, week after week, I wouldn't have believed I had stories worth telling.

Special thanks to:
John Lipscomb
Noel Barton
Rob Reeve
Jim Alvis
Steve Swinehart
Mike Mann
Nick Rye
Rick Marshall
Wayne Thelen
Luis Sanchez

And the many, many others who graced my table.

As always, my agent Lucienne Diver, who continues to champion my cause.

My editor, Helga Schier, for wholeheartedly endorsing these wacky yarns.

About the Author

BORN NEAR DETROIT, J. A. CRAWFORD WANTED to grow up to be a superhero before he found out it was more of a hobby. He's the first in his family to escape the factory line for college. Too chicken to major in writing, he studied Criminal Justice at Wayne State University instead, specializing in criminal procedure and interrogation.

Despite what his family thinks, J. A. is not a spy. When he isn't writing, he travels the country investigating disaster sites. Before that, he taught Criminal Justice, Montessori Kindergarten, and several martial arts. J. A. is an alum of the Pitch Wars program. In his spare time, he avoids carbohydrates and as many punches as possible. He loves the stories behind the stories and finds everything under the sun entirely too interesting.

J. A. splits his time between Michigan and California. He is married to his first and biggest fan, who is not allowed to bring home any more pets.

If you've enjoyed

J. A. Crawford's *King Me*,

consider leaving a review to help our authors.

And check out

Lisa Malice's *Lest She Forget*.

CHAPTER ONE

THE LOUD HEAVY BEAT of my heart echoes in my ears, pulsing in sync with the car's wipers as they furiously slap at the snow alighting the windshield. The frantic rhythm draws me in as I stare ahead into the darkening night and the thick snowflakes swirling in the beams of the headlights. The effect is almost mesmerizing.

My eyelids start to droop. I want nothing more than to let sleep come, let my mind shut off. Under slumber's spell, the ache in my heart would subside, the guilt in my soul would vanish, and, if I was lucky, I'd wake up to find that the words I heard earlier today were just part of a gruesome dream, an awful nightmare.

Your sister is dead.

I can't get those words out of my head.

My stomach lurches as my thoughts are pulled toward our last moments together. Fraught with suspicion, accusations, anger. My eyes tear up.

It's your fault.

The words reverberate in my ears and a wave of weakness washes over me for being so stupid and naïve, enough to have fallen for that man's lies, his manipulations. If I could go back in time and change everything, fix my mistakes, right a host of wrongs, I would. Things would have turned out differently. Two—*no three*—people would still be alive.

But I can't. There's no going back. Worse, I see no path forward, at least not one I can live with.

Please, God, have mercy on me. Make this all go away.

My gaze is drawn to a hazy pair of headlights reflected in the rear-view mirror. A shiver courses through me, even as a bead of sweat trickles down the side of my face. My chest tightens. My fingers, clenched atop the steering wheel, go numb as my foot presses down on the accelerator.

Calm down. I can't let fear trick me into imagining what is not there.

I squeeze my eyes shut for a second, then open them again and glance into the side mirror. They're still there, those headlights, keeping pace with me. I focus on the road in front of me, take a deep breath, and let it out slowly. "Get a grip," I tell myself. If he wanted me dead, I wouldn't have made it this far.

Staring ahead, a forest of tall pines engulfs the road. Its trees block out much of the remaining daylight, casting a gloom all around that grows blacker and grimmer with each fleeting moment. But I can't go back. Not now. I'd have to face the truth, accept my own culpability, surrender myself, my life, my future. I'm not ready to do that.

I turn on the radio and press the scan button, hoping for a distraction. Music pours through the speakers in short clips—Spanish, hard rock, country, polka, and then—

". . . *Would you know my name, if I saw you in Heaven . . .*"

My body flushes with sorrow. I punch the scan button repeatedly, desperate to put the song out of my mind.

"*. . . I know St. Peter won't call my name . . .*"

My hands, clutching the steering wheel, suddenly go weak and start to tremble. Those songs, their lyrics—words that never held any personal meaning—now haunt me. It's as if God, or some cosmic disc jockey in the heavens, knows what I've done and doesn't want—no— *won't* let me forget it.

"*. . . I would give everything I own just to have you back again . . .*"

A woman's voice pops over the speakers, a news program. "Thank you," I sigh, casting my eyes upward, relieved my prayer was answered. I poke the scan button to set the station and listen.

". . . it's time for a quick station break, after which we'll go to a weather update with WCVA's meteorologist, Alec Bohanan. Our weather team says this blizzard hitting Virginia and much of the East Coast, the first significant snow event of 2017, is a bad one. It could be a killer, so sit tight at home and keep your radio dial tuned to this station . . ."

She's right. The snow is coming down thicker, heavier with each passing mile. The roads will only get worse. But I need to press on. I must get home. I can think better there. Figure out what options I have left.

My attention is pulled back to the voice on the radio. "When the last segment of the June Jeffries Show returns, we'll join the Virginia State Police press conference with breaking news on the missing person case of—"

Your sister is dead.

The words echo in my ears, pulsing louder and faster with each echo, drowning out the newscaster's voice. I slam my fist down on the radio's power button.

It's your fault.

Suddenly, flashes of light bounce off the rear-view mirror. The muscles in my jaw tighten. My neck stiffens. My hands, locked in a death grip on the steering wheel, grow cold, numb.

The light intensifies inside my car. My gaze darts to the rear-view mirror. I'm unable to look away from the looming vehicle, even as its bright beams reflect directly into my eyes. I throw my left arm up to block the intense light and hear myself scream. The steering wheel jerks to the right, pitching the passenger-side wheels off the road. I clutch the steering wheel with both hands and pull to the left, but over-correct. The car careens across the snow-swept blacktop, skids beyond the centerline. When I finally pull the car into the right lane, my body is trembling, my heart pounding inside my chest, my grip on the steering wheel weak.

"Calm down. Breathe." I inhale, then exhale and count down with each breath released. "One . . . Two . . . Three . . . Four . . ."

The headlights explode inside my car once again. The rumble of a fierce engine pierces my ears. I can feel my chest tightening, my throat closing.

Just as quickly, the light dims inside my car. I hazard a glance in the rear-view mirror. The reflection of a large truck, its silver grill inches from my back window, sends my heart pulsing faster and faster.

A powerful growl fills the air once more, followed by the sound of metal on metal. Suddenly, the car lurches forward, jerking my head backward against the headrest. My heart jumps inside my chest as I punch the gas pedal to the floor.

The car accelerates, my heart races with it. Sweat bleeds into my eyes, burning and blurring my sight. A quick swipe at my eyes clears my vision enough to see I'm on the wrong side of the road. I veer back into the right lane. The headlights glowing inside the car tell me the fiend is still on my tail.

A glimmer of brightness in the driver's side mirror catches my attention—another pair of headlights drawing near in the distant blackness. The sight sends blood surging through me. "Help!" I try to shout, but the words catch in my throat, not that anyone can hear my desperate plea for help.

The monster truck bolts into the left lane, obstructing my line of sight to my would-be savior. The truck accelerates and pulls up alongside me. I return my gaze to the road ahead, as if blocking the dark beast from my eyes will make him go away.

But it doesn't. The roar of its ferocious engine penetrates the car and vibrates through my bones. My hands begin to shake. My body follows. Up ahead, I see a bridge, one too narrow for our two speeding vehicles to cross side by side.

With dread, I turn my head toward the truck. Its dark passenger-side window begins to slide down. I hold my breath and strain for a glimpse of the driver. In the shadows, a man's profile comes into view. He turns to me. My blood runs cold.

A gun appears, aimed at my head.

My chest seems ready to explode. "What are you waiting for?" I shout. "Just shoot me."

From the corner of my eye, I see the bridge looming. I turn my head and gape at the road ahead and, all too late, realize his plan.

———

My forehead pulses with a heavy ache, my nose with a shooting pain. A band of pressure pulls across my torso. I open my eyes but only see darkness. I feel water, cold and numbing, rising over my shins, my knees.

A faint glow appears from somewhere behind me, then quickly grows in intensity. I wince at the light and look away just as a loud crack pierces the silence. I make out a soft buzz, a hum—no, a muddled jumble of words. The deep voice is vaguely familiar. I'm both drawn to and repelled by it, making my heart pound.

The pressure across my chest suddenly dissipates. Two strong hands grab me from behind. Lodged under my arms, they lift me up, pull me to the side, then backward.

Don't look. Don't move. Don't speak. The frantic commands seem to come from somewhere deep inside me. Am I awake? Hallucinating? Dreaming?

I struggle to cry for help, but my lips throb with pain, too much to form even one word. I manage a moan. Struggling to open my eyes against a bright light, I glimpse a figure looming over me. A man with broad shoulders. He is speaking. I strain to understand his words, but only hear the echo of my own inside my head.

Keep hiding.

I heed the warning, squeeze my eyes shut, and allow myself to drift away into a welcoming blackness.